TO SEE
TOO MUCH

Suspenseful psychological thriller fiction

MARK WEST

THE
BOOK
FOLKS

Published by The Book Folks

London, 2024

ISBN 978-1-80462-270-4

www.thebookfolks.com

For Sue Moorcroft

Chapter 1

"So, when were you last in Seagrave?" Rita asked. She was driving my car because the doctors in the cardiac unit had advised me not to.

"I think Luca was in his early teens." My son was now on his university placement year, so it must have been the best part of ten years ago.

"A little while, then?" She pulled into traffic and someone honked their horn. She honked back. "Didn't he ever want to come to the seaside?"

"Not this one. When Dante and I got divorced, Luca spent a big chunk of his summer holidays in Italy, and however fabulous Seagrave might be, it's not going to compete with the Amalfi Coast, is it?"

"That's a good point."

We bypassed the town centre and drove by a run of large townhouses with expansive front gardens before joining the road that would take us up the coast towards Cromer and Sheringham.

Rita stopped at some traffic lights, and I glanced out the window. Four young girls, probably aged about twelve or so, were standing in the doorway of a boarded-up pub. Three of them were wearing what I took to be a school uniform of blazers and trousers, while the fourth wore cut-off jean shorts and a T-shirt with a blazing sun on it. The girls dressed for school shared a cigarette and ignored me, but the casually dressed girl looked at me with a sullen expression. I smiled. Her lip curled and she slowly and carefully drew her thumb across her throat, without once taking her eyes off mine. I looked away quickly, feeling a little disconcerted at the randomness of it. Had I been dealing with a client who wasn't happy, I might have expected it, but as I sat in traffic, it was unnerving. As welcomes go, this one felt like it needed some work.

The light changed and, as Rita pulled away, I glanced back to see the girl still glaring at me. I looked back towards the road.

"So," Rita said. She wasn't the kind of person who enjoyed a quiet car ride. "How're you feeling, Carrie? Really?"

I suffered my heart attack while on a house visit with a client of Rita's, after she'd been forced to withdraw. Since I'd stepped in at the last minute, she'd convinced herself that the related stress had caused my cardiac episode.

I put my hand on her knee. "Pretty much the same as when you asked this morning." I felt washed out and my wrist ached from the angiogram, but I didn't tell people that because it made them fuss around me. Luca had offered to come home straight away from Paris and I'd told him absolutely not. "I'm as well as I can be," I told Rita and hoped I sounded convincing.

"I just feel so guilty. You were already stressed enough with work, so I shouldn't have asked you to cover me."

We'd been over this before. "My myocardial infarction was probably a second minor heart attack, considering I'd been in pain all morning. You know this, Rita. It could have happened when I was driving or sitting at the office."

"Except stress is a major factor and you wouldn't have got that, sitting at your desk."

I wasn't aware of much after I collapsed. An ambulance took me to Norfolk and Norwich University Hospital where I had an angioplasty to fit a stent. The doctors assured me that, since I was relatively fit, I would be fine after some weeks of recuperation, and I was determined to prove them right. Just avoid stress, they told me, and I was signed off work for a month. I lasted a week of poodling around at home before I rang Rita, telling her I was going insane.

"But you're helping me with my stress," I told her now. She'd suggested I stay in her holiday home for the duration of my medical leave, to give myself a change of scenery.

"It's the least I could do, Carrie."

"If you keep whittling about me, you'll be next in line for a heart attack."

* * *

Miller's Point, a small and exclusive enclave of former fishermen's cottages a few miles outside of Seagrave, was to be my home for the next three weeks.

"Here we are," Rita said as she turned off the main road. "You'll love it here. I fell in love with the place straight away."

Patrick, her husband, ran an art gallery in Lowestoft and they'd had such a successful show with a new artist called Caroline Lake, who went on to win major awards, that they decided to invest in property with the windfall. Rita often talked about it, but I'd never been here before.

Trees and bushes shielded the road from view as we drove by a terrace of three well-maintained stone cottages with whitewashed walls and shuttered windows. Each of them had parking spaces in front.

"The neighbours," she said.

A natural stone wall blocked the way ahead, so we turned the corner by the last cottage. The road continued for a hundred yards or so and ended at a neat two-storey house, built in red brick with pebble detail in areas. It was old, but newer than the cottages, and the left side butted up to the stone wall. A small garden to the right was fenced in. Four parking spaces were marked out and, between them and the front door, was a bench. A young woman sat on it, with her legs pulled tight enough to her chest that her heels touched her thighs. She was holding a paperback but speaking to a much older woman, who was standing next to a knackered-looking moped. It was propped up on its kickstand and the old woman had one hand on the saddle.

A big hill rose sharply behind the house, its summit crowned by wispy summer cloud.

"This is us," said Rita as she pulled into one of the parking spaces.

"This whole house is yours?"

"Uh-huh. Like I said, it was a successful showing."

"And this is the end of Miller's Point?"

"It is. A footpath runs between my garden and the cottages to a footbridge that crosses the river. From there, you can go up the hill, which is a bloody good hike but well worth doing for the views. You'd love it, but you might want to give it a miss for a couple of weeks in your condition."

"I'm weak," I pointed out, "not incapacitated."

"Trust me," she said. "It'll be gruelling. If you go right at the bridge, there's a breakwater that leads to the beach. We get some walkers here, but no cars. One of the neighbours put a sign up saying it was a private road and that keeps most people out."

"You have a smart neighbour."

"Oh, Amanda's quite a woman and not to be crossed. I'll introduce you later."

"I can't wait."

"You might regret saying that," Rita said and got out. "Come on, we'll get you settled."

As I got out, the young woman looked up from her book, smiled at Rita, and stood up. She was tall and slim, with shoulder-length brown hair and didn't look much older than Luca. She wore a Foo Fighters T-shirt, Converse without socks, and cut-off shorts. She slid her paperback into a back pocket and said something to the older woman, who was watching us intently. Her hair was white and wild, but her eyes were lively, and she had a nice smile. Her leggings were a loud floral print, and she was wearing walking boots and a yellow cagoule that looked like it might have come from the seventies. The map pocket along the front was made bumpy by whatever items she had stored in there.

"Hi, Flo," Rita said. "And hello, Merry, it's been a while."

"Aye," said the older woman. Merry might have been eighty, or she might have been sixty. Her face was lined, but there was a youthful air about her or, perhaps more accurately, an air of refusing to be old.

Rita looked at the younger woman and gestured to me. "This is Carrie, who I told you about." Rita turned to me. "This is Flo and she's a proper gem, even if she doesn't realise it. She's the cleaner-stroke-caretaker for Miller's Point and effectively keeps the place running. And this charming lady is Merry Baldwin."

Merry thrust out her hand and we shook, briskly. "Merry as in Christmas," she said. "Lovely to meet you." She smiled widely. "I'm sure you'll love it here, because it's a wonderful place and who doesn't want to be beside the seaside?" She let go of my hand and looked at her watch. "I hope you don't think I'm being rude, but I'd best get off. Things to do, people to see and all that."

She waved at Flo and Rita and then walked towards the footpath and was soon out of sight.

"Well," said Rita, "that's Merry."

Flo tentatively held out her hand, as if she didn't know whether we should shake or not. "Pleased to meet you," she said.

I shook her hand.

"I've never met anyone who's had a heart attack before."

"I'm sure you have," I said. "People don't tend to advertise the fact."

"Maybe," she said. "You look well, all the same. Just a bit tired."

I could tell she was being honest, rather than cruel.

"No, I always look like this."

I smiled to let her know I was joking, and she returned it, her broad smile producing dimples.

"You had me going for a moment there."

"She had us all going, a week ago," Rita said as she opened the boot. "I went grey, I tell you…"

"But you wear it well," I said.

Rita laughed. "Well, just for that, I won't give you the Merry warning."

"The Merry warning?" I asked, intrigued.

"Oh, yes," said Flo and grinned conspiratorially at Rita. "You need that."

I smiled at their obvious enjoyment of the in-joke. "So, which of you is going to tell me, then?"

"Or maybe we could let you find out for yourself?" Flo said.

"We can't be that cruel." Rita laughed. "It's nothing terrible and, I have to say, Merry is a truly lovely lady, but what you just witnessed was a major exception. She's very friendly and she likes to talk."

"She *loves* to talk," corrected Flo.

"Yes, that's true. If she catches you and she's in the mood, you can be stuck for an hour or more."

"Does she live here?"

"No," said Flo. "She lives in Seagrave but walks a lot and this is one of her favourite places, or so she says. She goes up the hill every day." She gestured towards it. "Like clockwork. It won't always be the same time, sometimes it's in the morning, sometimes in the afternoon, but she'll be up there."

"Amanda told me," Rita said, "she even goes up there after dark, trekking along with her torch."

"Blimey," I said.

Rita opened the boot. "I mean, she's lovely and you'll like her a lot, but she can talk for England."

"Afternoon, ladies."

We all turned at the voice. The man who'd appeared from the path was about my age and his thick, salt-and-pepper hair was swept back from his forehead. Sunglasses hid his eyes but he had a nice smile. He also looked good in a short-sleeved T-shirt, cargo shorts and deck shoes.

Flo glanced at him and took a subtle step towards us. Rita didn't look overjoyed to see him but smiled anyway.

"Afternoon, Boyd," she said.

"Afternoon," he said and walked over to us. "It's been a while."

He smiled at me, and I felt something go ping in my belly. He seemed comfortable in himself and there was an air about him, the kind of charisma you didn't often encounter. Or, certainly, one that I didn't encounter very often with my dating app.

"And who's this?" he asked.

"This is my friend, Carrie Riccioni," said Rita. "She's going to be staying in the flat for a few weeks."

"Marvellous." He shook my hand. "I'm Boyd Manning, from the cottage at the far end. It's lovely to have you here, even if it's only for a short while." He held my fingers for a moment longer than I expected him to, but it didn't feel uncomfortable.

"Aren't you working today?" Rita asked.

"It's an admin day, so I decided to take a calming walk down to the beach." He turned his full attention to me, and I could feel it like a heat. "So where are you visiting us from? Your accent sounds fairly local."

"Norwich," I said.

"She's just here for a bit of rest," Rita said quickly, as if she didn't want me to reveal the real reason. "I told her Miller's Point was the place for that."

His phone rang. "I hope that's the case," he said as he took it out of his pocket. He checked the screen then looked at me and Rita in turn. "Excuse me," he said. "I need to take this. I'll hopefully see you later."

With a smile, he answered the phone and walked away. Flo watched him go without saying anything.

"I don't recall you mentioning him before," I said.

"He must have slipped my mind," Rita said.

"You didn't seem all that pleased to see him."

"Was it that obvious?"

"Probably not to everyone, but I know you, Rita. I've sat in enough meetings to be able to read your body language."

"Let's just say we've had our differences, eh?" she bristled. "Leave it at that."

"Fine," I said, not wanting to upset her. Whatever their issue was, it wasn't my place to pry, and I was here to relax.

Chapter 2

Rita hefted my case out of the boot and I moved towards her, intending to help.

"I've got it," she said.

"Rita, the cardiac people said I need to get back to normal with things."

"I'm sure they didn't mean carrying a suitcase packed for a month, though."

"Are you okay?" I asked Flo. "You seemed a little tense when Boyd came over."

She shrugged and the gesture reminded me of Luca and his friends when they were asked a question they didn't really know how to answer. "Yeah, it's just…" She chuckled. "I'm just not a big fan of his, that's all."

I glanced at Rita and frowned. "Is there something about this bloke I should know?"

"Not at all." When I didn't relax my frown, Rita said, "Come on, Carrie, have I ever lied to you?"

"No." She was the most honest person I'd ever met in my life.

She handed me an archive box. "Here, carry this and make yourself useful."

"Thanks," I said, happy she wasn't treating me like I was made of glass.

Over the preceding week, whenever I'd wanted to make a cup of tea, or walk to the shop, well-wishers kept jumping in to help. Although it was lovely, it wasn't really helping me. So I agreed to stay at Rita's place on the condition she gave me something to do while I recuperated. She ummed and aahed until I assured her I wasn't a workaholic but I just didn't want to get bored during my enforced leave. She relented and we agreed I'd work on safeguarding reports.

Rita slipped her arm through the strap of my rucksack. "There," she said. "That's everything."

"Is this all you've got?" Flo asked with surprise.

"Carrie travels remarkably lightly."

"I can wash my clothes, can't I? It's not like I'm going to go out and paint the town red every night."

"Paint it red?" Flo asked.

"It's an old person thing," I said and gave her a grin. She looked at me with confusion. "It means going out."

"Does it?"

I smiled at her. "It really does. Blimey, even Luca doesn't make me feel this old."

"Is he your husband?"

"No, he's my son. He's about your age and sometimes calls me a dinosaur."

"Oh, okay. Well, I promise not to call you a dinosaur, but I think it'd be hard not to make you feel old when I don't understand all your Victorian expressions."

I couldn't help but laugh. "I think we're going to get along fine, Flo."

"I hope so. If you have another heart attack or die of old age when I come in to clean, I'm really not going to be happy."

"Fair enough."

"Lead the way, Flo," said Rita.

Flo took some keys out of her pocket and Rita picked up the carrier bag of food and supplies we'd got from the supermarket on the way. All three of us walked to the front door together.

"I asked Flo to air the place, because Patrick and I haven't managed to stop here so far this year."

Flo opened the frosted-glass front door onto a small hallway and gestured for me to go in. There were two doors on either side of the staircase and a side table with a plant sitting on it that had seen better days.

"I might have killed the spider plant with kindness," Flo said as she slipped off her Converse.

Rita took off her shoes, so I slipped my trainers off too.

"Killing plants with kindness is one of my specialities," I said.

Rita gestured to the door to her left. "That's the downstairs flat. We haven't sorted it out yet, so it's a bit of a dumping ground." She pointed towards the other door. "That's to the garden. There's not a lot out there, but it's nice to sit and catch some sun, if you feel like it."

The idea of sitting outside and enjoying a cold glass of wine sounded very appealing. "Do you need me to do the weeding or mow the lawn?"

"Nope, I've got that under control," Flo said.

She led us upstairs to a narrow landing and opened the flat door. The lounge was at this end, with a large sofa, a couple of chairs, a small dining table and a television. There was a compact but well-equipped kitchenette at the other end, boxed off by an island. A window looked out over the hill.

"The bedrooms and bathroom are through here," Rita said.

Three doors opened off a narrow hallway. The first, on the left, was the bathroom, and the main bedroom, which looked comfortable and cosy, was at the end of the corridor. Through the window, I could see the backs of the terrace of cottages and their gardens. A line of trees at the end of each hid the river. The middle cottage had a boathouse.

Rita put my suitcase next to the bed then stood beside me. "What do you think?"

"I think it's fantastic."

"I'm glad you like it. I had the other bedroom prepared as your office."

We went into that room, which was about half the size. It had a sofa bed at the far end and a student's desk near the door.

"It's not much," Rita said, "but it's a separate workspace so you're not taking over the lounge."

"I like it."

"Good, just so long as you're sure this isn't going to be too much."

"I need to move on, Rita."

"I know," she said, cautiously. "You also need to be careful. Flo's blunt but she was right, you do look tired."

"Because I am. The doctor says my stamina will recover, but it's frustrating. I can't even power-walk." It was my favourite form of exercise, and I'd tried it once since leaving the hospital. By the time I got to the end of my street, I was gasping for breath.

"Just give it time, Carrie, it'll come back. I'll let you go now, so you can get sorted at your own pace."

"Do you want me to drive you back?" I asked.

"You're not allowed to drive for a fortnight, remember? I'll get an Uber. Take it easy tonight and I'll ring tomorrow, to see how you settled in."

She pulled me into a quick, tight hug then held me at arm's length, as if she wanted to remember how I looked. "You'll be fine," she said.

"I know."

Chapter 3

I was setting up my laptop in the office and glanced over my shoulder to look out of the open window. It was almost seven o'clock and twilight was settling in, the few clouds tinged pink. The cottages looked wonderful in the light, as did their gardens. The closest was laid almost completely to lawn, as was the one furthest away. The middle cottage had a garden filled with colour, with a small pond in the centre of it, in which several garden gnomes were fishing. The grass was rich and deeply green, and the borders burst with a variety of bushes and flowers. All three cottages had patios. It looked like the kind of scene you'd see on a postcard.

I decided to make a start on the archive boxes and went downstairs to get the second one out of the car boot. If Rita couldn't see me do it, she couldn't moan at me for exerting myself.

"No," I heard Flo say, loudly and firmly, as I opened the door. She sounded annoyed. "Harley, leave it alone."

Flo was standing with her back to me, midway between my flat and the cottages. A young man, about her height, was leaning in as if trying to invade her space.

"You're not listening to me, Flo," he said.

"No, *you're* not listening to *me*."

She was standing her ground, but I decided it wouldn't hurt to make my presence known. The young man glanced at me as I walked towards them. He had a long, thin face and a mark near his eye; his hair was shaved at the sides and curly on top. Flo looked over her shoulder and smiled tightly at me.

"How's it going?" I asked, as I got closer. "And who's your friend?"

"This is Harley."

He looked annoyed but didn't speak. The mark I'd seen was the edge of a bruise fading from his cheek. "What happened to your face?" I asked.

"Nothing," he said. "You should see the other bloke."

"That's what they all say," I said.

He frowned, like I'd ad-libbed from a script he'd memorised and now he'd lost his place. "Eh?"

"When you point out a bruise, a lot of people say, 'you should see the other bloke' rather than tell the truth."

He flared up. "Are you calling me a liar?"

"No," said Flo. "She's saying she's heard it all before."

He looked at us both and it was clear he didn't know if he was being made fun of or not.

"Harley decided to drop in to see me," she said, "but forgot to say he was coming."

"That's–" Harley said.

"He caught me unawares," Flo said, cutting him off. "And now he's leaving."

His annoyance became resignation as he realised she'd backed him into a corner. "Ring me later, yeah? We need to talk."

"I will," she said.

"You'd better," he said and turned on his heel to stalk away.

We both watched him go.

"You'd better?" I repeated.

Flo raised her eyebrows. "Harley's a real drama llama," she said. "But mostly harmless and useless."

"Are you okay?"

Her smile was quick and seemed genuine. "Yeah, I'm fine. But thank you."

We watched until Harley had walked out of sight.

"Are you going to be alright getting home?"

"I'll be fine, but I was on my way down to the beach to clear my head of the day. By the time I head off, he'll be long gone."

"If you're sure?"

"I'm sure," she said and, with a quick wave, walked at pace to the path and was soon out of sight.

I watched her go.

* * *

As I put the archive box in the office, movement caught my eye. I looked out as a woman came through the patio doors of the middle cottage.

She was thin, wearing an expensive-looking trouser suit and her hair was a yellow that didn't look natural but suited her. After throwing a box onto the patio table, she lit a cigarette and inhaled deeply, then tilted her head to blow smoke at the sky.

I'm not naturally voyeuristic and should have looked away because she didn't seem happy, but I couldn't. Instead, I moved to one side hoping that if she looked up, she wouldn't see me.

A man came timidly onto the patio. He had thinning hair and wore a cardigan and dark corduroy trousers. "Is that my package you threw on the table?"

"Well," she said sharply, "it's certainly not mine."

"You can't throw that, Amanda. It's a manifold for the—"

"I don't care," she said and sucked hard on the cigarette. She blew the smoke at him.

"We don't want to do this now, do we?"

"Don't you tell me what to do."

"What if Boyd and Scott are about? I'd rather they didn't hear…"

"Who cares? I want to know what you're doing, Will."

"You know exactly what I'm doing, love. I need that manifold to—"

"Don't 'love' me, you cretin. You told me that bloody boat would cost a grand to get back into the water and you've probably spent that amount this month."

He held up his hands defensively. "You know how these things go, Amanda. Costs escalate."

Amanda barked out a laugh that didn't sound at all amused. "My costs escalate, Will, let's get it right."

Will's shoulders sagged. "Yes, you're right, your costs escalate."

"Like they always bloody do."

"That's not fair, Amanda."

"Fair?" she demanded, with real venom in her voice. "Do you want to talk about fair, Will? Do you really want to drag all that up again?"

"No." He looked away, defeated. "Of course I don't."

"I'm not bloody surprised." She gestured broadly with her hands towards the house and the red tip of her cigarette drew a circle in the gloom. "I can't trust your ethics, and now I can't trust you not to lie about your finances. I wonder if I ever could. From now on, if you want to spend anything, even ten-fucking-pence, you bloody ask me first."

"Oh come on," he protested. "I'm not a child."

"Aren't you?" She picked up the package. "If you want to spend my money on shite, then at least have the decency to ask. If you have any decency left."

"Amanda, I've apologised for that a million times over. And if I don't rebuild the engine, the boat'll never get finished."

"I never noticed before how much you whine," she said and mashed the cigarette into an ashtray. "You're pathetic."

"Am I?" He pushed his shoulders back.

"Yes," she said and stepped closer to him. "This worm won't turn. You'll never leave me."

"Your money isn't everything."

"Isn't it?" She tossed the box, which he only just managed to catch, then stalked into the cottage.

He watched her go then looked towards the boathouse.

"Will!" she shouted.

As he turned, our eyes met. Startled, I stepped back into the shadows. He regarded me for a moment then went into the house.

A flush of shame warmed my cheeks, and I went into the kitchenette, unsettled by what I'd witnessed and the fact I'd been spotted. It's never pleasant to witness a domestic disagreement, but to be seen doing so would only make things more difficult. I hadn't even met Amanda and her husband yet and surely, now, he'd be on edge with me, knowing I'd seen his dressing-down.

I made a cup of tea and my phone beeped with a message. I smiled when I saw Luca's face on the screen.

> *Hey, Mum, hope you're well and taking it easy. Don't forget, you need to worry less and keep those stress levels down! I'm doing okay, so that should be a big worry off your mind (if not the biggest worry, since I'm your only heir!). Work's fine, Françoise is as gorgeous as ever, and she told me, on threat of death, to pass on her love and best wishes to you. We're off out for a meal soon, but if you need me, ring or text. I love you, Mama. Speak to you tomorrow.*

His message warmed me, and I texted him back.

> *I'm fine and I'm so happy that you are too. Please pass on my love to Françoise, and both of you should stop worrying. I'm taking care of myself, I'm not stressed, the flat is as lovely as Rita said, so everything's good. Enjoy your meal, my little patatino, much love.*

He was right about me getting stressed and I needed to work on that, so I decided if Will had an issue with me, then I'd deal with it when it arose and not fret now.

I made a ham and cheese sandwich and ate it in the lounge watching television. At nine, I had a nice, long shower then lay on the bed to read.

It didn't take me long to fall asleep.

Chapter 4

At home, on Aldwych Street in Norwich, the morning soundtrack was of people and vehicles. Here, all I could hear were the call of gulls. It felt like I was living in the middle of nowhere and I liked the peace and quiet.

I got up, feeling remarkably refreshed, went to the toilet then padded through to the kitchenette to make some toast and a strong cup of tea. I ate at the island, looking out at the hill. The light was glorious.

Iona, who ran the cardiac rehabilitation programme at the hospital, had advised me to walk as soon as I could "but take a steady pace". I decided this morning might be the time to properly start. Even if I only managed to get to the beach, simply watching the waves would do my mental well-being a world of good.

I put on a T-shirt and shorts, found my flip-flops, then left the flat.

There was the tang of salt in the fresh air and I breathed in deeply as I followed the path down to the bridge. The river was perhaps ten feet wide and flowing steadily. Someone had laid stepping stones in it but the water washed over them frequently.

I crossed the sturdy wooden bridge and looked back at Miller's Point from this vantage. The end wall of my flat was rendered, which made it blend better into the surroundings, and the three cottages were mostly obscured by the trees, though the wood panels and rear door of Amanda's boathouse were clearly visible.

Turning back, I followed a short gravel path until it split into two. The hill was steep and grassy, with a few rocky outcrops, and looked like the good hike Rita had said it was. Ahead was a concrete and stone breakwater that stretched along the base of the hill. The tide was out and the beach seemed to run forever before the glittering water. Far out to sea, almost on the horizon, a line of turbines turned lazily. There was no one else around and that added to my delight, as if this was my own private place.

I walked to the end of the breakwater and stood for a moment, tilting my face towards the sun. Breathing deeply of the sea air made me feel glad to be alive and I wanted more, so I skipped down the stone steps and jumped the last couple to land on the sand like an excitable kid.

To my left, the beach spread as far as I could see until the bluff obscured the view. Seagrave was visible to my right, and I could make out the pier and what looked like an old holiday camp.

I slipped off my flip-flops and the sand was cool and soft. It felt good between my toes and I jogged on the spot for a moment, enjoying the sensation. I felt a bit of a thrill at the thought of exercising again. If I did well, I'd be very chuffed, but even if I had to give up halfway through because I was knackered, nobody was here to see me fail, so it was a win-win situation.

Walking towards Seagrave seemed the best idea. The sand looked harder-packed there and the line of the river, as it turned down towards the sea, would give me a natural end point. Judging by eye, it was perhaps half a mile away from where I stood and something I could do before my heart attack without even thinking about it.

I set off as briskly as I dared, looking at my feet and willing them on. My pace slowed noticeably as I walked but it didn't take as long as I'd thought to reach the river. Even better – although I'd pushed myself, I wasn't particularly out of breath.

As I waited for my breathing to regulate, I looked around and saw, for the first time, faint wisps of smoke further up the beach. It was close to the line of trees that stretched from Miller's Point to here. Curious, I walked over to it and saw that someone had fashioned a rough semicircular wall of sand around a makeshift firepit. There was a spread of charred branches and a couple were still warm enough to smoke. I looked around again and, for a moment, thought I saw movement in the trees. Surprised, I kept watching but saw nothing else and decided it had probably been a bird or something, moving between the trunks or lower branches. There was no reason for anyone to be in the woods and, for all I knew, some locals had decided to come out and have a barbecue on the sand last night and left their fire burning. I kicked sand over the smouldering bits of wood and then started back towards the breakwater.

By the time I reached it, I could feel the exertion in my calves and thighs, but otherwise I seemed to be okay.

It felt like I'd taken steps in the right direction.

Chapter 5

I met Merry as I was walking up the footpath. She came striding towards me and today had paired her yellow cagoule with red-and-white-striped leggings. She smiled broadly when she saw me and the expression deepened the lines on her face.

"Good morning, Carrie. You're up bright and early."

"Morning," I said. "I could say the same about you."

"Ah," she said, "I get to places when I get to them. I leave the house at six every morning and sometimes I turn left and sometimes I turn right. So long as I get to Miller's Point and the hill at least once in a day, I'm happy."

"It looks like a good hike up there."

"Yes, it properly gets the lungs and muscles working. Have you been up yet?"

I tapped my fingertips against my chest. "Not allowed to, at the moment."

"Oh, that's a shame? Heart issues?"

I told her about my heart attack.

"You were lucky," she said. "My Ally dropped dead from his."

"I'm sorry to hear that."

"Me too," she said, and her smile faltered for a moment. "So, are you here to recuperate?"

"That's the plan."

"You'll love it here, I certainly do. And if Flo's looking after you, you've got it made. She's truly a lovely young woman and she looks after this old dear" – she jabbed a finger at her chest – "like I was her mother or something."

She grinned and I smiled. "Is that so?" I asked.

"It really is." She leaned in, as if to impart a secret. "Sometimes, when she's cleaning up after Mrs Ross, she'll slip me a Tupperware of finger food or biscuits. When they have a party, I eat well the next day, I can tell you."

"Flo really does sound like a lovely young woman."

"I tell you, if me and my Ally had been blessed with young 'uns, I would have been immeasurably proud if one of them turned out like Flo did."

"That's a lovely thing to say."

"Ah, I'm an old softy, don't mind me." She laughed. "So were you walking on the beach, or did you watch the sunrise?"

"I was attempting a brisk walk, because the people at the hospital told me I could start exercising and I want to get back into it."

"How did you do?"

I smiled. "Not as briskly as I'd hoped."

"But brisk enough that you've got some proper colour in your cheeks," she said. "You'll get your strength and stamina back, love, just think yourself lucky and keep going."

"I will."

"And now I suppose you're in need of a shower and strong cup of tea, aren't you?"

"Something like that."

"Then I'll let you get on. After all, if you're going to be here for a while, I'm sure we'll bump into each other again and we can talk more."

"I'm sure we will."

"And I look forward to it, Carrie." She patted her thighs. "Okay then, I'm off up the hill. You take good care."

"You too, Merry."

Chapter 6

After a shower, I made a cup of tea and was in the office for ten o'clock. The day was bright, the sky a perfect blue, and I opened the window to get the benefit of the fresh air.

I was looking forward to the work because I believed getting back into the groove of it would straighten my world a little more and a little quicker. I needed to get back to my old reality as another way of shrugging off the heart attack.

Several safeguarding cases were in the box, the files and folders held together by thick elastic bands. I took out the top batch, then put the archive box on the floor and kicked it to one side.

I switched on the laptop and opened a fresh Word document. Then I took out my notepad and pen because, as if to prove I am the dinosaur Luca sometimes calls me, I like to take notes by hand. Also, I like to doodle as I read.

It had been a while since I'd written safeguarding reports, but it was a task I enjoyed. Tapping my pen against my teeth, I put on my reading glasses and leaned back in my chair as I opened the first file.

* * *

The morning whisked by and when I broke for lunch, my shoulders and neck were stiff. Doing too much wouldn't be good for me, so I'd have to figure out a way to pace myself going forward.

I made a sandwich and ate it at the counter, drinking some water. The sun had warmed the flat and I was tempted to go out for another walk, but knew I'd exerted myself enough this morning. I went back into the office and glanced out the window as I sat down.

Flo was on the patio of Amanda's cottage, wearing a New Kids On The Block T-shirt and oversized headphones, the lead from them running into the left pocket of her shorts. She emptied an ashtray into a black plastic bag then stood upright and tilted her head back, her face to the sun. After rocking her head gently from side to side, she looked around her as if making sure she'd picked up everything she was supposed to do, and then paid particular attention to the table. A lighter sat on the packet of cigarettes by the ashtray and she palmed it neatly, quickly slipping it into her pocket. She glanced around and looked up and saw me watching her.

I smiled and waved then realised the lighter wasn't hers from the way her expression dropped. She sheepishly waved back, put her hand in her pocket as if she was going to return the stolen item but then pursed her lips, gave me a sad little shrug and went into the house.

I was surprised, because this didn't fit with what Rita had said about Flo. Had I really witnessed her stealing? Granted, the lighter probably cost less than a quid, but that wasn't the point. On the other hand, I had no context, and, in my line of work, context often means everything. I've met and worked with people who had virtually nothing and would still give it away if they thought it would help someone else. I've also worked with people who stole constantly; some for survival, some for spite. I also knew that Flo, knowing she'd been seen, would probably speak to me about it and all I had to do was wait.

It took her until three. The doorbell rang and, when I went downstairs, I could see her silhouette through the frosted-glass panel.

Flo gave me a little, half-hearted wave when I opened the door.

"Hey," she said, with a tangible air of nervous energy.

"Hello, Flo. How're you?"

"I'm okay but I think we need to talk."

"If you're sure," I said.

She tilted her head to one side as if considering an answer. "I am, but I don't have long as I'm on my break."

"Did you want to come up? I can get you a drink."

"That'd be good."

I closed the door behind her and we went up to the flat. "You can have a tea, coffee or tap water."

"Water would be great."

I poured her a glass, put the kettle on for myself and then sat across from her at the dining table. She took a long sip of water and delicately wiped the corner of her mouth.

"You saw me," she said, a statement and not a question. She picked at the cuticle of her thumb.

"I saw something."

"I didn't know you were there."

"I assumed that from your expression."

"Are you going to tell anyone?"

"I don't know," I said, honestly. "But I'm not going to make life difficult for you."

She blew out a breath. "That's fair."

"What did Rita tell you about me?"

"Not much, other than you're a friend of hers who'd had a heart attack and needed to get away from things for a while."

"That's all true, but she's also my boss."

Her shoulders sagged and she looked at the ceiling. "You're a social worker?"

"Uh-huh. So, I'm not going to be obnoxious, if you want to talk."

Flo licked her lips and leaned forward, pressing her arms against the table and linking her fingers. She regarded me coolly. "I don't do it a lot."

"Take things, you mean?"

"You didn't say 'steal'."

"No. I'm not a monster of a social worker."

"Clearly," she said, and the corners of her mouth twitched into a small smile. "I just do it every now and again, but this was the first time in ages. I take little things that people will never notice are missing."

This didn't sound like the set-up for a pickpocket ring. "Okay. So what do you do with the things you take?"

"Nothing, really. Sometimes it's bits and pieces I can use, or that my mum could use, sometimes it's just because it looks nice." She suddenly looked very serious. "But I never take anything that's valuable. You know, like jewellery or money or anything like that."

"You give some of the things to your mum?"

Flo's smile only touched the left side of her mouth, dimpling her cheek. "She doesn't have a lot and there's a few mouths to feed, so I get little gifts for my siblings to give her."

She could have been playing me expertly, or it could be that in my weakened state I was more susceptible to a sob story well told, but she didn't sound like she was going to carve out a career in theft. "Have you ever told anyone about this?"

"Nope. And, until now, I don't think anyone's seen me. Nobody's reported me, either."

"Do you think you're a kleptomaniac?"

She looked indignant for a moment and then her expression lightened. "That's someone who likes nicking stuff, isn't it?"

"Uh-huh."

"No. I don't nick stuff to sell on. I'm not a criminal."

"Good. I'm sure you don't need me to remind that you that young people sometimes do stuff that could potentially screw up their lives."

"It was a cigarette lighter, Carrie."

"I know, but kleptomania is an impulse-control disorder, so it can be tied into OCD and that kind of thing. It can be worked on."

"Oh." She reached into her pocket and took out the lighter. Up close, I could see it was a lot cheaper than I'd originally thought.

"Do you smoke?"

"Jonny sometimes has some weed, but I don't smoke ciggies."

"Who's Jonny?"

"You sound like a policewoman."

"I'm just naturally curious, so I ask questions to find out stuff." I wouldn't tell her this, but I also wanted to see if there was a way to help her. She was out of the age range of clients I encountered through work, but it was clear there was something else going on here.

"But why find out stuff about me?"

"Like I said, I'm curious and you're about the same age as my boy."

"He's at university?"

"He is, but he's on placement at the moment. In Paris."

"Lucky him." She didn't say it bitterly.

"He's worked hard to get where he is. As I'm sure you work hard."

"Oh, you wouldn't believe it." She leaned back in her chair and put an arm over her head. "Jack of all trades, my mum reckons. I don't know about that, but I'm willing to give most things a go."

"Do you work anywhere other than here?"

"Not really, this place takes up a lot of my time. During summer season, I help look after some holiday lets in Seagrave and work anywhere someone needs something done. The only thing I don't do is dance on the pier." She chuckled. "I have two left feet."

Other than the stealing, I found myself warming to Flo. She struck me as a resourceful young woman. "So do you have a plan for the future?"

"Millions, and all of them involve leaving this horrible town."

"You don't like Seagrave?"

"I hate it. If you don't own property then there's no money here, it's horrible during the summer and then the town dies on its arse in the winter. It's awful."

"So where are you going to go?"

"Away, anywhere." She shrugged and let her arm drop. "It doesn't really matter where, does it? Me and Jonny have talked about going, so we're trying to save up money. He works at a garage in town. I also have to think about my little sister."

That last part snagged my attention. "How old is she?"

"Eight. I have an older sister called Agnes, who's in her own place now, with a couple of kids of her own. Then I have two brothers, but they live with him. Mum had another kid, with her new boyfriend, so I need to make sure that Roxy's okay and not left out of things."

"That's a big family, Flo."

"Tell me about it," she said, with a slight smile.

It felt like she was pleased to be able to talk to someone about this. I wondered if anyone had just sat and listened to her in a while.

"She shares my room," Flo continued, "and Jonny wants me to move in with him, but I'm worried what'll happen to her if I take off."

There was no hint of sadness in her voice, she was just stating the facts as she saw them. I'd heard similar stories in the past and, like then, had no easy answer. "It's not down to you to worry about this kind of thing."

"Probably not, but that's not how it works in here, is it?" She tapped her temple.

"No," I said, "I agree. What we should do and what we actually do are often worlds apart."

She glanced over my shoulder then clicked all her fingers against her thumbs. "I need to be getting back." She finished the water. "Thanks for the drink, Carrie." She stood up. "Are you going to say anything?"

"No," I said because, really, what would it gain? But it seemed like she'd got something off her chest. "Anytime you want to drop in and talk, please do."

"What about your work?"

"I'm writing reports, Flo, I can always spare you some time."

She looked taken aback. "Are you serious?"

"Of course. I'm only working to stop myself from going insane from boredom, so I don't feel guilty about having so much time off."

"She told me what happened." Flo glanced out the window. "It's been a long time since anyone said they have time to spare for me. You're going to wish you'd never said anything."

"I'm sure I won't," I said and meant it. I worked hard to ensure Luca and I had the kind of relationship where he was never afraid to talk to me, and it was sad Flo hadn't been given the same opportunity.

"You're really not going to say anything?" she asked quietly.

"So long as I don't catch you doing it again."

"Agreed," she said and this time she gave me a two-dimple smile. She pulled her phone out of her shorts and checked the screen. "Bollocks, I'd best get back."

Chapter 7

I kept glancing out the window as I worked and saw Flo a couple of times, but she didn't look my way. Amanda and Will came into the garden in the late afternoon and Amanda sat at the patio table, after having to go back inside briefly to find a lighter. Will spoke to Flo, who was hanging out washing on the line. I couldn't make out what was said, but her answers seemed short and to the point. He kept looking at Amanda, as if worried he was going to get into trouble. She didn't seem to be paying any attention, as she smoked and read a glossy magazine.

I shut down the laptop at six and my lower back protested as I stood up. Since my legs felt stiff, I decided to have a stroll before eating.

There was a pleasant haze to the light, and gulls cawed high above me. I walked barefoot, the paving slabs warm on my soles, until I reached the path when I put my flip-flops on.

Then I heard the raised voices and Flo telling someone to leave her alone. I walked briskly to the bridge, where Harley was leaning over her. She'd been backed against the handrail, but didn't look like she was giving up. She gave me a quick wave and when Harley turned and saw me, his shoulders slumped.

"Hi," I said, loud and friendly. "How's it going with you two?"

"We're fine," he said.

"Doesn't seem like that to me," I said, keeping the same tone. "Did you want to step back there, mate, and give Flo some room?"

"I think we're good, missus. You can leave us alone, thanks."

"Flo, are you okay?"

"Not really," she said, watching Harley's face.

He glared at her then looked back at me. "Do you make a habit of nosing into other people's business?"

"Not usually," I said. "Just when you're about."

He took a step back and she pushed away from the handrail.

"Why don't you just go, Harley?" she asked. "We've got nothing to talk about."

"So, you say," he said.

"And I meant it. Just leave me alone, alright?"

Harley bit his lip, looking at her then me. He grunted and walked to my end of the bridge. I held my ground.

"Do you want to move?" he asked me.

"Are you leaving?"

"Seems like it, doesn't it?" He glanced over his shoulder at Flo. "I'll see you again, I promise you. And we will talk, if it's the last thing we do."

"Is that a threat?" she asked, jutting her chin at him.

"It sounds like it to me," I said. "And you really don't want to make threats in front of witnesses."

"And who're you," he asked, but there was no bravado in his words, "some kind of cop or something?"

"I'm a concerned friend of Flo," I said and moved to let him by.

He glared at me then looked over his shoulder. "I'll see you later, Flo."

"No, you won't," she said.

He stalked away and, once he was out of sight, she let out a huge and shaky breath. I felt a bit light-headed.

"Are you okay?" I asked. The situation over, she now looked fragile and young.

"I'm fine. I had it under control but, still, you're like my guardian angel, Carrie."

"I could see you had it under control," I said. "But he was out of order."

"He always is. Harley's a knob."

"What did he want?"

She shrugged. "To talk about us being together."

"That's a weird way to get into a relationship."

"Yeah, you're telling me."

"Did you want to talk about it?"

She shrugged again. "You must be tired of me by now, surely? I must seem like such a mess to you."

The way she said it made me think she'd been told that a few times in the past.

"If you're willing to tell me, Flo, I'm happy to listen."

She smiled, with a touch of shyness. "I've known him since we were little kids at school and then, in Year 11, we started going out. It was lovely but, once we left school, he kept getting his head turned and I kept finding out. Sometimes it was girls we both knew, sometimes it was girls on their summer holidays and I wouldn't see him for a week or more, then he'd turn up with love bites on his neck."

"So what did you do?"

Flo looked away. "I put up with it for longer than I should have, then told him to fuck off. He thought I'd cave in, but I haven't, so whenever he splits up with his latest flame, he comes sniffing back around. He doesn't get it that even if I wasn't seeing Jonny, why would I go out with some dickhead who messed me around countless times in the past?" She folded her arms. "This is my life; I get to choose who I spend it with."

"I like that line of thinking," I said.

"Anyway, he'll stop bothering me when he falls for the next girl." She took out her phone and checked the screen. "I'd better get going."

"Okay, Flo. Just take it easy."

She walked over to me. "Thanks, Carrie. I appreciate you not judging me."

"You're young," I said, because she really didn't need a lecture, "that's what life is supposed to look like."

Flo smiled and walked away. I watched her go then crossed the bridge onto the breakwater. The tide was in, so I sat on the steps and listened to the water lapping at the concrete, trying not to think about too much.

When my bum started to get cold, I went back to the flat and made some dinner.

Chapter 8

A pale mist lay over Miller's Point, muting the colours around me, and it put a nip into the air that you could almost smell.

I liked mornings. I'd been an early riser since I was a kid, when my dad worked shifts and told me he didn't like to waste any precious daylight. It drove Dante, my ex-husband, mad. He'd been a night owl – and, more than likely, still was – and he used to moan that I was up by six and usually in good cheer. It didn't seem to matter that he sometimes woke me up when he came to bed at all hours of the night, even though I often complained about it.

There was still enough of a chill in the air by the time I reached the breakwater that I was glad I'd put my fleece on. I was wearing trainers, rather than flip-flops, because I knew the sand would be colder than the day before.

I never used to feel the cold, even before the menopause delivered the delights of the hot flush, but that changed since I now had to take aspirin daily to thin my blood, because of the stent.

I went down the steps and did some stretches. I could barely see the river and it felt like I was on another planet. I heard the low rumble of a foghorn but couldn't tell which direction it came from.

Using the breakwater as a guide, I set off towards where I thought the river would be at as brisk a pace as I could. I tried to spot the firepit from the previous day and it took a while before it materialised from the mist. There didn't seem to be anything smouldering in it today.

Soon, I got to my finish point. My breathing wasn't too heavy, yet it felt like I'd covered the distance quicker this time, and that felt really good. I hadn't thought to time myself, though, and decided I'd do this walk every morning and clock it, to check on my progress.

* * *

The doorbell rang a little after midday and I opened the door to Amanda. Up close, I guessed she must have been in her late sixties but looked good for it. Her pale-blue silk blouse and tweed skirt appeared expensive.

"Hello," she said and tucked some daffodil-coloured hair behind her ear. Her hand was large with a pronounced vein network. "I'm sorry to bother you, but I wanted to introduce myself. I'm Amanda Ross, I live in the middle cottage over the back there."

She offered her hand and we shook. Her grip was firm.

"I'm Carrie Riccioni. I should have come to introduce myself, really."

"Nonsense, it's down to me to be the welcoming committee and I did exactly the same thing when Rita bought this place last year." She leaned in closer. "She told me about your situation," she said, then raised her eyebrows. "I'm sorry if that makes it sound like we were gossiping, because we really weren't. You see, my husband Will and I were both doctors at the Norfolk and Norwich."

"Oh. Did she ask you to keep an eye on me?"

Amanda laughed, a charming tinkling sound. "Not at all. According to her, you're as strong as an ox and twice as stubborn."

I couldn't help but laugh too. "Well, at least I know where I stand now."

"You do, indeed, though if you have any issues, then please don't hesitate to come over. In fact, we'll exchange phone numbers. I semi-retired at Christmas but still go in a few days a week to consult. I was there today as it happens, and since I was out and about, I thought it an ideal time to call on you."

I suddenly realised she'd made the effort to introduce herself and I'd left her standing on the doorstep. "I'm sorry," I said, "would you like to come in for a cuppa? I was about to break for lunch."

"No, but thank you. As well as introducing myself, I wanted to invite you to a little get-together at our cottage this evening. We have them every now and again, and it'd be a great opportunity for you to meet everyone."

I'm not the most outgoing of people and 'everyone' made it seem like I'd be the only person in the room who didn't know anyone. "That's a very nice offer, Amanda," I said.

"I detect a 'but'," she said. "When I said 'everyone', I may have made it sound grander than it really is. I understand your trepidation; I'm not a fan of being dropped into company I don't know, but that's not the case here. It'll be Will and I, along with my brother, Scott, and his wife, Zoe, and maybe our other neighbour, Boyd."

That was a lot of names. "I met Boyd when I arrived."

"Well, in that case, since you've now met me, that's only three new people. That's not too bad, is it?"

"No," I agreed.

"Come to us, at number two, for about seven. We'll have food so please don't feel compelled to bring anything." She held up a finger, as if something had just occurred to her. "In fact, you can't drive anyway, can you? So, please, don't worry about turning up empty-handed. It's an informal do amongst friends."

"Thank you for the offer, Amanda," I said. "I do appreciate it."

Chapter 9

I had a shower then put on the one summer dress I'd packed and examined myself in the bedroom mirror. I still looked washed out, but not as bad as before. Since I didn't have any smart shoes and my trainers would look silly, I wore my flip-flops and put a light cardigan over my shoulders.

There were a couple of bottles of wine in my supplies, so I took one of those with me. I knocked at number two and it took Amanda a few moments to answer.

"Hello, Carrie," she said, and I watched her appraise my appearance in a second or so. "It's wonderful to see you, and that dress is lovely."

"Thanks." I took a compliment whenever it was offered. "So do you."

Her cream linen blouse and trousers were offset by espadrilles with a low heel. My flip-flops seemed low rent in comparison.

"How lovely of you to say."

I handed her the bottle.

"You really shouldn't have," she said.

"I know, but Rita picked it up for me when I moved in."

Amanda leaned in conspiratorially. "I won't tell anyone if you won't."

"Agreed."

"Anyway, do come in."

I stepped into a small, square hall with a closed door to my left and a staircase on the right. An open door behind Amanda led into the kitchen and I could hear Linda Ronstadt singing.

"Come through," she said. "Scott and Zoe just got back." She said the word 'Zoe' as if it was something unpleasant and I looked at her. "Don't mind me. I always think we judge our siblings' spouses, don't you?"

I got on really well with my brother-in-law but nodded anyway.

"Zoe's lovely, but she's young and Scott needed someone a little more stabilising."

I wondered why she felt he needed stabilising.

"They live next door and have just come back from London."

With a hand in the small of my back, she subtly guided me into the kitchen. It was a bright and airy room, the back wall all glass and patio doors. A door on the left was open and I could see the edge of a dining table through it.

"There's so much light in here," I said.

"It's lovely, isn't it?" She gestured towards a collection of bottles on one of the worktops. "Would you like a drink?"

"A white wine would be lovely, thank you."

She was pouring my glass when a man came in from the garden. He was about six feet tall, with dark hair starting to grey at the temples and eyes that almost looked black. I guessed he was in his late thirties or early forties. He didn't look happy.

"Hey, sis," he said and then saw me. He smiled and his face brightened considerably. "Hello," he said. "I don't know you, do I?"

"No," I said.

"This is my brother, Scott," Amanda said. "This is Carrie. She's staying in Rita's place for a while, as she recuperates."

"Recuperates?" He looked me up and down. "Everything okay, I hope."

"I had a heart attack. I have to take it easy for a while."

"Understandable. Well, you're in the right place, with these two doctors close by."

"We're not cardiologists, Scott," Amanda said.

He pursed his lips with an exasperated look. "I'm aware of that." He smiled at me and shook his head. "Amanda doesn't always get humour."

"I've never got *your* sense of humour," she said and handed me a glass.

"It's an age thing," he said and smiled.

"Where's Zoe?" Amanda asked.

"Out in the garden, being bored by Will."

He said it matter-of-factly and I glanced at Amanda as he did so. Her lips pursed but she didn't say anything.

"I came to get my cigarettes," he said, and it looked like the ghost of a smile was playing at the corners of his mouth. Whatever this needling was, he seemed to be enjoying it.

He went into the dining room and came back a few moments later, holding a pack of Marlboro and a Zippo. "See you later," he said to me as he went out the patio doors.

"I keep telling him he ought to stop," she said. "Unfortunately, I'm one of those 'do as I say, not as I do' doctors, and I've been smoking since the seventies. I couldn't stop if I wanted to. Do you smoke?"

"No, I stopped cold turkey when I found out I was pregnant."

"You're either lucky or have incredible willpower. Unfortunately, Will and I were never blessed with children, so I didn't have that drive."

"I'm sorry to hear that."

"Don't be," she said, with a wave of her hand. "I came to terms with it a long time ago. Plus, I had Scott. He's a lot younger than me, as you could probably tell."

"I did notice," I said.

"It's quite obvious, isn't it? I have no idea what our parents were thinking of. I was leaving for medical school when he came along and I wasn't his biggest fan for a long time, mainly because his upkeep dug into the savings they'd put aside for my education. I ended up working a couple of jobs and it made life difficult, then I'd come home and have to babysit him."

"That can't have been easy," I said.

"It wasn't. And I'm still babysitting him now." She laughed sourly. "Some things never change, eh? Anyway, you're getting a crash course in my history here. How about you? You mentioned you have a child."

"I do," I said and told her about Luca and Paris.

"I like your name. Are you Italian?"

"No, it's through marriage."

"I thought so. You don't have that Mediterranean colouring."

"You mean I'm a pasty English woman?"

That made her laugh. "I didn't mean that, but you and I are cut from the same cloth. So is your husband around?"

"No, we divorced some time ago. He's back in Italy now."

"That's a shame. Divorce is such a nasty business."

"Ours, thankfully, was fairly amicable. Things hadn't been good for a while and Luca was old enough to see it, so it made sense. Dante went home to Italy and Luca visits him every summer and winter. I kept the name because I liked it and everyone knew me by it at work."

"So are you a local?"

"We moved to Norwich when I was a teenager and I've been there ever since. How about you?"

"I'm a dyed-in-the-wool Seagraver," she said, with a hint of pride. "I was born on the far side of town, went to medical school in London, then came back here to live and work."

"You picked a lovely place to settle."

"Didn't we just? I was aware of Miller's Point for a long time because Will and I would sometimes walk the coastline, and when the first of these old fishermen's cottages came up, we bought it. Then we bought next door." She jerked her thumb towards Boyd's cottage. "And then, finally, we got the other side last year."

"You own all three?"

"Of course. I wouldn't want to live out here with any old rag, tag and bobtail, would I?"

"Weren't you interested in buying Rita's property?"

"Wasn't quick enough," she said and there was a hint of annoyance behind her words. "We were away when it went up and Rita got in quick. Luckily, she's a pleasant lady and she's not renting it out to the dreaded holidaymakers."

I smiled. "Not a fan of them?"

Amanda regarded me with a tilt of her head. "They have their place because Seagrave would fall over without them, of course, but I don't want them here. This is our place of peace."

It sounded harsh to me, but then, I didn't live in a town whose population doubled in size during the summer.

"To be honest," she said, "I'd be quite happy without some of the locals too, but I know that's unreasonable. Other than Merry Baldwin, who's lovely though best taken in small doses. Have you met her yet?"

"I have, on my first day here. I met her again yesterday, as I was walking back from the beach."

"Her heart's in the right place, but I don't think all her marbles are lined up. Her one issue is that she could talk the hind legs off a donkey if you don't stop her."

I could see what Rita meant about Amanda being formidable. I wouldn't want to be a random holidaymaker straying into Miller's Point.

We went out onto the patio. Scott and a dark-haired woman were sitting on the chair to the left. On the right, Flo was setting up some nibbles on a table and smiled when she saw me.

"Haven't you got that sorted out yet, Flo?" Amanda demanded, in the voice a schoolteacher might use with a truculent pupil.

"Almost," Flo said and turned a little too fast, knocking a glass. It teetered on the edge of the table and seemed to fall in slow motion. Flo grabbed for it but missed and it smashed on the paving slab.

"Oh, for goodness' sake," Amanda said curtly.

"I'm sorry," Flo said, clearly flustered.

The dark-haired woman stood up and Amanda turned to her. "No, Zoe, sit down."

Zoe looked at her as if unsure of whether she should comply.

"Sit down," Amanda repeated and watched Zoe until she did. Then, turning to Flo, she said, "You know where the dustpan and brush are."

"Yes, of course," said Flo and rushed into the kitchen.

I was so surprised, it took me a moment to respond. "I'm sorry, but that seemed a bit harsh."

Amanda looked askance at me. "Harsh? I hired her to help out this evening and breaking our glassware is hardly helpful, is it?"

"I'm sure it was an accident."

"It's okay," said Flo, as she came out with a dustpan and brush. "Amanda's right, it's my fault. I'll get it tidied up, just be careful where you step." She looked at me briefly and shook her head once.

I was more than ready to fight her corner, but she clearly didn't want any trouble.

Amanda regarded me, as if expecting me to say something. When I didn't, she said, "Let me find Will."

"He was down near the boathouse," Scott said and walked towards us. "And you," he said and gave his sister a light punch on the arm, "should go easy on the staff."

Amanda brushed it off and walked away. Flo swept up the glass and took it into the kitchen. Scott put some sausage rolls on a plate.

"Don't mind Amanda," he said. "She's spent so much of her life being in control that she's become a narcissist."

I couldn't tell if he was joking or not and his wan smile didn't help. "She was a bit over the top with Flo, just then," I said.

He shrugged. "Maybe, but she didn't hire Flo to break glasses, did she?"

"She hardly did it deliberately."

"Of course," he said and took my elbow. "Can I introduce you to my wife, Zoe?"

Zoe was slightly shorter than me, with thick black hair tied back into a tidy ponytail and the willowy physique of a runner.

"Ah, you're the lady in the holiday flat." There was the slightest lilt of a West Country accent. "You're the one recuperating."

"The social worker," Scott said, as if it wasn't an honest profession.

"That's right," I said. "What do you do?"

"A bit of this, a bit of that," he said. "I'm my own boss and I prefer it that way."

"He works from home or the pub, whichever he feels like doing when he wakes up in the morning."

"I boarded out the loft and put up a dividing wall between us and Amanda's place," he said. "It's my office and my sanctuary."

"I'm not allowed up there," Zoe said.

Scott grinned at me. "Of course she is. Just not when I'm working."

He clearly wasn't going to clarify what he actually did for a living.

"I'm an office administrator in Norwich," Zoe said.

"So where did you two meet?" I asked.

"In Bristol," Scott said, "where Zoe comes from. My career hit a few rough patches and we needed somewhere to stay, so it made sense to prevail on sis and move in here."

"Well, it must be nice living next door to your sibling."

"You'd think so, wouldn't you?" He drained his can and crushed it. "Did you want another?" he asked and gestured toward my glass. I'd barely touched it. He looked at Zoe and her glass seemed equally full. "I'll be back in a minute," he said and went into the kitchen.

"Amanda threw you then, didn't she?" Zoe asked.

"Just a bit."

"She still does me, especially when she does something good, like letting us live here until we get back on our feet."

I wondered if Zoe knew how Amanda felt about her. I moved the conversation back to safer waters. "It's a nice part of the world to live."

"We've been lucky. I grew up in Filton, which is okay, but it's not the seaside and it certainly wasn't a cottage." Zoe's smile was wide and contented. "I feel like I fell into one of those reality shows, like Real Housewives of Seagrave or something, including having a bitchy woman living close by. She's pleasant most of the time but does have her mood swings and she never misses a chance to rub Scott's nose in his failure, which is unfair." She shrugged. "It could happen to anyone that one minute you're fine and then next you're on the floor." She looked aghast. "Oh, I'm so sorry. I didn't mean…"

"I know you didn't," I assured her.

"Did I see you on the beach earlier today?"

"Probably. I used to walk a lot and I'm starting to get back into it."

"A girl after my own heart," she said, with the kind of smile you have with people who share a similar passion. "I'm a runner."

"You run on the beach?"

"It's perfect when the tide's just gone and the sand's compacted. Plus, if I go early enough, I don't bump into anyone."

"Not another exercise nut," Amanda said, close enough that she made me jump. "You two will get along just fine then." She touched my elbow. "This is Will, my husband. I'll leave you three on your own while I check on Flo." She tilted her head towards Will. "Don't bore the ladies, okay?"

I didn't hear any humour in her comment.

Will was in his late sixties with a kindly face, but a little frown crinkled around his eyes when he looked at me. "You're our new lady, then?"

"That's me," I said. We shook hands.

"Why don't you show Carrie some of your borders?" Zoe asked.

"What a good idea," he said. "If you'll excuse us."

"Of course," Zoe said.

Will and I walked into the garden. "I saw you the other night," he said, his voice low even though nobody was anywhere near us. "I'm sorry about the entertainment you witnessed."

"Please don't apologise," I said and my cheeks heated with embarrassment. "I shouldn't have been eavesdropping."

"You were spying on us?"

"No! I was trying to get my office sorted and heard voices and…"

"She can be a bit loud."

It didn't seem like a good idea to respond so I kept quiet.

"She likes to be in control," he said quietly. "It happens so often I barely notice anymore, but I'm sorry you had to see it."

My opinion of Amanda was slipping all the time. "What was it you'd bought?"

"A part for my boat, and she had a good go at me until I pointed out that if I'm tinkering away in the boathouse, I'm not in her way." He laughed quietly but didn't sound amused. "She looks after our finances, you see, so she knows when I'm wasting money. She hates wasting money."

"Most people do," I pointed out.

Will scratched the back of his head. "Apart from Scott. And he's the root cause of her issues, I'm afraid. He spends money like water and then shifts to credit when the cash runs out."

"Well, it happens," I said. I was uncomfortable with how much he was sharing.

"It does. Anyway, listen to me droning on. Let me talk you through the blooms."

Will spent five minutes showing me the various flowers he'd carefully cultivated, and it was clearly something he delighted in doing. His knowledge and enthusiasm, even to someone like me who could kill a cactus, was infectious.

"I'd show you my boat, if you were interested, but I've got a little family in there at the moment."

I wasn't sure I'd heard him right. "You've got…?"

"A little family. I can't stand cat shit in the garden, so I keep a close eye out for the beasts and then, a few weeks back, I noticed a pregnant stray. I managed to coax her into the boathouse, and we fashioned a bit of a nest. An old friend of mine is a vet and he came over when Amanda was out, to check on the expectant mother. She's fine, apparently, and the litter is perhaps days away."

"Will!" Amanda's voice carried down the garden. "Will!"

"Bugger," he said. "I'd better go and see what she wants."

After he rushed away, I looked up at the office window of my flat and could see into the room clearly. If I was going to watch again, I'd need to stand to one side.

I made my way back towards the cottage, enjoying the evening air, the scent of the flowers and the gentle sound of the sea. Movement caught my eye and I saw the patio doors of Boyd's cottage open.

A woman in her mid-twenties, wearing a dark trouser suit, stepped onto the patio. She saw me and raised a hand in greeting. I waved back.

Boyd came out and said something to someone who I presumed was his daughter, that made her smile wider. He saw me and looked surprised, then glanced at the fence panel separating his patio from next door. He touched the woman's arm and held her back, then looked at me and put his finger to his mouth. I looked at him curiously and he smiled, shook his head and stuck his thumb up. He said something softly to the woman and both of them waved before they went back into the cottage.

Amanda was on her patio wearing a thunderous expression. "That bloody man will be the death of me."

"Is everything okay?" I asked.

She answered with a brisk shake of her head and walked past me and into the garden.

"I shouldn't worry about it," Scott said. "They wind one another up like a pair of kids."

His comment had just enough petty spite that I realised I didn't want to be there anymore. "I'm going to head off, actually."

"Are you sure?" asked Zoe.

"Yeah." I fluttered my hand in front of my chest. "You know, I need to take it easy."

"Uh-huh," said Scott, as if he didn't believe me.

"It was lovely to meet you both," I said.

As I went into the kitchen, there was a noise from the dining room, as if someone had knocked a chair hard against the wall.

Chapter 10

"Leave it, Will," Flo said. She didn't sound happy.

"Come on," he said, clearly exasperated.

"You'd better leave me alone, or I'll…"

"What?" he asked. "What're you going to do?"

My mentor had drummed into me the importance of trusting my gut instinct, saying "if something's wrong, you'll feel it before you can see it" and she was right. I called it my sixth sense and, right now, it was tingling.

I looked through the doorway. The room ran the length of the cottage, with a lounge area at the front. Flo was standing on one side of the dining table, against the wall, penned in by a chair. Will was directly across from her. Neither of them appeared to have seen me and, when he licked his lips, I got a bad feeling about what I was looking at.

"Don't do this to me, Will."

"I just want to have a word," he said and moved around the edge of the table, "so we're both on the same page."

I'd heard enough and went into the room briskly, startling them both.

"Hi," I said. "Amanda's looking for you, Will."

He looked at me with concern, but Flo seemed happy to see me. It might have been nothing, or I'd grasped the wrong end of the stick, but everything about this scenario looked off.

"Carrie," he said.

"That's me." I looked at Flo and she held my gaze steadily. I felt the adrenaline rush, like I'd kicked into work mode, and it was good. "Have I interrupted something here?"

"Not at all," he said, too quickly for my liking.

"Flo?"

She pursed her lips and shook her head once with the slightest of movements.

"Well, that's good," I said. "So, I think me and Flo should be going now. I need you to take three paces back, Will."

"What?" He pulled a face. "Are you ordering me about in my own house?"

"You can take it however you want, but I need you to take three paces back."

"I don't know what you think is going on here, Carrie, but I can assure you…"

"You don't need to do anything other than take three paces back so Flo can come around the table."

"I'm not stopping her."

"Except she's penned in from this side and you can see that." I held up a hand. "Or you could both stay exactly where you are and I'll call the others in then you can explain to everyone what's going on."

Will moved like he'd been scalded and made a sweeping gesture with his hand. Flo edged past him and came towards me.

"Regardless of what she tells you, Carrie, it's not what you think."

"I'm sure that's true," I said. Flo stood beside me. "Are you okay?" I asked her.

"I'm fine."

"What time do you get off?"

She took out her phone. "In about five minutes."

"I'm sure Will won't mind you going off a little early, will you?" I raised my eyebrows, and he shook his head. "Excellent. Let's go." I put my hand gently on her shoulder to steer her out the room.

"I promise this isn't whatever you think it is," Will said quietly.

"If you say so," I said, keeping my voice level. "Please thank Amanda for me."

I followed Flo out of the room and into the hallway. She opened the door and looked over her shoulder. "We're alright to go?"

"Of course."

I closed the door firmly behind me.

Chapter 11

My chest felt a little tight as we walked away, and I tried to convince myself it was adrenaline and nothing else to worry about.

Once we were around the corner, Flo visibly sagged. As I focussed my attention on her, my chest suddenly felt less restricted.

"I feel like all my energy has gone," she said.

"You were frightened and running on adrenaline back there. It's normal to feel drained."

"Do you?"

"Uh-huh, I feel drained a lot." I smiled. "Let's sit on the bench and get our breath back."

We flopped down next to one another, and I leaned back, my head against the brickwork.

"Are you sure you're alright?" Flo asked with genuine concern.

"Absolutely, I just got a bit worried because my chest hurt a little."

"Oh my God, were you having another–?"

"No," I said, cutting her off. "I just got a bit stressed, that's all."

"You and me both," she said and leaned forward, elbows on her knees. "That wasn't nice."

"What was going on?"

"Are you asking as Carrie, or as a social worker?"

I looked into her eyes. "I'm asking as an older woman who's been around the block a few times and is concerned for her young friend."

Flo's cheeks went pink, and she pulled a face. "You consider me a friend?"

"Why wouldn't I? And I hope you'd consider me one, too."

"I do," she said and took a deep breath, exhaling slowly. "I was sorting out some bits and pieces when Amanda bellowed for Will, but she does that a lot, so I didn't pay much attention. He ran in, like he always does, and they had a few words in the hallway."

"Did they know you were in the dining room?"

"I doubt it. After she went out, he came into the room and jumped when he saw me. He made a bit of a joke about it and then said he always feels better when I'm around. But, like, in a way that made my skin crawl." She cleared her throat. "Then he came towards me, like he wanted a hug or something, and I backed up and then managed to get myself trapped. It was probably nothing, but I didn't like it and I'm glad you came in when you did. And I'm really touched that you stood up for me."

"How could I not? The question is, what do you want to do about it?"

"What do you mean? It's just the way he is."

"He's done this before?" I asked with surprise.

"Not that openly, but he often makes uncomfortable comments." She looked at me without expression, as if we were discussing the weather or what she had for breakfast.

"You're a smart young woman," I said, "and I don't want to insult you, but you don't have to accept this."

"Oh, he's harmless really. He went further today but, normally, I hear worse from lads in town on a Friday and Saturday night."

"That's doesn't make it right, Flo."

"I know that, I'm not dense."

"I'm not saying you are, but if you don't stop this now, it'll only get worse."

"You think he wants to do stuff to me?" She looked as if she'd stepped in something unpleasant. "Yuck, the bloke's fifty years older than me."

"Does Amanda know he makes comments?"

"I've never told her. The horrible woman scares the life out of me." She bit the corner of her lip for a moment. "If you were me, would you tell her?"

"Yes," I said, without hesitation. "If her husband trapped me behind a table and made uncomfortable suggestions, I'd go straight to her."

"She wouldn't believe me. I don't think she even likes me and they've been married for donkey's years, so it's not going to end up well for me, is it? She'll let me go and I can't afford to lose this job, Carrie, even though it doesn't pay a fortune. It's a nice area that's clean and smells nice and I don't get shouted at much."

"Apart from today."

"Yeah, but it's just one of those things, isn't it? Loads of my friends have had the same kind of thing and it could be worse."

"Could it?"

"Of course. If I worked in an arcade, I might get stuck with a handsy manager and I'd have to deal with the public too. These things happen. I even had it at home, once."

Surprised, I looked at her. "What?"

"Yeah, it was one of Mum's first boyfriends, after she and my dad split up." Her face scrunched up momentarily, as if her tongue had accidentally caught a sensitive tooth. "He'd been out, had a bit to drink and he was overly friendly."

"When was this? How old were you?"

"It was three or four years ago. I told him that if he didn't back off, I was going to tell Mum, and then Agnes came into the room and overheard, and she actually went and told our mum. So that was the end of Kev, the lecherous boyfriend."

She said it like it was nothing, just something to be dealt with on the path to womanhood, and my respect for her increased. "You're a smart girl, Flo, and you know none of that is right, don't you?"

"Of course, and I can normally handle Will but today, he got the better of me. So, I really do appreciate you standing up for me."

A moped chugged along the road above us, ridden by someone wearing jeans and a blue-and-white leather coat. They wore a helmet and another was tied to the back seat. The rider made a clumsy three-point turn, then turned the engine off.

"That's Jonny," Flo said and stood up. "He's come to pick me up."

"I thought you had your own bike."

"The bloody thing packed up yesterday and he's going to look at it for me." She waved but he didn't notice. "I swear, he doesn't pay any attention to anything around him."

"He's expecting you to come out of Amanda's."

"True. I've got to go." She started walking backwards towards the corner.

"Are you sure you're alright?" I asked.

"Don't worry about me, Carrie, I'm as tough as nails." She smiled. "But thank you. Nobody ever stood up for me like that before."

She waved then jogged up to Jonny. He handed her the second helmet and she said something to him. He looked at me and waved, so I waved back. Flo got onto the moped, clutched Jonny around his middle as he started the bike and they roared away.

I slipped off my flip-flops and stretched my legs out as I tried to decide what to do about Will. It wasn't really any of my business and Flo seemed content the issue was resolved, but I could see predator red flags and didn't want to ignore them. Her comments comparing him to lads in the town made me hope she'd had some self-defence lessons.

Then again, maybe I was showing my age and not giving her enough credit. Were things really that different thirty years ago, when I was hitting the nightclubs and late pubs in Norwich? Back then, I had my fair share of older men commenting on my clothes and looks or making lewd suggestions. My friends and I might have been scared but we stood up for ourselves and that's what Flo was doing.

I had to respect her wishes and just keep an eye out for her, even if I wanted to do more. With a sigh, I picked up flip-flops and went up to the flat.

Chapter 12

My mind circled around Flo all evening, partly because of the incident but also what she'd said about no one sticking up for her before. That really snagged me because, despite her saying she was as hard as nails, I could also see a young, vulnerable woman. But perhaps I was doing her a disservice; she had her own plans and way of dealing with things and didn't need me to save her. My assumption, in effect, was an insult.

"She can save herself," I said and, oddly, it made me feel better to hear it verbalised.

I had a shower and got into bed. While I was in hospital, I picked up a Sue Grafton novel from the charity trolley at the ward entrance and quickly became enthralled in the mystery. When I got home, I ordered several of her books and was now working my way through them. I was currently on *C is for Corpse* and was really enjoying it.

My mobile rang and Luca's handsome, smiling face filled the screen. While it was a bit late for him to be calling, it wasn't exactly unusual, so I ticked the FaceTime app. I ran my hand quickly through my hair and made sure my nightshirt wasn't gaping open.

"Hi," I said.

"Hey, Mum, I'm sorry it's late, but I wanted to check how you were doing."

"I'm doing okay and all the better for seeing you, *amore mio*."

He was sitting on the sofa in his apartment, holding the phone far enough away that I could see his head and chest. The top button on his crisp white shirt was undone and his tie was loosened. His jet-black hair was swept off his forehead.

"The same to you," he said.

"You're looking very dashing."

"We've just got in. One of Fran's oldest friends got engaged and her fiancé arranged a meal out."

I heard a rush of French and Luca glanced away from the camera. "*Maman*," he said and smiled, then moved the phone as Françoise flopped on the sofa next to him. She beamed a smile and waved.

"*Allô*, Carrie." I'd spent a chunk of my life listening to Italian people say my name – Dante's *nonna* had real trouble with it, for some reason – and it was nice now to hear it said with a lovely French accent. "How are you feeling?"

"I'm doing okay, *merci*."

We talked about my day and evening, and she told me about the engagement dinner and how delighted she'd been at her friend Noémie's surprise.

"Anyway," she said, "I shouldn't hijack Luca's call. It's *merveilleux* to see you looking so well and I hope we can see one another in person soon."

"So do I, Françoise."

She blew me a kiss, pecked Luca's cheek then moved off camera.

"And there you have our evening," he said with a grin. "So you're taking it easy with the walking?"

"Of course," I said, anticipating his concern. "It wasn't as brisk as it could have been." He raised his eyebrows. "I'm being careful, Dad, I promise."

He laughed. "Just make sure you are."

Raised voices sounded outside and I looked towards the window.

"What's that?" he asked.

"Can you hear it?"

"It sounds like someone shouting."

"It's my neighbours. Maybe they're a little the worse for wear after the party." They sounded more argumentative than loudly drunk, though.

"Old people drinking, eh? What's the world coming to?"

"I know, it's terrible, isn't it? Now go and have a nice evening and stop worrying about me."

"It doesn't matter how much you tell me not to, I will worry, you know."

"I know, *amore mio.*"

We said our goodbyes and Françoise leaned in to blow me another kiss before Luca ended the call.

The argument was still going on. I knew I shouldn't look, but my curiosity was too much. I got out of bed and walked into the office, closing the door behind me to make the room as dark as possible. Just to be sure, I stood to one side where I knew I wouldn't be seen.

Amanda and Scott were standing on her patio.

"So, what if I tell him myself?" he demanded.

Amanda jabbed her finger at him. "If you do that, it'll be the last thing you do."

"So now you're threatening me?"

"I don't need to threaten you, little brother. You know which side your bread's buttered."

He looked away, his lips pursed tight. "Every single time," he said. "Every single fucking time."

The bedroom curtain of his cottage twitched, and Amanda looked up at it. The curtain quickly settled. Amanda glanced towards me and I froze, even though I knew I was effectively invisible.

When she spoke again, her voice was quiet. "We're not doing this now. You always were an ungrateful brat."

"And you've always been a controlling bitch, so we're probably even."

"You don't know the fucking half of it," she said and turned on her heel. She stalked back into her cottage and the patio doors slammed shut.

Scott climbed over the garden fence and went into his own cottage. He didn't turn on the kitchen light.

I was about to move away when movement on Boyd's patio caught my eye. A moment later, the person's face was lit by the glow of a phone screen and his daughter moved towards the cottage.

I let the curtain drop and went back to bed.

Chapter 13

There was no mist on Saturday morning, just a clear sky and a low sun that filled my world with a golden light. Seagulls circled overhead as I sat on the breakwater steps and opened the health app I used, so I could set my target this morning. To walk the half-mile to the river, at my old pace, would take about six minutes – I couldn't expect to get anywhere near that in my current state and I'd promised Luca I wouldn't push myself too hard.

As I did some stretches, I noticed someone running up the beach towards the bluff. When they disappeared from view, I took a couple of deep breaths, set the timer and pressed Go.

It took the best part of nine minutes to reach my target and, by then, I was sweating and my breathing was slightly ragged. I didn't feel half dead though, and I took that as a win. I did some warm-down stretches and looked across towards Seagrave, where the sun reflected off a few windows. Turning slightly, I saw movement in the corner of my eye and felt a jolt of surprise. I looked more intently and, yes, someone seemed to be walking between the trees. I followed their progress as best as I could until they reached what looked like a red stripe beside a tree and then they were gone. I squinted, trying to make out what the red thing was. Could it be part of a tent? Was someone camping in there?

I looked along the sand for the firepit and saw there was fresh, charred wood there. So, perhaps my theory of if being locals coming to the beach for a barbecue was wrong and, in fact, the cook was some of kind of traveller. That did make sense, I supposed – if you were on a walking holiday, staying somewhere like this would be free and private.

I decided to leave them to it, finished off my stretches and then walked back to the breakwater. I took it slower this time round. By the time I got back, I could see the runner was Zoe on her way back. I waited by the steps for her.

She ran with a natural grace and long strides, arms and legs pumping with ease. When she was a hundred yards or so away, she slowed and pressed something on her watch before walking to me.

"Hey," she said, breathing quick and hard. Her face glowed with exertion. "It's good to see you."

"And you. You run well."

"Thanks. It looks like you had a pretty good pace with your walk."

"I'm setting my target," I said. "So long as I knock off a few seconds a day, I'll be happy."

"Good idea." She leaned on the breakwater to do her stretches, and her breathing was already steadying; she was clearly fit.

"Do you run every morning?"

"Only at the weekends, because I hate rushing around before work." She lifted the hem of her T-shirt to wipe at her face. I don't think my belly was ever as flat and toned as hers, even before I had Luca. "I'm heading home now, did you want to walk together?"

"I'd like that."

"It's a shame you had to get away so early last night," she said as we went up the steps. "It would have been nice to talk to you some more."

"Maybe next time," I said. "Meeting so many new people was a bit overwhelming."

"It would have been for me," she said, agreeably. "It's probably for the best though, because Amanda and Will had a bit of a falling-out and he stormed off somewhere."

Was that fallout from what I'd involved myself with, I wondered. "They did seem a little volatile," I said.

"That's one way of putting it. I left after a few more drinks and then she started on Scott."

That must have been what I'd overhead. "Really? What happened?"

"The same thing as always." She wiped her face again. "I'm not a back-stabber, especially when someone's giving us a place to live, but Amanda's not the easiest of people to get along with. And Scott, well, he knows which buttons to press and takes great delight in doing so. I know siblings don't always get on because I hated my little sister for years, but you either move on or stop seeing one another."

"My sister and I used to fight like cat and dog," I said, but that wasn't the case now. She lived in Brighton with her family and, even though we didn't see that much of one another, we spoke at least once a month. "I got the sense the age gap between them didn't help."

"True. I can't imagine being almost twenty and off to university when a little brother arrives and soaks up all the money you've been promised to live on." She did a stretch on her arm that made her grimace. "I'm being horrible, aren't I?"

"Not really because, to be honest, I thought she treated Flo horribly. I know the girl broke a glass, but she deserves some respect."

"I don't know how Flo keeps her cool, because Amanda treats her like a skivvy." Zoe put her hands on her hips and twisted her torso slightly with each step.

"How is she with you?" I asked.

"Let's just say she hasn't gone out of her way to make our relationship easy since we got married. It's almost like she prefers to exist in a state of tension. I mean, she can be nice, like letting us live in the cottage, but she also uses it as a weapon. She reminds Scott he's in her debt every chance she gets."

"Do you get on with Will?"

Zoe linked hands behind her back, pushing her chest out. "He's fine," she said, with obvious affection. "He puts up with a lot too. I know he's made his mistakes, but he's always been pleasant and kind to me."

We crossed the bridge and started up the path.

"Did you want to come in for a coffee?" I asked.

"I'd love to, but Scott wants us to go into Cromer, so I need a shower. I'll take you up on your offer another day though."

"I look forward to it."

* * *

I had a shower and, as I got dressed, glanced out the window.

Boyd's daughter was sitting on their patio and looking at her phone. He came out, wearing shorts and a T-shirt, cradling a cappuccino mug. He smiled at something she said then went back into the cottage.

Will was weeding a border at the end of his garden and a small radio was on the ground next to him. The door to his boathouse was propped open.

Being outside seemed like a good idea, so I made a drink and got my book and went down to the garden. The aspect made it a suntrap at this time of day and the air was warm. A patio had been built under my bedroom window, with a small bistro table and two chairs on it. I sat and put my bare feet on the spare seat, wiggling my toes in the sunshine. I could hear the sea, some gulls and the faint hum of music from Will's radio.

It was pretty much perfect and, aside from making lunch, I spent the day out there. Even when the sun moved behind the building, the air stayed warm.

Will's music stopped around lunchtime. A couple of cars left Miller's Point and one of them came back an hour or so later. In the middle of the afternoon, a group of people walked along the footpath, talking in German. I saw flashes of them, wearing brightly coloured T-shirts or anoraks, through the slats in the fence. They didn't show any signs of seeing me and I wondered if they could.

It was late afternoon when I heard Amanda and Will coming down the path.

"Have you seen Flo today?" she asked.

"No," he said. "Why would you ask me that?"

"Why not? You've been here all day and she could have come round when I was out."

"As far as I know, she hasn't been here."

"So where the bloody hell is she? That's twice the silly girl has let me down now. First, she disappears from the party yesterday and leaves me to tidy everything up. Then today, she hasn't cleaned the windows like I specifically asked her to. I despair of her sometimes, I really do."

I wondered what he'd told Amanda about us leaving last night because it certainly didn't appear to have been the truth.

"We could get rid of her," Will said.

"And then we'd just have to teach some other girl from Seagrave everything? Do you want to do that?"

He coughed but didn't say anything.

"No, I didn't bloody think so."

"So what are you going to do?"

"Punish her. I'm not going to pay her full rate for Friday night and, if she wants to keep the job, I'm going to deduct ten per cent of her money this week."

"That seems a bit harsh." He sounded worried, which made sense. If Amanda threatened her, then Flo might be persuaded to tell a few home truths.

"And I wasn't impressed with Carrie disappearing like that. She didn't even say goodbye."

"Perhaps she was unwell," Will offered.

"Well, that's just rude. She could at least have told someone."

"You're not going to say anything to her, are you?"

"Hardly, Will. She seemed quite pleasant, other than her leaving, and it'd make a nice change to have decent company around here."

Chapter 14

I was making a sandwich for my tea whilst singing along to a Spotify playlist when the first flashing lights reflected across the splashback. I looked out the window and saw a police car arrive and park next to an ambulance and another police car. As I watched, another ambulance came around the corner and pulled to a halt. The driver and paramedic got out, consulted with their colleagues and then began taking stuff from the back of the van.

Why would they gather at my place? There must be some mistake, surely. I found my flip-flops and keys and rushed downstairs, expecting someone to knock at any moment, but no one did. I opened the door and one of the policemen looked at me. He didn't seem surprised or concerned, which only confused me even more. What was he expecting to find?

"Hello," I said. "Are you here to see me?"

"Not at all," he replied.

We looked at one another and I didn't want to be rude, but it seemed like I needed to point out the obvious. "But you're outside my house," I said.

"That's as maybe, but it's not you."

"I don't understand," I said.

The ambulance crew rushed over to the footpath and out of sight.

"We're here because there's been an incident on the beach."

"An incident?" My mind conjured images of Zoe, slipping and bashing her head on the steps. "That doesn't sound good."

"It isn't," said the policeman and he went to talk to one of his fellow officers.

As he clearly wasn't going to tell me more, I locked the door behind me and went down the path to the bridge. Amanda and Will were standing just on the other side. Two red Land Rovers were parked on the beach and a group of men were working at the far end of the breakwater with some kind of pulley system.

Amanda jumped when I reached them and said hello. She turned, with a hand pressed to her chest.

"Sorry to frighten you," I said. "What's going on, do you know?"

"Someone came off the hill," said Will.

"What?" I glanced up and, from this angle, the face of the hill looked sheer. "They were climbing up it?"

"Who knows?" he shrugged.

The summit seemed so far away it made me feel giddy for a moment, so I looked away. "I got worried when the policeman said there'd been an incident."

"You were right to," said Amanda and pointed towards the group of men. "I was talking to one of the rescue team and he reckoned the body had been there for a while." She shook her head sadly. "Can you imagine? It's a terrible way to go, anyway, and then not to be found for hours."

I didn't want to imagine and felt ghoulish, standing at the edge of the breakwater and watching the emergency services do their jobs. I managed to stay for a few minutes and then it became too much. "I'm going to head back," I said.

"Sure," said Amanda.

"There's movement," said Will.

The rescue team at the pulley started an engine and the rope jogged a couple of times. One of the men shouted, "It's good!"

The edge of a stretcher appeared a few moments later. The body on it was covered by a sheet and now I really did feel ghoulish.

"Oh shit," said Amanda. "That's a yellow cagoule sleeve."

* * *

Amanda went to introduce herself to the sergeant and he allowed her to check the body. She confirmed it was Merry Baldwin. All three of us were interviewed then, but there wasn't much I could add to what the female officer already knew except that, yes, I'd been on the beach early this morning and no, I hadn't seen anything untoward.

The experience shook me. I didn't really know Merry, but she seemed like a good sort and it was no way for anyone to go. What made me feel worse was the thought that she'd been lying there when Zoe and I walked along the breakwater, deep in conversation.

"You can't let that get to you," Amanda admonished me, as we walked back along the footpath. "That kind of guilt doesn't help anyone, especially since there wouldn't have been anything you could have done, even if you had seen her."

I let her talk, but she didn't need to tell me that. It hasn't happened often in my career but, occasionally, there are horrible incidents where things don't always work out the way you assume they will, and if you felt the weight of guilt after each one, you'd soon stop being able to function.

"I don't understand how it happened," said Will. "I mean, she walked up the hill every single bloody day, come rain or shine, night or day."

"It could be any number of reasons," said Amanda. There was a clipped quality to her speech, as if she'd clicked back into medical professional mode. "I think she probably lost her bearings and that's what the sergeant I spoke to suggested as well."

"Could be." He shrugged. "Still seems odd, though."

Amanda rolled her eyes. "Not everything is odd, Will."

He shrugged again but said nothing.

We came to the end of the path. The ambulances had gone but the two police cars remained, and a scene-of-crime vehicle had arrived at some point. I wondered if an officer was going to draw the short straw and have to stand guard at the site overnight.

"Are you going to be okay, Carrie?" Amanda asked with what sounded like genuine concern, though I couldn't be sure she wasn't still in medical professional mode.

"I'll be fine."

"Good, well, we'll see you around. Just remember, there's nothing to feel guilty about."

"No," I said and let myself into the flat.

Chapter 15

A scream startled me awake that night.

I sat up, heart pounding and the hairs on my arms and the nape of my neck standing to attention. The scream came again.

"What the fuck?" Was I dreaming? Had someone else fallen?

I stumbled out of bed and pulled back the curtain. The bedroom light in Boyd's cottage was on, and the kitchen light in Amanda's. As I watched, the light went on in Zoe and Scott's bedroom.

Was it a scream of distress, or someone messing around?

A security light on Will's boathouse flashed on and he was caught in the beam, holding a small tin. He was looking towards Boyd's bedroom window. I followed his gaze and saw the curtain twitch.

Will stared at the window for a few moments then shook his head and walked towards the boathouse. He took off the padlock, opened the door and went inside. The security light went off.

Boyd's kitchen light went on and, a moment later, the door opened. His daughter sat at the patio table with her back to me. She was barefoot and wearing a dressing gown pulled tight around her. She looked at her phone. Boyd came out, carrying two tall glasses. He handed her one then sat across from her. They both seemed okay and I wondered if one of them suffered with night terrors. Perhaps the screams happened every so often, which is why Will hadn't seemed too worried.

As I turned away, my attention was caught by a sense of movement on the path by the corner of my garden. Surprised, I took a step back so I wasn't exposed in the window, then crouched slightly to stare intently into the darkness. It took a few moments to acclimatise to the gloom and then I saw the movement again. There was someone down there, standing with their back to me and looking over the fence into the cottage gardens.

The person moved and I lost sight of them, but watched for another minute or two, until I was convinced they'd walked away. I wished I could have seen whether they went down towards the beach or back up towards the cottages. It might have been anyone, but I'd have felt slightly better knowing it was one of my neighbours taking a midnight walk, rather than a random stranger doing the same.

I got back into bed, but it took me a while to drop off.

Chapter 16

Despite my disturbed sleep, I was up and out of the flat by six thirty. As I walked onto the breakwater, I found myself glancing up at the sheer face of the hill and thinking of poor Merry. I shuddered and kept walking, trying to focus on exercising.

The beach was deserted and I managed to shave twenty seconds off yesterday's time, which I was thrilled with.

After doing my warm-down exercises, I angled my walk towards the firepit and saw that someone had already kicked sand over the remains of the last fire. I was closer to the trees now and looked along them but couldn't see any sign of the red tent, or whatever it was I'd seen before. Maybe the traveller had decided to move on.

I had hoped to bump into Zoe, to ask if the screams were unusual, but didn't see any sign of her. Perhaps she took Sunday mornings as a rest day.

I saw Boyd's daughter after I'd had my shower. She was at the patio table again, staring at her phone. Something in her posture made me think she wasn't happy and when Boyd came out and spoke to her, she shook her head and her shoulders rocked. He squatted awkwardly next to her and tried to put his arm around her shoulders, but she shook him off and went back into the cottage.

Will had been working on his borders again but was now looking over his shoulder. "Morning," he called. "Is everything okay?"

"Yes, thanks," Boyd said then went inside.

Will shrugged and went back to his gardening.

* * *

The doorbell rang mid-afternoon and, when I answered, Rita was on the step. Her husband, Patrick, was in the car and we waved at one another.

"I'm sorry to drop in on you like this," she said.

"Don't be silly, it's good to see you."

"How are things? I heard the news this morning, about the person who fell down the hill. Did you see anything?"

"Only when the emergency services turned up," I said and told her what had happened.

She listened intently and, when I mentioned seeing the yellow cagoule, she shook her head. "Oh, no, was it Merry?"

"I don't think it's been confirmed."

That's such a shame." She touched my arm. "But you're okay?"

"I'm fine, I was just a little shaken up at the time. I mean, Zoe and I were on the breakwater that morning."

Rita bit her lip. "That's just the way it goes," she said. "You know that."

"I do."

"Good. So, what've you been doing today?"

"I was just reading in the garden."

"I'm jealous, because it's the perfect weather for that. But, unfortunately, I'm playing the dutiful and attractive spouse." She gestured expansively at herself. "Patrick's lined up a meeting with some investors for the gallery, so we're wining and dining them at the Hilton on the edge of town." She didn't look happy at the prospect.

"You'll have a great time. Just focus on the wine and nibbles."

"I always do." She took a USB out of her clutch purse. "You have absolutely no need for this, but I needed an excuse because I wanted to check in and make sure you're okay and coping."

"I am. I even survived one of Amanda's parties."

She looked impressed. "Lucky you, that's a difficult ticket to get. So, what did you think of her?"

"That what you told me was spot on. Her husband isn't much better."

"Will? I always thought, if anything, he was a bit too nice."

"He was intimidating Flo."

"What?"

I told her what had happened, and she seemed genuinely surprised.

"How did Flo cope?"

"She was a bit frightened and angry, but also touched that I'd stepped in to help her."

Patrick tooted the horn. Rita threw him a glare and then turned back to me. "That arse would have a right fit if I honked my horn at him," she said through gritted teeth. "Actually, that reminds me. Monday is Flo's day in here, from ten to four. I'm sure she'll work around you, but you might want to get up and stretch your legs when she does the office."

"I never turn down a break."

"That's not true and you know it."

Patrick tooted the horn again and she waved her arm at him in a sharp angry gesture without looking.

"I saw Boyd and his daughter on Friday, and they missed Amanda's party on purpose. Doesn't he get on with her either?"

"Probably not, but then, she is his landlord." She paused. "Did you say his daughter was with him?"

Something about how she said it made me cautious. "Well, it's a young woman, mid to late twenties, so I assume it's his daughter."

"Yeah," Rita said, "she's not." She put her finger to her lips. "I'll tell you sometime, okay?"

"You said that before."

Patrick opened the car door and started to get out. He looked at me and shrugged resignedly.

"She's just coming," I called.

Rita didn't turn around. "The bugger's got out of his car, hasn't he?"

"He has. Go on, go and do the dutiful spouse thing and drink some wine on the company. And next time I see you, I want to be told everything about Boyd Manning."

"I'm not sure I can do that," she said and touched my arm. "You know where I am if you need anything."

She walked back to the car and shooed Patrick into it. He waved and I watched them drive away then went back into the garden.

* * *

Luca rang as I was browning mince.

"I can't stay for long," he said. "We're going to Fran's parents for dinner and her brother and sister will be there, *en famille*."

"That's okay, I'm just making spag bol for myself."

"Did you snap the pasta?"

"Of course." Dante taught me spaghetti should be cooked long, to be wrapped around the fork, and I'd adjusted my methods until our marriage was on its last legs, when I went back to my old way of snapping the strands. It used to drive him nuts.

"You know Papa was right, don't you? It is so much easier to eat."

"Don't you start," I said, good-naturedly. "Now, I'm fine and took it easy today, so go and enjoy your meal *en famille, amore mio*."

"I will. You enjoy your snapped pasta too. Take care, Mum. Fran sends her love."

"And mine to her," I said, and we ended the call.

Chapter 17

After my morning walk, where I cut another five seconds off my time, I showered, had breakfast and resisted the urge to look out at my neighbours. I wasn't voyeuristic at home and couldn't quite understand why I felt an almost compulsive need to look now. What did I expect to see that was so interesting?

I worked until nearly ten thirty when I took a mouthful of tea and discovered it had gone cold. After making a fresh cup, I worked through until lunchtime, when I made myself a sandwich and switched on the radio to catch the local news.

The lead item on Seagrave Sound was confirmation that the person who fell off the hill was Merry Baldwin. The reporter said that it was a terrible and tragic accident and that the police weren't treating her death as suspicious.

I switched the radio off and looked up the hill. I didn't really know her, but I felt a sense of sadness. Nobody deserved to die that way. My appetite had faded but I forced myself to eat my sandwich and read my novel while I did.

I put the plate into the dishwasher and avoided glancing at the hill, before going back into the office. I looked out the window and saw Scott on his patio, eating a Big Mac meal as he checked his phone.

That reminded me to check my own phone, but there were no messages or missed calls. I wondered when Flo would turn up.

Rita rang at a little after four. "How are you?"

"I'm okay."

"I heard the news at lunchtime, about Merry."

"Yeah."

"It's awful," she said. "She was up there every day, but I suppose she must have missed a step or something."

"I know. I've tried to avoid looking up there today."

"On the other hand, at least she passed away in a place she loved." She clicked her tongue. "That wasn't as positive when I said it as it sounded in my head."

"We'll change the subject then," I said. "How was the investors meal?"

"Too long and painfully pretentious, but I had half a bottle of wine to myself, so I was happy. Patrick said the investors were happy to meet me."

"That's a good result then." I checked my watch. "Did you hear from Flo today? I've been home all day and haven't seen her."

"That's odd. Give me a minute and I'll ring her."

She rang back two minutes later. "No answer, so I left a message. It's not like her to miss a session."

"Maybe she got a better offer."

"Yeah," Rita mused. "I'll let you know when I hear anything."

We said our goodbyes and I worked through until five. When I got up and stretched, I saw the gardens were empty, but Boyd's bedroom window was open.

"Bloody hell," I muttered. "I'm even aware of when people open their windows."

I packed away, sneaked one last look out the window and the doorbell rang, making me jump. For one weird, delirious moment, I thought it might be Will or Scott, coming round to tell me off for spying on them. I went downstairs and saw my caller through the frosted glass, wearing a blue-and-white jacket. I opened the door and he backed away a couple of steps as I opened it.

"Hi," I said.

Jonny was about six feet tall, with a strong jawline and those striking cheekbones some young men get when they lose their teenage puppy fat. His hair was shaved at the sides and wild on top, but partly flattened, probably by the crash helmet he held under one arm. His jacket and jeans looked too big for him. He didn't look much older than Luca.

"I'm really sorry to bother you, but are you Carrie?"

"I am. You're Jonny, I take it?"

He looked surprised, as if I'd pulled off a grand magic trick. "Yes, I'm Jonny Stewart. How did you know?"

"I recognised your jacket. It's quite distinctive."

"Thanks. Anyway, Flo told me what happened on Friday and said you'd helped her out."

"I did what I could."

"No, you did a good thing," he said firmly. "Flo's lovely but doesn't always stand up for herself."

"I think, in that situation, it might have been difficult."

"Yeah, you're probably right."

We looked at one another for a few moments and I wondered if he'd called round to thank me but now didn't know what to say. "Is there something I can do for you?"

"Actually, there is." He sounded a little apprehensive. "Have you seen Flo today?"

"I'm afraid not. She hasn't turned up."

He shook his head and bit his lower lip. "Oh, shit."

"Is everything okay?"

"I don't think so," he said. "I think Flo's gone missing."

"Are you sure?

"No, not exactly. I dropped her off on Friday and we were supposed to go out later that night, but she cancelled and said something had come up. I figured it was her mum, because she's always cramming Flo's plans. So I said I'd pick her up on Saturday to go bowling, but when I got to her house, her mum asked me where she was. I said, like, I didn't know but, apparently, she went out Friday and didn't come home. She sometimes stays over at mine, so her mum didn't think there was anything odd, except Flo didn't turn up on Saturday morning to take Roxy out."

"Her little sister?"

"Yes, and that's really unusual because Flo always takes Roxy to her swimming lessons. Never fails. She does everything for that kid and would never let her down. I said as much but her mum didn't believe me and reckoned it was all my fault."

I got the sense there was something else he wanted to say, so I kept quiet.

"I get that a lot," he said after a while and shrugged.

"You mean, people not believing you?"

Jonny shrugged. "I was a badman, you know?" He ran a hand through his hair, fluffing it up, then shook his head. "Nothing serious, just a bit of thieving and some drugs, but that was the old me. I got myself sorted when I met Flo and we're doing things differently."

He sounded proud of his efforts. "Good for you," I said. "It's not easy."

"It wasn't, but she steered me right. So, if you see her, can you let me know?"

"I could, if you give me your number."

"Tell me yours and I'll call you."

I told him and he dabbed the number quickly. My phone, sitting upstairs on the countertop, rang. "There we go," I said.

"Mint. If I hear anything, I'll let you know." He pulled the moped off its kickstand. "Thanks for being so nice about this, Carrie."

"You're welcome. I'm sure you'll find her quickly."

"Hopefully," he said. He pulled on his helmet and started the moped.

I watched him go, feeling a little tingle of my sixth sense. My mind was trying to find a link between what he'd told me and what I knew about Friday evening. Ordinarily, I wouldn't have tried to make a connection because Flo perhaps needed some space to get her thoughts together, but that didn't make sense with the Roxy situation. From what Flo and now Jonny had said, she'd never let her little sister down.

Chapter 18

On Tuesday morning, I paused on the breakwater and looked at the loop of police tape, strung between two poles at that base of the hill, then moved onto the beach. To keep my focus and up my pace, I was wearing headphones and had cued up Donna Summer, so I could walk to the beat. I shaved ten seconds off my previous best, though it made my legs ache.

The day was bright and clear, with few clouds in a cerulean sky. I worked in the office during the morning and checked out the window every now and again, to see if there was any sign of Flo doing her cleaning. I didn't see anything of her at all and, while that didn't necessarily raise red flags, it felt off.

After lunch, I took my laptop downstairs to work al fresco and was enjoying the sun on my face when Rita rang.

"Hi," I said and decided to rub it in. "I'm working outside in this glorious weather."

"We need to get you back into the office sharpish then, to suffer with the rest of us. It's horribly stuffy here today."

"That's not a very nice thing to say to an employee on sick leave."

"You're probably right, but she's being a smug cow. Anyway, I rang to see if Flo came in today."

"Nope, and I've been looking out for her."

"That's very odd, because she's still not answering her phone or responding to voicemail."

"Her boyfriend came by last night and thinks she's gone missing."

"Does he think she's missing or run away?"

"He's not sure," I said and told her about Roxy. "Bearing that in mind, I doubt she'd run away."

"She wouldn't be the first person to do so," Rita said.

We both knew the statistics, even if Flo was edging out of the age range. Every year, thousands of people are reported missing, with a considerable number being under eighteen. The figures were higher from coastal towns.

"True," I said.

"Either way, there's not a lot we can do. She's an adult and can take off for pastures new if she wants."

"I know. And she comes across as a tough cookie, but I think there's a soft centre there too."

"You're right." Rita sighed. "But as much as we'd like to, we can't save everyone, Carrie. Listen, I have to go, but let's keep one another posted on the situation, yeah?"

* * *

"Hey, Carrie!" Zoe took me by surprise, peering through a gap in the fence. "Hope you're not working too hard."

"Trying not to."

"Good. I'm just off for a run but wanted to see you. Do you have any plans for tonight?"

"No, though I'm open to the idea of a handsome, witty man in his fifties inviting me to dinner."

"Well, I can't promise that, but Scott's doing a barbecue and it'd be great if you could join us."

While I was touched to be invited, I wasn't so keen to spend another evening with her in-laws. "Will you have enough food?"

"Easily," she said, as if anticipating my question. "I picked up the meat from Seagrave on my way home and planned to freeze half of it, because it'll just be the three of us. We don't do everything with Amanda, you know."

That was a much better proposition. "I think I could make it."

"Excellent. See you at our place for seven."

"I look forward to it. Enjoy your run."

"I'll try."

After I clocked off, I took the laptop and reports up to the flat and put them on the office desk. A murmur of conversation drifted through the window, and I looked out to see Amanda and Will on their patio.

"You were the one who said he could use the cottage," Will said, "when he got into his latest round of trouble."

"So it's my fault he's leeching off us?"

"I didn't say that, my love, you did." The way he said the word 'love' sounded like it had been marinated in sarcasm.

"And speaking of leeching, where the hell is Flo?"

Will glanced furtively at the office window and I took a step back.

"I haven't seen her, and Boyd told me this morning she hadn't been to his place, either."

"Well, these bloody windows aren't going to clean themselves," she said and took a step towards him. "What did you do, Will?"

"What're you talking about?"

"You know what I'm talking about."

"I really don't, Amanda."

She seemed to scrutinise his face then turned on her heel and went into the cottage. He followed her a few moments later.

Chapter 19

I didn't have any more wine, so I picked some wild flowers from the garden and fashioned a little bouquet, which I presented to Zoe when she opened the door.

"Oh, they're lovely," she said and invited me in.

We went into the kitchen where Scott stood at the range, dunking chicken breasts into a marinade. The room smelled gorgeous.

"Hey, Carrie," he said, glancing over his shoulder. "I hope you're ready for some great food."

"I am."

"Good stuff. Grab a drink and some sun."

Zoe and I went out onto the patio. A smart speaker in the middle of the table played rock music I couldn't quite place, and several plastic bowls were filled with salad. Some thick burgers were cooking on the grill.

"Red, white or a beer?" Zoe asked.

"A white would be nice."

She poured us each a glass and then gestured for me to sit down. I chose a chair with my back to the fence separating their patio from Amanda's. Zoe sat next to me.

"Cheers," she said, and we touched glasses. "It's so nice to have pleasant female company, for a change."

"Now, now," said Scott as he came out carrying a Pyrex dish. He put it on the table and turned the burgers. Fat hissed on the coals. "Just because your usual female company is my sister."

"You see," said Zoe. "I told you their relationship was a bit strained."

"It has its moments," he said and put three chicken breasts on the grill.

We watched him cook and talked about our exercise routines. Zoe seemed impressed that my walk times were speeding up so quickly.

"We're ready for the rolls now, love," Scott said.

Zoe went to get a plate of buttered rolls from the kitchen and stood by the barbecue as Scott laid burgers on three of them.

"Here you go," he said and handed me a plate. "Tuck in."

The burger tasted as good as it looked. We ate in silence and, after Scott finished his, he checked the chicken. "A breast each?" he asked, and we agreed.

"What about us?" asked Amanda.

Startled, I looked over my shoulder and saw her leaning around the fence. She didn't look happy, and I felt caught in the middle of something I didn't want to be in, with tension almost tangible in the air.

"I called round," Scott said, sounding panicked, "but no one answered."

"Well, I was in," she said. "In fact, I was cleaning the windows because Flo hasn't bloody turned up."

"If I'd seen you leaning out the window, I would have come in and shoved you through."

"You're not funny, Scott," she said, drily. Her *s* was a little soft, like she'd already had a glass or two.

"We'll have to agree to disagree on that," he said and offered her a thin-lipped smile.

Will appeared behind Amanda. "Hello," he said, but blanched when he caught sight of me.

"Evening, Will," Scott said. "I suppose you'd like to join us?"

"I wouldn't want to put you out," Amanda said, pointedly.

"You aren't," Scott replied, sounding very insincere.

Amanda made a harrumphing sound and she and Will walked away. A few moments later, the doorbell rang and Scott went to open the door.

"I'm sorry about this," Zoe whispered. "You can leave if you want to."

"It's hardly fair, you'll be on your own then."

"This always happens," she said.

Scott came back through with Amanda and Will. She stumbled on the step, and he caught her arm. Once she regained her balance, she shook him off and sat in the chair opposite mine. After nodding to Zoe, she smiled warmly at me.

"How's the ticker, Carrie?"

"Holding up, Amanda, thanks for asking. How are you?"

"Feeling unloved," she said. "Zoe tells me you're walking on the beach in the mornings. Don't forget to take it steady as you rebuild your stamina."

"I'll do that," I said.

She glanced at Will. "And what're you doing, standing around like a spare part."

"I'm just–"

"Sit down," she said dismissively, then turned to Scott. "How's that chicken coming along?"

"It's cooking," he said.

Amanda stood up and held the back of her chair as if steadying herself. "Can I have a word, baby brother?" she said, as if it was a foregone conclusion she could.

"Can't it wait?" Scott turned one of the breasts over. "I'm a bit busy."

"No, darling, it can't wait."

He turned over another breast then looked at her. "Why don't we do this another time, eh? Perhaps when you've not had a little drinky in the afternoon."

"I'm not drunk," she said, indignantly.

Zoe and I exchanged glances then looked back at the warring siblings. It felt horribly like watching an accident in slow motion.

"Well you sound it and you're embarrassing yourself and me." He sounded like he was struggling to stay calm. "We have a guest."

Amanda barked a laugh. "I don't think you really want to talk about who's more of an embarrassment, do you?"

They looked at one another for a moment and the tension seemed to ratchet up.

"You're a bitch," he said.

"And you're a bastard. Now, can I have a word?"

"For fuck's sake," he muttered and gave the tongs to Zoe who stood up and moved towards the barbecue as Scott led his sister into the kitchen.

When we'd moved far enough away that Zoe probably wouldn't hear him, Will leaned over and touched my elbow gently. "Can I have a word?"

My skin bristled and I moved my arm away. "Please don't touch me."

"What?"

"If you touch me again," I said, feeling uneasy at his proximity, "I will slap you."

"I'd like to talk about Friday night."

"I'd rather not." I resented being put on the spot by him.

"Listen, Carrie, whatever you think you saw or heard, it's not what you think it was."

"You know what I saw and heard, *Will*." I put emphasis on his name.

"What you *think* you saw and heard, you mean?"

I felt a flash of anger that warmed across my chest. "I saw you speaking to a young woman you'd trapped and who clearly didn't want to be there. So, which part of that do I have wrong?"

"So, you're not willing to listen to my point of view?" He shook his head sadly. "I thought, as a professional, that you'd keep an open mind, but I was wrong. I understand you're a do-gooder, Carrie, but you and your Wonder Woman cape aren't needed here."

"A do-gooder?"

"Yes, you lefty social workers are all the bloody same."

The blanket dismissal almost made me laugh. "You're not the first person who's made that mistake, Will, but if you do believe that, then you won't be listening to my point of view either, will you?"

He looked as though I'd slapped him and I was about to stand up when someone pounded on the door.

"Shit," Zoe muttered. "What now?"

"I'll get it," I said.

Scott beat me to it. I was only halfway across the kitchen when he stepped into the hall and opened the door.

"What do you want?" he asked.

"Can I come in?" I couldn't see him but I knew it was Jonny.

"We've got people here, mate. Can it wait?"

"Not really, no."

Scott paused for a moment then let Jonny in and gestured for him to go through to the kitchen. Amanda came out of the lounge.

"What does he want?" she asked.

"No idea," said Scott.

Jonny nodded when he saw me.

"Come on," Scott said. "Everyone's outside."

We all went out onto the patio and I noticed Will had moved down the garden, as if worried about what was going to be said.

"What's up?" Scott asked. "We haven't got enough to feed you."

"I'm not hungry," Jonny said. He looked nervous.

"Have you been drinking?" Amanda asked.

"A little," he said.

"And you rode that shitty moped of yours? We should call the police," said Amanda.

"Oh, pipe down," said Scott.

"Why don't we let him talk?" I asked. Jonny looked like a man who knew he'd made a bad decision and wanted to back away from it.

"I need to know about Flo," he said.

"Well she's not here," said Scott.

"She hasn't been here since the weekend," said Amanda. "I had to clean my own bloody windows today."

"She's not here, Jonny," I said.

"I know that," he said and fixed his gaze on me. I didn't mind. I was probably the only person here sympathetic to him, and if he needed that focus, then so be it. "But I need to know where she is."

"Don't you know where she is?" Scott asked. He held out his hand and Zoe gave him the tongs. "I mean, she hasn't turned up for work in two days. Did you two have an argument or something?"

"No, we were fine. But I'm worried about her."

"Yeah, I'm sure you are, but we haven't seen her since the party."

"That's right," said Amanda. "Carrie left with her, so maybe you need to ask her."

"I already did," said Jonny. "They were talking when I came to pick Flo up."

"Hold on," said Zoe. "That means you saw her last."

"Yeah, but that was Friday night. I wanted to make sure she hadn't come back to work."

"You're an idiot," said Amanda. "She hasn't been here since Friday and when she does show her silly little head again, she's not going to like what I have to say to her."

"Hey," said Jonny and took a step toward Amanda.

Scott moved between them and so did I. Jonny might think he was being chivalrous to Flo, but he was likely to get himself into real trouble if he tried anything.

"Okay," I said. "This isn't helping anybody. Let me take Jonny away, then everyone can get back to their barbecue."

"What about you, though?" Zoe asked.

"I had the burger, I'm fine." I held Jonny's arm. "Come on, let's go."

He looked at all of us without moving.

"Come on," I said, more forcefully. I pulled him towards the patio doors. "Thanks for the food, Scott, and thanks for inviting me, Zoe."

"That's fine," she said. "We'll talk tomorrow."

I led Jonny out of the cottage and closed the door behind me. He stood, staring into space, and his eyes glistened with unshed tears. His moped was across the road, at an angle to the kerb that made it look like he'd abandoned rather than parked it.

"Hey," I said. "Are you okay?"

He swallowed and shook his head lightly.

"I didn't think so. Let's go back to my flat and I'll make you a strong coffee."

Chapter 20

Jonny sat on the sofa and picked up my book.

"Is this good?" he asked.

"I'm enjoying it."

"What's it about?"

"A private detective called Kinsey Millhone, who has to investigate when someone gets killed."

"Oh," he said and put it down.

The kettle boiled and I made him a strong coffee and me a cup of tea and carried them through to the lounge. I put them both on the coffee table then sat at the opposite end of the sofa.

Jonny looked at the hot drinks. "Thanks, but I don't really need this. I only had a couple of beers."

"And rode your bike," I pointed out. "That's risky if you're a mechanic, isn't it? It's hard to move cars around if you're banned from driving."

"Yeah, but I thought the beer might chill me out. Flo's been on my mind all weekend, I'm worried sick about her."

"You still haven't heard anything from her?"

"Nope. Nor has her mum."

"Have you reported her missing to the police?"

He looked at me like I'd asked the stupidest question in the world. "Of course I did. Not that they seemed all that bothered."

"So why come here tonight? Did you really think she'd come to work and not let you, or her family, know she was okay?"

"Where else would she be? She didn't take anything from home, no clothes or nothing and Roxy's still there and there's no way she'd leave her." He looked at me intently. "She wouldn't leave me, Carrie. We had plans to get away. This place hasn't done either of us any favours, so once I'd got some experience and we'd saved some money, we were going to leave."

"So she would have left Roxy then?"

"No, Flo's mum said we could have her at weekends and in the school holidays."

"What?" The very idea chilled me.

"It's awful, isn't it?" he asked, shaking his head. "But there's a lot of noise in that house."

I couldn't condemn the woman because I didn't know her reasons or situation. "That doesn't explain why you came back here."

"Because I don't think she ran off." He stood up abruptly and walked over to the window. The low sun coloured his face amber. "I don't think she's missing by choice."

I hadn't expected him to say that. "You think someone is holding her against her will here?"

"I don't know." Jonny threw out his arms and stalked over to the kitchenette. "It all seemed to make sense in my head, but it sounds fucking stupid now you've said it out loud." He leaned against the counter for a moment or two. "You must think I'm some kind of nutter, but I'm really not."

"I don't think that at all," I said. He didn't sound drunk or seem paranoid. "But I'm curious as to how you came to the idea she's here."

"Okay." He came and sat on the coffee table, hands on his knees. He looked at me intently. "Flo told me that everyone here is a bit odd and, cleaning their houses, she learned all kinds of things. All their secrets."

"Like what?"

He shrugged. "She never told me exactly, just bits and pieces. Like the woman doctor is a real cow."

"I wouldn't disagree with that," I said, then decided to push my luck. "What did she say about her husband?"

"He made her uncomfortable, because he was weird and looked at her oddly sometimes. She didn't like it when it was just him and her in the house. Then there's the bloke at the end, not the one who had the party."

"Boyd?"

"Yeah, she said he was slimy."

That didn't surprise me, given her reaction to him when I first arrived, though I didn't get any sense of him giving off a vibe that would make young women uncomfortable. But then, Rita had her issue with him too, didn't she? "Did she say why?"

"No. I did ask about him because, well, he's a good-looking bloke and he's single and he's clearly got some serious money."

He couldn't hide his jealousy and I wondered if Flo had called him slimy or maybe Jonny was projecting onto Boyd.

"He gave her the creeps," he said. "She found handcuffs in his place and the kind of whip a jockey would use. I mean, who does that in real life?"

I wanted to tell him that plenty of people probably did. I'd even indulged once or twice, though it didn't do much for me. But who cared if Boyd was into bondage? It didn't necessarily make him a bad person.

"How about Scott?"

"She liked him because he was nice to her. Nicer than his wife was, at any rate."

"Zoe wasn't nice to Flo?" That definitely didn't sound right.

"So she said."

"And you think one of these people had a hand in her going missing? Are you sure she wasn't depressed or worried?"

He threw his arms up in despair. "I don't know," he said sharply.

"Could she have gone to visit someone and forgot to say?"

"She's not answering her phone, plus her moped's knackered and her mum takes so much rent off her, she can't afford to fix it." He shook his head. "She's gone, Carrie, and I think something's happened to her. We need to find her."

"We?"

"Yes, if you'll help me. I'm rubbish at doing anything like this, my idea of finding her is just riding all over Seagrave and looking. Flo said you were a good person and, with you being a social worker and all, I thought people might tell you stuff they wouldn't tell me."

"I don't know if you've ever met a social worker before, Jonny, but we're not private detectives. I only read crime; I don't solve it."

"But social workers are always on the news getting involved with people and helping out." He looked at me intently. "Isn't there a thing that, if I tell you someone's in trouble, you have to help?"

It took a moment to figure out what he meant. "I don't have a duty of care to Flo, Jonny. Professionally, people leave the system when they're eighteen so she's out of jurisdiction."

"Professionally, but what about as a friend?" He bit the inside of his cheek. "I know you've only known us a couple of days but, if you knew Flo was in trouble, you'd help her, wouldn't you?"

He'd played me into a corner. "You little shit," I said. I wasn't sure I believed him, but he seemed so sure, and I'd definitely witnessed something untoward with Flo and Will. "I can't really turn that down, can I? But if I help you, there must be caveats."

"I don't know what that means."

"They're conditions on me helping you. I need to look after my health, so I can't do anything too energetic and won't be able to chase all over town with you. Plus, I'm not allowed to drive at the moment, so don't expect a taxi service."

"I have a spare crash helmet," he said, as if that solved everything. "We're golden, Carrie."

"So, what's your plan?"

He shrugged. "We can use some of your contacts and some of mine and try to figure it out."

It wasn't much, but it might be enough to make a start.

Chapter 21

I watched Jonny ride away and wasn't quite able to shake the feeling I'd got dragged into something I wouldn't be able to help with. I was concerned for Flo but, surely, the odds were far more likely she'd gone somewhere of her own accord.

Fresh air always helped me to think better, so I put on my trainers and went out. The evening was drawing in and the sky was a glorious mix of oranges and pinks. There wasn't much noise coming from the barbecue, just a low murmur of conversation. As I walked over the bridge, I thought it might help to get a second opinion, so I rang Rita.

"Is everything alright?" she asked with concern.

"Yes, I'm fine, thanks. I just wondered if you'd heard anything from Flo."

"Not a word, which does feel odd. How about you?"

"Nothing," I said and told her everything, including Jonny's fears.

"Please don't tell me you got yourself involved, Carrie."

"I didn't see that I had a lot of choice, to be honest."

"Nonsense, you always have a choice. Come on, Carrie, you need to take it easy."

"Once he sees I'm not an ace investigator, I'm sure he'll find another assistant, but I can't leave it." I walked onto the breakwater. The tide was in and lapping at the walls. "And you wouldn't be able to in my position either, would you? I mean, you yourself said it's odd that she's just disappeared."

"You're right," she said and sighed, perhaps recognising that she couldn't change my mind. "It does seem out of character for her and the issue with her sister is a niggle."

"Do you know if she's ever been in the system?" I wasn't sure if that would be a help, but it would give me somewhere to start.

"I could have a look."

"Thank you," I said. "You do understand why I can't turn my back on this, don't you?"

"Of course I do and now I can't turn my back either, can I?" Rita sighed again. "I'll check in the morning but don't turn all *Magnum PI* on me. I want you back to full health as soon as possible and back in the office."

"Yes, boss," I said briskly.

"Good, that's what I like to hear." I heard another voice, muffled enough that I couldn't make out what they said.

"Yes, I'm just on the phone to Carrie." Another muffled noise. "She's fine. Patrick sends his love," she said.

"Any news on the potential gallery investors?"

"No idea. Unless I'm being wined and dined, I'm not too bothered."

We said our goodbyes and ended the call. I watched the sky until it faded into darkness and my legs got cold enough to make me shiver.

I had to use my torch app to get safely across the bridge and, as I walked up the path, I saw someone come around the corner of the cottages. It took a moment to realise it was Boyd and we met just outside my front door.

"How's the beach?" he asked.

"Underwater. It'll be good if you're planning to have a paddle."

"I hadn't planned to, I just wanted to get some air."

"Same here." The chill had increased, and I rubbed my arms.

"Did you hear the argument at that party earlier?"

"Some of it," I said.

"It didn't get any better when Amanda and Will got home, though that's not unusual. I don't know how he puts up with her, to be honest. She seems to take great delight in picking fault with everything he says or does, though she's not much better with Scott." He rubbed his chin. "Each to their own, though, eh? I mean, she's alright with me, so I'm alright with her."

"That didn't stop you avoiding her party on Friday though, did it?" I teased.

"Yeah, thanks for not dobbing me in." He smiled. "I couldn't face it. I hadn't seen Kay all week and I didn't feel like sharing her."

"Is that your daughter?"

He laughed. "No, she's my partner, but I get that a lot. Amanda's not impressed with the age gap and has made it plain I was in my early twenties when Kay was born, as if I didn't know that." He tilted his head and the streetlight caught the contours of his face. He was a very handsome man. "But, hey, age is just a number, isn't it?"

"I suppose."

"Amanda doesn't make her feel welcome either, which can be awkward. And Will gives her the chills, for some reason."

"He seems harmless enough to me," I said, because it seemed like a good way to fish for information.

"And me, but she reckons he's creepy, even though she can't quite explain why."

I shivered strongly enough for him to notice.

"I'd better let you go. The nights get cold quickly this close to the water, so if you're out for a walk it's best to wear your layers."

"You sound like my dad."

"That's what Kay says and she's probably right. It was lovely to see you, Carrie. I hope we get a chance to talk again, when you're not shivering."

Chapter 22

I stood on the breakwater as dawn broke, looking out to sea and feeling a little unsettled.

I'd spent a lot of time the previous night trying to make sense of the Flo situation but hadn't come to any conclusions and I didn't have any now either. I hoped my power walk would reinvigorate me.

A light mist swirled around my feet, but the morning wasn't as chilly as I'd expected. I tied my fleece around my waist, put on my headphones, set the timer and walked. I managed to shave off another fifteen seconds and had built up a light sweat by the time I reached the river. Unfortunately, I still didn't have any conclusions.

Zoe was running towards me as I walked back to the breakwater, and she waited for me at the steps as she did her warm-down stretches.

"Morning," she said brightly.

"Morning. I didn't think you ran early on weekdays."

"It's a slight change of plan. Since Scott was so wound-up last night, he suggested I take a day off and go up to Cromer with him. He's got a business meeting for an hour or so, then we can have some quiet time to ourselves and go for a walk, and just take it easy." She gestured for me to go up the steps first. "In fact, I need to apologise to you too. I absolutely did not expect that to happen."

"It's hardly your fault."

"But you wouldn't have got involved if you weren't there. Flo's boyfriend would have still turned up, though, and things would have been worse if you weren't there to guide him away." She touched my arm. "So, what happened with him?"

I told her about taking him back to my flat, but not what we discussed. Partly because she was involved with the people he was suspicious of, but mostly because he trusted me and I didn't want to betray that.

"As annoyed as I was at him turning up, I felt sorry for him," she said. "He seems like such a lost soul."

It was the perfect description. "You're right."

"It's just a shame he's a little misguided."

The spike in her voice made me look at her. "What do you mean?"

"I probably shouldn't say this, because I didn't know her particularly well, but Flo isn't the angel he thinks she is. I saw her being very flirty with Scott and Boyd."

"Really?"

"Yes. I was reading on the patio and Boyd was in his garden. He'd taken his shirt off and, I'll admit, looked good, but Flo was all over him, complimenting him on his abs and asking if she could stroke them. He did his level best to change the subject, but she trailed around after him and it made me cringe."

It didn't seem in keeping with the Flo I recognised but what would Zoe gain by saying something untrue?

"Worse than that, though, was when I came home early from work one day. Flo and Scott were on our patio, sitting so close their legs touched and she was laughing too hard at his jokes. She's also very tactile with him."

"Did he try and stop her?"

Zoe acknowledged the question with a tilt of her head. "I know, it takes two to tango and he wasn't trying to push her away, but it almost felt like I'd stumbled across something that had already been established. When I appeared, she moved like someone had shot her. Scott and I had a row that night – he said I should trust him, I said he needed to set boundaries."

Had Zoe misread the situation? Flo hadn't struck me as being flirty but if she was, would I have seen it? The Boyd situation raised questions too, because it didn't fit with what Flo told me and how I'd seen her react to the man. Or was that reaction because Boyd had turned her down?

"I didn't realise she was like that," I said.

"Why would you? And even if her boyfriend did, he'd hardly broadcast it, would he?"

"Probably not, plus he wasn't thinking straight, and Amanda didn't help matters."

"She can be a spiteful bloody cow, especially when she's got a drink in her." She glanced at me. "I shouldn't say that, really, should I, but she thrives on being unhappy."

"Did Scott tell you what she wanted to discuss last night?"

"Nope, as per usual."

We crossed the bridge and I tried to circle the conversation back. "Did you ever see Flo flirting with Will?"

Zoe pulled a face. "No, yuck, I didn't. And knowing what Amanda's like, why would you put yourself in the firing line?"

"She could have done it on the quiet."

"That's true. I mean, he's pleasant enough but" – she shuddered – "the bloke must be fifty years older than her."

"Scott doesn't seem overly struck with him."

"I think some of that is due to Amanda, and then Will got involved in something at the hospital and had to retire with immediate effect."

"That doesn't sound good."

She shrugged, clearly not interested. "It didn't affect me, so I never pressed Scott to find out what happened. I thought, for a while, it's why Amanda runs him down, but Scott reckons she's always been like that. My mum always used to say this phrase, 'there's nowt as queer as folk', and it seems perfect for Amanda and Will."

We'd reached my flat and I got the sense there was more we could talk about. "Did you want to come in for a cuppa?"

She checked her watch. "No, I'd better get showered and sorted. I think Scott's planning to buy me breakfast when we're out."

"Lucky you," I said. "Enjoy your day."

"You too, Carrie."

Chapter 23

Jonny rang me mid-morning. "Can you spare me an hour or so today?"

"Why?" I asked, with suspicion. "You do realise we're both supposed to be working today, don't you?"

"Yes, but I rang Flo's mum and she's agreed I can take you round to speak to her."

"What? You can't spring stuff like that on people."

"I'm sorry, Carrie, but I couldn't think of anything else to do."

"What am I going to talk to her about?"

"I don't know, but you'll think of something, and it'll make her see I'm serious. And if you meet Roxy, you'll know Flo didn't go off on her own."

His assumption I'd do it annoyed me and I couldn't imagine Flo's mother was happy having a random stranger enquiring why her child had gone missing. Plus, there was the question of how the visit would be viewed, if this project overlapped with my professional life. "Did you tell her I was a social worker?"

"No," he scoffed. "Even I'm not that stupid, Carrie. I told her you were a friend of mine who might be able to help."

I sighed. It didn't seem like that great an idea, but I still hadn't had a better one. I checked the calendar on the laptop. "I can go now but I'll need to be back in a couple of hours for a Zoom meeting."

"You will be. I can come and get you in about ten minutes. Thank you so much for this, Carrie."

He ended the call before I could respond.

* * *

It had been a long time since I was a pillion passenger, but Jonny was a good rider, and I didn't feel unsafe. We followed the main road into Seagrave, and he weaved between cars at traffic lights, only having to stop once or twice, but expertly balancing us each time. He cut through a run of side streets until we came to a large estate on the far side of town near the docks.

"It's the Duncan Jackson estate," he said, turning his head to one side so I could hear him.

"Okay," I replied. It didn't mean anything to me.

We followed a series of roads through the estate, some made narrower than others by badly parked cars and vans. A lot of the houses were well maintained while others looked like they were on the verge of dereliction; I recognised the look from estates in Norwich.

We pulled up at the kerb in front of a row of five slim houses and curtains twitched at several windows with our arrival.

"That's the one," he said and pointed to the house at the far end.

The front garden grass was short and mostly hidden by bright, plastic children's toys that were old but well-loved. Next door's garden had a motorbike skeleton in it with grass and weeds growing around the metal.

Jonny helped me off then pulled the moped onto its kickstand. I gave him my helmet and ran my fingers through my hair to try and give it a bit of life. "After you," I said.

He held the helmets by the chin strap, and I followed him up the path. There was a small piece of faded cardboard taped in one corner of the glass panel on the door.

Jonny rang the doorbell then stepped back to stand next to me. "Val's not overly keen on me," he said, sotto voce.

"I assume Val is Flo's mum."

"She is."

"Why isn't she keen on you?"

He didn't have a chance to answer because the door opened. A woman who looked like a slightly older version of Flo, but with long dark hair, regarded us coolly. "Alright, Jonny?"

"Uh-huh, how're you Agnes?"

"Been better." She turned her attention to me and raised her eyebrows, as if in a prompt.

"I'm Carrie Riccioni," I said.

"She's a social worker," Jonny added unhelpfully.

I glared at him.

"We don't need a social worker here," Agnes said. "And I already have my own."

I held up a hand. "I'm not here officially."

"Shit, Jonny," she muttered, as if she hadn't heard me. "What're you doing?"

"He's concerned about Flo," I said.

"Like we aren't?" she asked.

"Of course you are," I said. "Do you have any idea where she might be?"

"No."

"It's okay," Jonny said. "I spoke to your mum. She knows I'm coming."

Agnes looked like she didn't believe him and it took her a few moments to stand to one side and push the door wide. "If you're fucking about, I'll kill you." She gestured for us to go through and I followed Jonny through a porch overloaded with coats and shoes into a lounge.

The room was dominated by a couch and easy chair with a big television mounted on the chimney breast. The alcoves to either side were filled with toys and DVD cases. Two little girls, who looked to be three or four, sat in the middle of the room playing a game with some dolls. They only gave us a cursory glance.

"Mum's through there," said Agnes.

The room was open in the far corner and led to a small hallway, from which the stairs rose sharply on my right. The hallway ended at a kitchen-cum-dining room the same size as the lounge. A woman who looked my age sat at the table with an infant on her knee. The child was chewing on a teething ring and looked happy enough, even though her bib was soaked with saliva.

"Here we go, Mum," said Agnes as she sat next to her mother. "Jonny's brought a social worker to see us."

"Has he now?" She looked at me suspiciously. "I'm Val."

"I'm Carrie and I'm not here as a social worker."

Val's eyes narrowed for a moment, as if she was assessing whether I was a liar or not. "Agnes, clear one of those chairs so Carrie can sit down."

Agnes put a handful of papers and toys on the floor. "Do you want me here or shall I go and watch the girls?"

"Go," said Val.

Agnes went through to the lounge and Jonny leaned against the wall like a spare part.

"You might as well bugger off and have a smoke or something," Val told him.

"Okay," he said, amiably enough. "See you in a bit."

He followed Agnes out of the room and Val jogged the child on her lap for a moment or two.

"Thank you for seeing me," I said.

Val shrugged. The child looked at me as she chewed noisily on her ring. "Jonny said you were going to help him look for Flo. He didn't say you were a fucking social worker."

"I am only trying to help. I talked with Flo, and she seems a lovely young woman, but Jonny seems sure she hasn't just left Seagrave."

"That's as maybe, but Jonny's a bit of a romantic fool and that sometimes changes the way you think."

I frowned. "In what way?"

Val ran her thumb down the side of her mouth. "Flo's a good girl. She's not booksmart, but she's got her head screwed on and knows how to take care of herself. Our Agnes already had Dottie by the time she was Flo's age and, believe you me, having a baby when you're in your teens doesn't exactly set you up for the better things in life." She raised her free hand as if gesturing to her own house. "I did try to warn them. But our Flo's always said her future lay somewhere other than Seagrave and, I have to say, I agree with her."

"So where did she think it lay?"

"How should I know?" she asked and shrugged one shoulder. "Are you a mum, Carrie?"

"I am. My son's on his placement year in Paris."

"Fancy," she said. "Have you been out to see him?"

"No. He doesn't want me out there, cramping his style."

"Do you talk much?"

"More so since my heart attack, but probably once a week before that."

"You had a heart attack?"

"A couple of weeks back. I'm recuperating at Miller's Point, that's how I met Flo."

Val visibly relaxed, as if my issue made me more human. "Me and Flo don't talk much anymore but then, it's difficult to have quiet conversations in a full house like this." She gave a quick, humourless smile. "I don't know her plans and I know how it must look, me not knowing and her living in a house full of kids, but she was loved. If she has run away, it's not because she wasn't loved."

She sounded sincere and anguished. "I don't doubt it, Val."

She jiggled the baby and tickled under her chin. "Plus, we see a lot of Ruby and Dottie too…"

"Ruby?"

"This little munchkin."

"Oh," I said. "I thought this was Dottie."

"No, Dottie's in the other room, with my littlest."

I tried to tamp down my surprise before it showed. If it did, Val didn't react. Maybe I'd got her age all wrong.

"Agnes brings them around most days," she continued, "which is why it gets a little bit crowded here. Normally, it's three kids, including Flo, plus me and my partner."

"Is Agnes your eldest?"

"Uh-huh, and she's repaid me telling her to be careful by making me a grandmother. She's twenty-one now." So even if Val was twenty when she had Agnes, that made her only forty-one now. "Flo was next and then we had Peter and Richard." She looked pained for a moment. "They live with their father. He wasn't interested in girls and after we had Roxy, he decided he'd had enough, so we got divorced and he took the boys with him. Then, with number two, I had Maddie, who you saw in the other room."

"Flo talked fondly of Roxy."

"Oh, she loves that girl beyond all reason and has no problem sharing a bedroom with her. I can't imagine it's easy, having an eight-year-old all over your stuff, but Roxy absolutely idolises her big sister."

Ruby, grinning at me, bit down hard on her teething ring and, judging by how her face screwed up, it hurt. A second or so later, she started grizzling.

"She's probably hungry," said Val.

I was struggling with where to take the conversation and wondered how Sue Grafton would deal with it. "Could I come back when Roxy's here and speak to her?"

"She's upstairs, in her room."

I glanced at the clock but didn't ask why she wasn't at school. "Could I go up, while you sort Ruby out?"

"I don't see why not, but she doesn't know anything. I talked to her about it when we realised Flo wasn't coming home."

"I won't upset her," I said.

"I'm sure you won't. I imagine you lot get taught how to deal with this kind of thing all the time."

Val lifted the baby to smell her backside and pulled a face. "Okay. You sit with Roxy while I change this monster." She stood and swooped the baby onto one hip. "Then," she said, not unkindly, "I can keep an eye on you."

"That sounds fine to me," I said.

I followed her out of the kitchen and up the narrow staircase. Three doors opened off the small landing, one at the front and two at the back.

"Maddie's in with me and my partner at the moment, so all the gear's in there. Roxy's room is to the left. Just go in."

Val went into the front bedroom and left the door open. I knocked lightly on the back bedroom door and pushed it. It was a small room with bunk beds against one wall and two wardrobes across from them. The window was wide and let in a lot of light and a young girl lay in the pool of it, wearing shorts and a T-shirt. Her nut-brown hair was tied in a ponytail. She was colouring carefully and, when she looked up, I could see an ink stain in the corner of her mouth from where she'd chewed her pen.

"Hi," I said. "Are you Roxy?"

"Yes. Who're you?"

"My name's Carrie, I was just sitting downstairs talking to your mummy. She said it would be okay for me to talk a little to you about Flo. Is that alright with you?"

"Yes."

"Can I sit down?"

"Sure."

I sat on the lower bunk. The page of her colouring book was filled with panda bears chasing each other around on a football field. Roxy had completed the grass and was now working on the blue sky.

"Do you know Flo?" she asked.

"I do. She seems very nice."

"She really is." Roxy put the pen down and sat up quickly in that fluid way children have. She leaned against the wardrobe door. "Do you know where she is?"

"No, I'm sorry, I don't. But I'm trying to help Jonny find her."

Roxy's face brightened when I mentioned his name. "I like Jonny. He always makes me laugh and he buys me colouring books."

"Yeah, he seems nice. Do you and Flo talk much?"

"I talk more than she does. She sometimes puts me to bed, if she's not out with Jonny. I'm too old for bedtime stories, really, but I haven't told her that yet, so she reads to me and we have a talk. She's really interested in what I'm doing at school, and she knows the names of all my friends."

"Do you know all her friends?"

Roxy pulled a face, like I'd asked her to fly into space. "How could I? I'm only eight."

"Good point. So did Flo tell you she was going to go away for a few days?"

"No, not really."

"Do you mean 'no' or 'not really'?" I asked. I'd been caught out by Luca on that technicality a few times.

"She said she might go away, but that she'd come back to get me."

I leaned forward. "Did she say that before the weekend?"

"Yes, but she says it all the time. If she goes away, she said, she'll come and get me so we can live somewhere different and nice. I don't know what she means, really. Why wouldn't I want to live at the seaside, where I can go on the beach every day? I've seen people on television who don't live near the sea, and they can only go to parks. I have parks and the beach."

"You're right," I said. "So, Flo didn't say she was going away before this weekend?"

"No. We read a story, and she kissed me goodnight and told me to always be good and that I smelled." She grinned. "I don't really smell, but she says it sometimes. I tell her she's got a horrible big nose and that makes her laugh."

"I'll bet it does."

"I'm all done," said Val, standing in the doorway with Ruby on one hip. "How's the colouring going, Roxy?"

"Alright."

"Good." Val tilted her head, indicating she wanted me to go downstairs with her.

I nodded. "Okay, Roxy, thanks for talking to me."

"That's okay." She lay back down in the pool of light and picked up the blue pen.

I stepped carefully over her and followed Val downstairs. Ruby watched me the whole time. Val went into the kitchen and sat down. She put Ruby onto her lap and handed her the teething ring.

"So," she said, "do you think Roxy knows where she is?"

I stayed on my feet. "No, I don't think she does."

"Me neither, which is the only thing that makes me worry a little." She gave me a weary smile. "But Flo's an adult who can make up her own mind and she can take care of herself."

"I'm sure. Thank you for seeing me, Val, I do appreciate it."

"Are you really going to help him?"

"I'm going to try. Please say goodbye to Roxy for me."

I waved at Ruby, who gave me a big slobbery grin, then I made my way through to the lounge. Agnes was sitting on the chair, checking her phone and ignoring the dolls' tea party. She glanced up at me.

"Nice to meet you," I said.

"Uh-huh," she said and went back to her phone.

I let myself out.

* * *

Jonny took a different route away from Val's house and we ended up on Marine Drive. Just after we passed a big building made of steel and glass, he pulled over in front of a caravan selling fresh seafood.

"Are you hungry?" he asked when he took off his helmet.

"Not really, why?"

"Because this place does the best scallops in Seagrave and I wanted to ask how it went. Whenever I see people do that in films, they always stop and eat and have a chat."

"I don't want scallops but if they do hot drinks, I'll have a tea."

"Got you. Unfortunately, we both need to get off the bike."

We did. He pulled it into its kickstand then went over to the caravan, where he chatted amiably with the man behind the counter.

I sat on a bench that, oddly, faced away from the sea. Maybe the locals liked to use it because they were fed up of looking at the water.

There were only a few pedestrians and most carried shopping bags. A tall, thin man dressed all in black came out of the Lucky Strike arcade directly across the road from me. He looked to his left and right then across the road and our eyes met. He smiled, his teeth white in the depths of his beard, and folded his arms as he regarded me. We looked at one another for a moment or two before it became uncomfortable. I glanced over my shoulder to see Jonny still talking to the man frying his scallops. When I looked back across the road, the stranger was still staring at me, legs apart, arms folded high on his chest. Maybe he thought he knew me, maybe he had few social skills, but whatever it was, he made me feel uneasy.

A van went by slowly, wiping him from my view for a moment, then it was gone, and he was still watching me. He hadn't moved, hadn't stop smiling. I looked away, towards the Winter Gardens building but I could still feel his gaze on me, like a cold hand stroking my skin.

"Here we go," said Jonny, coming around to sit next to me on the bench. The man across the street finally broke his gaze and walked away.

"Are you okay?" Jonny asked. He handed me my drink.

"Yes," I said. The man wasn't leaving in any great hurry, but he wasn't looking back either. "I just got a bit spooked by that bloke over there."

"Which bloke?" He looked across the road. "What do you mean?"

"That one there, all dressed in black. He came out of the arcade and just stared at me."

Jonny shrugged. "Perhaps he fancied you," he said, as if he didn't really believe it himself. I felt every year of my age at that. "Or, maybe he's just weird. You get a lot of weird people in Seagrave, it's like we grow them in a field or something." He looked towards the sea. "It's partly why

I'm worried about Flo – what if it is some weirdo who's got her? He comes here, keen to see the water or whatever else it is that draws all these oddballs, and then he catches a glimpse of Flo and decides she's just right."

"I'm sure that's not the case, Jonny."

"But we don't know it, do we?"

He offered me a scallop. I shook my head but thanked him all the same.

"Your loss," he said and ate one. "So, what do you think?"

I took the lid off the tea and watched steam rise. "I think Val is worried but knows Flo can look after herself. I got the impression she's not used to worrying about her, which isn't surprising considering what she's got to deal with."

"There is a lot going on in that house."

"How old is she, do you know?"

"I think she's forty next year." He ate another scallop. "Did you get to speak to Roxy?"

"Yes. I think she knows there's something wrong as well but isn't quite sure what."

"So, what do you reckon?" he asked and looked at me expectantly, as if I'd be able to solve the mystery now.

I sipped the tea and it wasn't as hot as I'd expected. "I'm not sure. It seems out of character for Flo to disappear, but why shouldn't she when things weren't great at Miller's Point and there's not a lot of freedom at home? But it's the Roxy situation that niggles me."

Jonny pulled a moue face and ate another scallop. "We're not much further on then, are we?"

"Not really, except that somehow, it doesn't feel like she's run away."

"So you agree someone took her?"

"No," I said, quickly. "And I think you need to consider other options, too."

"Like what?"

It seemed too obvious a point to make, but he clearly wasn't willing to think about it. "Like someone didn't take her."

"Oh, like you mean she ran away?"

"Why not? Could she be staying with friends?"

"I don't know all her friends."

"Do you know her best friends?"

"Uh-huh."

"So get in touch with them and ask. They might be able to tell us something."

"That's a great idea." He finished the scallops and put the tray in a bin. "Shall I take you back now?"

"That'd be good," I said. I drained my tea and dropped the cup in a bin. "My fitness is improving, but I'm not sure I could walk several miles."

Chapter 24

"It's nice to see everyone," said Rita, "and thank you, Carrie, for agreeing to join us."

Four of my colleagues waved from their small boxes on the laptop screen and a couple said I was looking well. I thanked them and waved back. It was good to see them.

"And to remind you all, Carrie is still on medical leave, so don't anybody get any funny ideas about ringing her up and asking for things." A couple of my colleagues laughed nervously, as if that was their plan after this. "But since the news is going to affect our office, I thought she needed to be involved."

"I'm happy to be here," I said.

Rita shared her screen, showing a memo discussing budget cuts due to hit our department in the next quarter.

I quickly scanned it to check safeguarding was going to be ring-fenced and it was.

I heard raised voices and glanced out the window. Will was in the garden with a small cardboard box under one arm, his face like thunder.

"Where the hell do you think you're going?" Amanda demanded, stepping through the patio doors.

Will turned to face her. "None of your business," he declared.

"What the hell is that?" asked one of my colleagues. "Who's shouting?"

"It's my neighbours, sorry," I said.

"Amanda and Will, I assume?" Rita asked.

"Uh-huh."

"What's going on?" asked my colleague. "Are you okay, Carrie?"

"I'm fine, I'll shut the window."

I muted my microphone then stood up to pull the window closed. Amanda was stalking towards Will, who was edging back to the boathouse. He'd put his hand protectively over the cardboard box.

"What did I tell you before about buying crap for that bloody boat?"

Will glanced up at the office window. I didn't have time to move out of the way and his gaze swept over me before turning back to Amanda. "Why do you have to be like this?"

"Are you saying this is my fault?" Her stern expression made it look like she was ready to do him some damage.

"It's my money, Amanda." His foot slipped off the edge of the lawn and he almost lost his balance. He dropped the box and it bounced towards her. She scooped it up. "Give it back, Amanda."

"We can't afford fripperies for your bloody stupid boat, Will."

"We have more money than we know what to do with."

"No," she said viciously. "*I* have more money. Without me, you're nothing."

He held out his hand. "Please, Amanda, just let me have the box."

"Tell me you agree with me." She clasped it to her chest. "Tell me that you're nothing."

He rubbed the back of his head vigorously enough to make his hair stand on end. "Please, give me the box."

"Just fucking say it, Will."

"Give me the box, please."

She glared at him. He stood his ground and didn't say anything, but his hands were twitching.

"You're pathetic," she said and threw the box over his head. It landed near the boathouse and bounced into a flower bed. "I'm going for a bath."

Amanda turned on her heel and strode back into the cottage. Will watched her and I sat at the desk, feeling a little shocked at what I'd seen.

Rita finished explaining the last paragraph. "So, is everyone clear?"

My colleagues agreed and I was glad I'd thought to read it on screen beforehand.

"Good," Rita said. "That's it. Thanks for giving us some of your time, Carrie."

"You're very welcome, thanks for including me."

We said our goodbyes and Rita waited until my colleagues had left.

"I'll call you," she said.

"Thank you for making me feel like I was still part of something."

"You weirdo, why wouldn't you be? Now get out in the garden and enjoy the sun while the rest of us slowly bake in these offices."

We laughed and she ended the meeting. I glanced out the window as Will opened the padlock on the boathouse. His shoulders were slumped and he was either dejected or very good at acting it. He opened the door and went in.

I had little sympathy for either of them, even though they seemed locked in a horribly toxic relationship. It'd be easy, based on what I'd seen, to make assumptions on the power dynamic, but sometimes what you saw wasn't always the truth it appeared to be. Indeed, the truth could hide in plain sight while the noise of volatile arguments and demeaning language shaded the illusion.

I made a drink and took it down to the garden with my book and sat at the patio table.

"I'm going for a walk," Will called.

"I hope you slip off the breakwater and drown," Amanda yelled back.

Charming, I thought.

A front door slammed and, a minute or two later, I saw glimpses of him through the fence as he walked down the path. He was muttering to himself, but I couldn't hear what he was saying. A flash caught my eye and I looked up to see the bedroom window of his cottage being pulled closed.

* * *

It was the best part of an hour before Will came back from the beach.

Caught up in my novel, I hadn't noticed the time and was surprised when I looked at my watch. My tea had long gone, so I went up to the flat to make a fresh cup.

I'd just clicked the kettle on when I heard a shriek loud enough to make me jump. I rushed into the office but couldn't see anyone on the path or in the gardens.

The shriek came again and was coming from one of the cottages.

"Help me!" Will called. "Please, help me!"

With my heart racing, I rushed downstairs as quickly as I could. One of my flip-flops got tangled, so I kicked them both off and went outside. The ground was warm against the soles of my feet and I ran.

Boyd came out of his own cottage as I went around the corner. He was tying the cord of his dressing gown around him, and his hair was wet.

"Did you hear that?" he asked.

"It's coming from Amanda's," I said.

I reached their front door first and banged on it. "Hello!" I called. "Amanda! Will! Are you okay in there?"

Will shrieked again, as if in response.

Boyd pushed open the door and rushed into the hallway. We heard sobbing from upstairs. Boyd went first, two steps at a time and I followed as quickly as I could. The stairs ended at a narrow landing with three doors opening off it. The back one was the bedroom, the door to the front was closed. In the middle was the bathroom, the door ajar, and that's where the noise was coming from.

Boyd raised his eyebrows, as if to say 'what do we do?'

"Hello!" I called.

"Carrie?" Will shouted. "Help me."

Boyd pushed the door open but it only went so far. He tried to push it further but couldn't.

"Will?" he called. "It's Boyd. Step away from the door and we'll come in and help."

"I can't," Will said.

I tucked behind Boyd and slipped through the gap into the bathroom.

Chapter 25

Amanda was in the bath and the water was tinged pink. Blood had run from her hairline and there was more around her right eye. Her head was slumped to one side so her nose and mouth were submerged. There were no bubbles. Halfway up the wall was a single palm-sized splat of blood.

"Shit," I said, and my belly made a queasy roll.

I'd seen a few recently deceased people in my career and, as unpleasant as it seems, the best way I'd found to deal with looking at death was to be as objective and professional as possible. The situation needed to be assessed so I stepped toward the bath.

"No," said Will. He had his hands pressed to his cheeks. "Don't do that."

"I need to check something," I said and hoped I sounded calm.

The water wasn't dark enough for it to have been suicide, but I checked both of Amanda's wrists all the same. There were no cuts on her body that I could see, which meant the blood was coming from her face and hairline.

Boyd managed to slip through the gap. "Fuck," he said and gagged. He put his hand to his mouth. "Is she…?"

"Yes," I said.

Will made a peculiar mewling sound. Boyd put his fist against his mouth and swallowed hard.

"Go out, if it's too much," I said to him.

"I'm fine," he assured me.

Will began to sob. He was probably going into shock. "I need to cover her up and give her some dignity."

"I understand," I said, "but you can't do that. Have you called an ambulance or the police?"

"No," he said. "I only just got back. She said she was going for a bath when I left, so I came up to check."

"Have you moved her?"

"Of course I did, she was underwater. I told her if she kept that up, she'd drown." He held out his hand and his sleeves were sopping wet. "It was difficult to move her and she kept slipping back. It was horrible. All those years at the hospital and I didn't know what to do for the best." His breath hitched. "Then I couldn't stop shrieking."

"If you hadn't, me and Boyd wouldn't have come to help."

"So, what do we do?" Boyd asked.

"You get him out of the bathroom and I'll call the emergency services." I took my phone out of my shorts pocket and dialled 999 as Boyd took Will's hand.

"Come on, Will," he said. Boyd moved him enough to open the door fully and guided Will out. "Are you going to be okay, Carrie?"

I nodded as the operator asked which service I required. I told her as much as I knew and she took the details and promised an ambulance was on the way.

As we talked, I found my eye drawn to the bloody mark on the tiles. How had that happened? Did she get into the bath and somehow knock her head before falling? That would make sense but didn't feel right somehow. I looked at the floor and turned in a tight circle but couldn't see any blood on the carpet.

I went out onto the landing. Will was sitting on the top step, his head in his hands, his shoulders shaking every now and again as he cried. Boyd was halfway down the stairs, facing him, and his hand was on the back of Will's head. Boyd looked up at me expectantly. His face was very pale.

"An ambulance is coming," I said.

Will whimpered and Boyd stroked his head. "Sorry, mate."

"We need to get him downstairs and make a cup of really sugary tea," I said.

"Does that really work?" Boyd asked.

"That's what they gave me when I saw my first dead body and it made me feel better."

* * *

Boyd went home to get dried and dressed then we sat with Will until the ambulance arrived. I opened the door for the paramedic, explained who I was, and he went upstairs in a flurry of equipment and heavy boots.

"What happens now?" Boyd asked.

I shrugged. "I suppose we wait."

The police arrived ten minutes or so later, closely followed by another ambulance. Seeing the patrol car arrive agitated Will so I made him another cup of hot, sweet tea. Soon, a male officer in his early thirties came into the lounge where we were all sitting.

"I'm PC Digby," he said, and we introduced ourselves as he took out his notebook. "Who found Mrs Ross?"

"Me," said Will. "She's my wife."

"Can you tell me what happened?"

With hitching breath, Will managed to do so, right up to me and Boyd coming in. He also admitted he'd moved the body.

A female officer peered around the door and called PC Digby into the hallway. They talked quietly for a few moments before Digby came back into the room.

"We need to have a SOCO team come in," he said, and Will made a quick sobbing sound. "Is there anyone we can call for you? Do you have any family living nearby?"

"My brother-in-law lives next door."

"I saw Zoe earlier," I said quickly. "She said they were going out for the day."

"I did wonder why he didn't come in when I started yelling," Will said.

* * *

The female officer came in to collect us, leaving Will in the lounge alone with PC Digby. She'd set out three chairs on the patio, so Boyd and I sat next to one another, and she faced us.

"I'm PC Trish Moss," she said, "and I'm perfectly happy for you to call me Trish. First of all, are you both feeling okay? It's never a nice thing to find a body."

"I feel a bit queasy," said Boyd.

"I'm just a bit unsettled," I said.

"Both understandable," Trish said, with a sympathetic smile. "But are you both okay to answer some questions?"

We both agreed and she took out her notebook. "Thank you. So, you two were first on the scene after Will?"

"Yes," I said.

"What were you doing before you heard him?"

"I was having a shower," Boyd said.

"I'd been reading in the garden. I heard Will go out for a walk."

"How did you hear that?"

"There's a path that runs along the back of the flat I'm living in."

Trish looked confused. "I thought you were in the other cottage?"

"No, that's where Amanda's brother lives with his wife. I'm in the flat over the back."

"Okay, so can you talk me through what happened?"

Being as methodical and precise as I could, I told her everything from hearing the first shriek to calling the ambulance. Boyd then gave his side of the story.

She finished writing then looked at us. "Thank you both for being so thorough and clear, I think that'll be everything for now." She closed her notebook. "Neither of you are planning to go anywhere, are you?" She waited until we both shook our heads. "That's just a precaution, obviously, but we might need to speak to you again."

"Is that likely?" Boyd asked.

Trish pulled a moue face. "I can't say, because it depends on what our SOCO people find."

I thought of that splat of blood on the wall. "I think we're both happy to talk more, if you need us to."

"Thank you, Carrie. And you too, Boyd, I appreciate this isn't easy."

"It's really not," said Boyd and stood up. He waited for me to get up.

Trish gave us both a card. "If you do recall anything else, let me know."

"Thanks, Trish," I said.

"Yeah," said Boyd. "And, in the nicest possible sense of the phrase, I hope we never see you again."

Trish smiled. "You wouldn't believe how many people say that to me."

We went outside and stood awkwardly by the door.

"I'm not sure what we're supposed to do now," Boyd said.

"We go home."

"Do you really find dead bodies at work?"

"Not that often. It's not the nicest aspect of the job."

He rubbed his hands together. "It feels weird, doesn't it? Like we should do something to remember her."

"That'll come later," I said. "Are you going to be okay?"

"Probably." He tried to smile brightly but just looked as queasy as before. "Kay's coming round, which'll help, but what about you? Are you okay going back to an empty flat?"

"I'll be fine."

He took out his mobile. "Give me your number and if you need anything, ring me."

I told him my number; he rang the phone and I saved him as a contact. "Sorted."

Chapter 26

My mobile startled me out of a doze. The television blared to itself and I had no idea what I'd been watching. The clock told me it was a little past eight.

A number showed on the screen and it seemed familiar but I couldn't place it. "Hello?"

"Hi, Carrie, it's Jonny. You sound a bit weird, did I wake you up?"

"Kind of. It's been a weird day."

"Yeah, I'm sure, so what's going on? There's a cop car and an unmarked van up by the cottages."

"Like I said, it's been a weird day."

"So what happened?"

"Amanda died this afternoon, Jonny."

"Are you serious?"

"Why would I lie about it?"

"I'm sorry, I don't know why I said that. Listen, if you're home, can we talk face to face?"

"I don't want company, Jonny."

"I know, but I'm here now and it'll be easier to talk face to face."

I got the sense he wouldn't give up. "I'll be down." I rang off, found my flip-flops and went down to open the door. He was standing near the bench, looking up towards the emergency vehicles.

"Wow, you don't look so good." His gaze drifted to the left side of my chest and then, as if realising he'd been caught looking at my heart, he locked eyes with me. "Are you feeling okay?"

"I'm just drained. It's the after-effects of seeing Amanda."

"I'll bet. So where was Will? Did they take him in?"

"Not so far as I know."

"Did he kill her?"

"I don't know, Jonny."

"I suppose that's what they'll have to investigate, isn't it?" He shook his head. "Are you sure everything's okay with your heart and stuff? You don't look so good, if you don't mind me saying. If you need anything, I'll happily go and get it for you."

His genuine concern was charming, but I didn't feel up to this. "I appreciate it, Jonny, but I'm going to head in now."

"Yes, of course, you need to get back to your company."

I frowned and then realised he'd misunderstood what I'd said earlier. "Thanks."

"Are you still going to help me?"

"Of course I am."

"Good, good." He rubbed his hands together, as if he was trying to gather the courage to say something. "Can I tell you something that sounds really weird?"

"So long as you promise to make it quick."

"I will." He cleared his throat. "I don't want to start a conspiracy theory, but does anything about this strike you as strange?"

"In what way?"

"What if Flo is being held here and Amanda saw who took her?"

If he hadn't looked so serious, I'd have laughed. It was a ludicrous thought and didn't even make sense. "So you're saying someone here killed Amanda?"

He shrugged. "I said it was strange."

"I think you're thinking too hard, Jonny."

"Not many people say that to me. But do me a favour, yeah? Lock your door, so I know you're safe."

"Nobody's hanging around, Jonny."

"That's probably what Amanda thought," he said and gave me a little salute.

I locked the front door, checked the garden door was locked then locked the flat door too. I knew he was being paranoid and that his theory was ridiculous, but it buzzed around my head like a fly trapped behind glass.

Amanda had drowned and Flo had run away. That's all it was – a terrible coincidence.

Or was it?

Chapter 27

It would have been easy to avoid going to the beach that morning, but I forced myself out into the grey day because I knew the endorphin rush would do me some good.

The fact I was able to cut another five seconds off my previous best also gave me a lift. As I walked back to the breakwater, I saw Zoe running towards me and waited for her.

She looked sad and I held out my arms.

"I'd love to give you a hug," she said, "but I'm all sweaty."

"So am I," I said and we embraced. When we let go, I said, "How're things?"

Zoe grimaced and leaned against the wall to do her warm-down stretches. "We got back late and the police were waiting for us."

"How's Scott taking it?"

"As well as you'd expect. They didn't get on but, at the end of the day, she was his sister." She pulled a knee tight to her chest, let it go then did the same with her other leg. "The policewoman was really nice but we were both shell-shocked, I think, because our last interaction with Amanda was at the barbecue. We went to see Will and he feels terrible because they had a big fight and he stormed out and…" She let the sentence fade and stretched her hamstrings. "He sounds like he's already forgotten how horrible she was to him." She looked at me. "I think you're the only person I could say that to."

"I think it's completely natural to feel conflicted."

"Really?" she asked, with a hopeful tone.

I wondered if she'd fretted all night about being a horrible person for not fawning over Amanda. "Yes, I've seen it a lot. If you have a rocky relationship, the memories of that aren't always wiped clear when the other person passes away."

"Thank you," Zoe said with a relieved smile. We walked up the steps. "You're so helpful. And how about you? Will said you and Boyd helped him after he found her. That can't have been easy."

"It wasn't too bad."

"I always thought drowning would be an awful way to die, but Will said she looked quite peaceful."

I wasn't sure she had, but Zoe wasn't really asking me to clarify that. "She did."

We crossed the bridge and walked up the path. "If you or Scott need anything, or want to talk, you know where I am."

"Thank you, Carrie." She gave me a quick hug. "You have no idea how much I appreciate this."

"You take care. And please pass on my condolences to Scott."

* * *

After my shower, I made some toast and ate it standing at the office window. The sky looked greyer, and I could almost smell rain in the air. I looked towards the cottages and thought of yesterday and that splat of blood. I knew it had to have come from Amanda bumping her head but wouldn't falling have made a splash? The bathmat, as I remembered, was dry.

That train of thought led, of course, to Jonny's wild theory, trying to make sense of what was nothing more than a coincidence of timing. Except for the fact that I, as a woman in her fifties who believes in love and the joy of simple things, am also a realist who doesn't believe in coincidence.

His theory was full of holes but my sixth sense was tingling. What if there was a grain of truth in it? What did that mean, in terms of the people living here in Miller's Point?

My mobile rang and Rita's smiling face greeted me from the screen.

"Hey, boss, how are you?"

"I'm fine, how're you? I just heard the news. Why didn't you tell me?"

"I didn't think to," I said, honestly.

"Well, you should have, rather than waiting for Mike to tell me." Mike was a mutual friend of ours, who worked in the ambulance service. "Are you okay?"

"I'm fine. It was a shock seeing her, obviously, but you knew her better than I did."

"So what happened?" she asked.

I told her everything.

"That's terrible," she said. "I know she could be a pain in the arse, but drowning in your own bath is a terrible way to go." She made a sound, and I could imagine her shuddering. "Is there anything I can do for you?"

"No, I'm fine, honestly."

She left a pause long enough for me to picture her shaking her head as if she didn't believe me. "Okay," she said. "And not to change the subject, but I did that search on Flo and the family is listed, mainly because of her sister, Agnes. But there was also a custody issue."

"I spoke to her mother, and she mentioned it."

"You saw Flo's mother?"

"Jonny engineered an introduction. I didn't find out much beyond what I already knew, other than the relationship with her younger sister is as strong as everyone suggested."

"I've heard that it's a very strong bond."

"I did wonder whether there would be mileage in speaking to her father, to see if he knew of her whereabouts. Do you know if he's still on the scene?"

"He's about, certainly, but it wasn't a pleasant divorce and, from what she's said, Flo doesn't have anything to do with him."

"Val said he took the sons and left the girls."

Rita clicked her tongue against the roof of her mouth. "That's true, but I've heard the reason for that might also have been the reason for his leaving."

"Oh, yes?"

"Uh-huh. There's a question of parentage with young Roxy, and Flo refused to leave her little sister, so Mr Adler had to leave her behind."

"That's terrible."

"That's life," Rita said.

I heard the call waiting beep and checked the screen. A number I didn't recognise with a Seagrave dialling code was flashing. "I have a call."

"Take it then, I need to crack on anyway. I just wanted to catch up on everything and make sure you're okay."

"You're lovely, Rita."

"I know."

We rang off and I took the next call. "Hello?"

"Hello, is this Carrie Riccioni?"

"Yes."

"This is PC Moss from Seagrave police station. How are you?"

"I'm doing okay."

"I'm happy to hear that, after your experience yesterday, which is what I need to discuss. I know you gave me a full statement, but would it be possible to come into the station and talk to one of my colleagues? There's no issue, we're just looking for a bit of clarification. I'd offer to send someone, but they might turn up in a marked car and…" She laughed. "That doesn't always go down well."

"I'm sure it doesn't. I'll get there myself, rather than tie one of your people up. When did you want me?"

"Can you do it today?"

"Of course."

"Thank you. Ask for me when you get in."

"No problem, I'll see you as soon as I can get there."

I finished the call and ate the remainder of my toast. The phone rang again, and it was Boyd this time.

"How are you feeling?" I asked.

"I've been better, I'll be honest. Have you had a call from the Seagrave rozzers?"

"I have."

"Does she want to speak to you, too?"

"Uh-huh."

"That's a relief. I was worried I'd done something wrong. Listen, did you fancy coming in with me? We could leave in twenty minutes or so."

Chapter 28

Boyd's top-of-the-line BMW was ridiculously comfortable and as quiet as a mouse.

"Nice car," I said.

He glanced at me. "Do you mean that, or are you winding me up? People either like BMW drivers or think we're knobs."

"I don't think you're a knob."

"Well, there's that, at least."

We lapsed into a comfortable silence and, as he drove with a quiet assurance, I looked out to sea. The sky was so grey now it was difficult to properly see the horizon.

"What do you think this is about?" he asked once we got into Seagrave.

"I'm not sure, unless the situation has changed from when they originally spoke to us."

"It looked pretty straightforward to me," he said, not taking his eyes off the road. "I can't get the image of her lying in the bath out of my head."

"It's not easy, is it?"

"Do you think we're in trouble?"

I looked at him in surprise. He seemed serious. "In what way?"

"They think we had something to do with it?"

"What makes you think that?" Perhaps he was troubled by the blood splat too.

He shrugged. "I don't know, I don't have much experience with the police." He paused then held up a finger. "Sorry, that makes it sound like I'm asking you because you're clearly a master criminal."

"Bollocks, you've discovered my secret identity." His sharp laugh surprised a laugh from me. "Which is a shame, because I was going to steal your car later."

* * *

Seagrave Police Station was a long, two-storey building that took up a good part of Howard Street and Boyd managed to find a parking spot close to it.

Steps led down from the pavement to a small car park where the spaces were designated to high-ranking officers. We crossed that and went into a reception area with institutional green walls and dark floor tiles that looked like they hadn't been cleaned properly for a while. A fake plant stood in one corner next to a line of chairs.

A desk sergeant sat behind a counter that stretched across the far end of the area. Behind him were two windows that overlooked an open-plan area filled with desks.

"Can I help you?" he asked.

"I hope so," I said and introduced us. "PC Moss asked us to come to the station."

The sergeant glanced at something on the desk in front of him. "That's right," he said then lifted a receiver.

"Mrs Riccioni and Mr Manning are in reception." He listened for a moment. "Okay, fine." He put the phone down. "PC Moss will be down shortly, if you want to take a seat." He gestured towards the chairs, then went back to reading whatever he'd been reading when we came in.

"I don't really want to sit down," Boyd said to me.

"Neither do I."

We milled around until the door behind the counter opened. PC Moss came through, said something to the desk sergeant then held the door open for a stocky man in his late thirties with a strong jaw and very black hair. He lifted the counter hatch, let PC Moss through then followed her out to us.

"Thanks for coming," she said and shook my hand first, then Boyd's. "This is DS Samuelson." He shook our hands. "You're with me," Trish said to Boyd. "Carrie, DS Samuelson will be speaking to you. Do you want to follow me?"

We went through the hatch and into the open-plan office. A narrow corridor branched off it, with several doors along the length. Trish stopped in front of the door marked 'Interview 1'.

"After you," she said to Boyd and opened the door.

"We're the next one down," said Samuelson. He opened Interview 2 and held the door so I could go in. The room was small and featureless, with four chairs around a table that was screwed to the floor. A digital recorder sat on a small shelf and a window overlooked a car park half-filled with police vehicles.

"Take a seat," he said and gestured towards one of the chairs facing the window. He sat opposite me and put a thin file on the table. "Are you feeling okay?"

"I'm fine."

"Good. I understand you had a heart attack recently."

I nodded.

"How are you coping with it?"

"Okay, I think. A bit tired, now and then, but otherwise pretty robust."

"Glad to hear it." He took my signed statement out of the file and turned it so I could see. "Am I okay to call you Carrie?" When I nodded, he said, "This is the statement you gave to PC Moss yesterday, at Miller's Point."

"That's it," I said. My curiosity was growing. "Is there a problem with it?"

"There's no issue with what you said at all, it's just that I need a little clarification on a certain detail of it."

"In what way?"

Samuelson read from my statement. "You said Will Ross walked by your garden after you'd overheard a heated discussion or argument between him and his wife, Amanda, which was also witnessed by colleagues on a Zoom call you were involved in."

"That's right."

"And you stayed in your garden until you saw him come back, approximately an hour later."

"Yes." Was he questioning me being outside? "It was warm, so I sat on the patio and read my book."

"You didn't go indoors at any point, to make a drink or have a comfort break?"

"No."

"How can you be sure it was an hour later?"

"I checked my watch, because I was surprised to see the time had elapsed."

"Did you doze off at all?"

"I'm pretty sure I didn't."

"Did you see anyone else walk along the path in all that time?"

"No. It doesn't seem to be used very often."

"Then, soon after he returned home, you heard Will Ross screaming and shouting and went to his aid, along with Mr Manning?"

"That's right." I leaned forward, very curious now. "I'm sorry, DS Samuelson, but I haven't said anything to you I didn't say to PC Moss last night. So what was the clarification you needed?"

He pulled a face and rubbed the side of his neck. The light caught his cheek and although he was clean-shaven, his hair was so dark a five o'clock shadow was already evident.

"There is doubt as to cause of death."

"Really? Is it anything to do with that blood splat on the tiles?"

"It might do," he said, cautiously. "It seems Mrs Ross had blunt impact trauma and fell into the bath after that."

The surprise hit me in the belly. "Do you think somebody hit her?"

"I didn't say that, Carrie, and, obviously, it's not something I could discuss with you when our people are still conducting their investigations."

I knew I wasn't going to get any farther with him on that, so I tried a different tack. "The blood in the water was coming from her hairline, wasn't it?"

"You notice a lot, Carrie."

"One of the aspects of my profession," I said and then it clicked what the clarification was. "You think Will did it, don't you?"

Samuelson looked at me blankly and gave nothing away at all. He'd have been a bastard to play poker against.

"But my statement has him being out of the cottage when it happened."

Samuelson drummed his fingers on the tabletop. "There's no sign of forced entry and nothing's missing, which would suggest it wasn't a random burglar or attacker."

"And my statement makes that impossible."

"I can't comment on that, Carrie, for obvious reasons."

"I understand. This hasn't really helped you, has it?"

"Please don't think that. I'd rather know the truth than have to make assumptions. And you've been very thorough, as I was told you would be."

"Really? Who told you that?"

"A mutual friend of ours called Ted Hunter."

I groaned, inwardly. Ted Hunter was a DS at Norwich, who I'd had several run-ins with in the past. He was good at his job and, so Rita told me, believed the same of me, but we always seemed to be on different sides and thus a problem to the other. "Ah," I said. "How much did he tell you?"

Samuelson gave me a tight smile. "Enough that I feel I should advise you not to over-involve yourself with this. Ted says you have a bit of a habit of throwing yourself into things full force."

"I don't see that as being an issue."

He held up his hands. "It isn't necessarily, but I wouldn't want us butting heads, especially while you're recovering from a cardiac episode. So, please, don't get involved with the Amanda Ross investigation."

As much as I was curious and concerned, I didn't see how I could get involved, even if I wanted to. There was, however, something else that he might be able to help me on. "I won't," I said and saluted three fingers to my temple. "Scout's honour."

He returned the gesture. "I take that vow seriously and I hope you do too."

"Dib dib indeed," I said. "So can I ask you a question?"

He pulled a face. "Why do I have the feeling this isn't going to be good?"

"I don't know, are you naturally a negative person?"

"No," he said. "So, what do you need?"

"There's a young woman I know, who's been reported missing."

"That's hardly my area of expertise," he said.

"I know, but perhaps you could ask some of your colleagues about the situation. Her boyfriend didn't get the impression anyone was taking him seriously."

"I'm sure that's not the case, Carrie."

"I know and I'm not knocking anyone, but I've promised to help him look for her."

He bit the inside of his cheek. "This isn't usual."

"I know, but call it one professional asking another for some assistance."

Samuelson looked at me intently, for long enough that it started to feel uncomfortable. "Okay," he said finally, with a nod. "Give me the details." He took a pad and pen from an inside pocket, and I told him Flo's name and the date we'd last seen her. "You know I can't promise anything, don't you?"

"Of course."

"Do you know anyone else here at the station, like a contact through work?" he asked.

"The only other person I know is PC Moss."

"She's a very good officer. I'll get her to give you a little update, but I will also advise you not to get involved with that investigation either."

"Okay, Dad, but I promised I'd help."

"I can imagine. But please don't take this as an invitation to badger Trish Moss. This isn't going to be a constant dialogue." He smiled thinly. "In fact, call it professional courtesy."

Chapter 29

Boyd suggested we go for a drink and took me to a cafe called Horner's, which was between a cheap jeweller and one of those shops popular with tourists, that sold whatever tat was big news that year.

Horner's was narrow, with orange walls festooned with posters for old shows at the Hippodrome. The checkerboard floor tiles sparkled in the light. All the tables and chairs were mismatched and the ketchup bottles were shaped like tomatoes. Four tables had pension-aged couples sitting at them and an old man and a decrepit-looking dog occupied the fifth.

"I can recommend the millionaire shortbread, if you're peckish," Boyd said.

"I'll have one of those and a cup of tea, please."

The woman who served us had 'Amy' sewn into the breast of her polo shirt. She had a lot of facial piercings and a bright smile. Boyd paid and Amy told us she'd bring everything over.

We picked a table near the window and sat across from one another. Our drinks and biscuit arrived a few minutes later.

"Do you suppose we can talk about what happened?"

"I don't see why not," I said. "So, what did you need to clarify?"

"It was about my CCTV. I have it on the front of the cottage and sent them a copy of the recording from yesterday afternoon."

"Did you watch it yourself?" I asked and took a bite of the millionaire shortbread. It was as lovely as he'd promised.

"I fast-forwarded through, because it records all the time rather than when there's movement. It seems like nobody came into Miller's Point and nobody left, though of course the image doesn't cover everything. You can only see a bit of me, for example, as I go tearing outside."

"Could anyone come in without being seen?"

"Yes, if they knew the camera was there. It's angled so my car is in full view and people walking along the road are pictured, but if you were close to the cottages or by the guest parking, you'd be out of sight." He drank some of his coffee. "How about you?"

I told him what I'd discussed with Samuelson. "You can see why they asked us in, can't you? Between your CCTV and me saying Will didn't walk back from the beach, how does that explain Amanda dying in what might be suspicious circumstances?"

He looked surprised. "That makes it sound like we did it."

"Yeah, that's not very reassuring, is it?"

Boyd shrugged. "Did you do it?"

"No," I said. "Did you?"

"Nope," he said, and I believed him.

I like to think I'm a pretty good judge of character and he sounded worried, not guilty.

"Do you have an alibi?" he asked.

"I was in my garden, on my own, reading a book. What about you?"

"I was showering, on my own."

"I'm not sure either of those would stand up in court."

"Which means it was either a tragic accident or someone came into Miller's Point without you spotting them and knew where to go to avoid being on my CCTV."

The idea of that seemed to give both of us a little chill and we sat quietly for a few moments.

Boyd drank some coffee. "Shall we change the subject?"

"Good idea," I said and considered how to ask what I needed to without being too abrupt. "How did you get on with Flo?"

He looked at me placidly. "That's an odd jump of subject and sounds, if you don't mind me saying, like a bit of a loaded question."

Maybe it was unfair to put him on the spot, but I'd started now. "Not at all."

He didn't look convinced. "I never had all that much to do with her, really, because I was usually at work when she cleaned. If I was working from home, she worked around me and I'd go for a walk when she wanted to do the study." He put his elbows on the table and steepled his fingers. For a moment, a cloud seemed to pass over his face and then it was gone. "We got on okay, I think, until one day when I caught her going through my wife's drawers."

"Oh," I said, surprised at the mention of her. "I didn't realise you were married."

"Well," he said, with a guarded smile, "now you do."

I frowned, wondering if he was going to say anything else about her, but he continued to talk about Flo.

"I don't know what she was doing and told her I didn't want to know, but she got very defensive and then a little bit bolshy."

I thought about Flo taking Amanda's lighter. Had she tried to steal something from Boyd too? "Bolshy?"

"Yes. She tried to turn it around and said I was spying on her, which is ridiculous. She was in the bedroom with the door open and I was heading to the bathroom when I saw her."

"What exactly was she doing?"

"I keep some of my wife's things in the top drawer of my dresser and Flo had it open. I didn't like the idea of her going through my wife's jewellery box."

"What happened after that?"

"Nothing, really. I said I wasn't spying on her and that I'd appreciate her leaving that drawer alone and she nodded, went downstairs and got on with the cleaning."

"Did you ever talk about it again?"

He let out a nervous little laugh. "You sound like PC Moss."

I smiled. "Sorry, I don't mean too."

"Is this to do with the fact that Flo seems to have gone missing?" He frowned. "Do you think I had something to do with that?"

I realised I didn't, however much Jonny's conspiracy theory had him as part of the suspect pool. "No, I don't."

"Good. That incident was just after Christmas and we've been fine since then. I was as surprised as anyone when Amanda said she'd gone."

"Did Amanda have any idea where she went?"

"Not really, other than saying she'd probably gone to London to make a new life for herself."

"Do you think that's what she did?"

"I have no idea," he said. "We talked, but I'd never say we were close, so it's not something we discussed."

I got the painful idea that if we were starting a friendship, I'd just put a little dent into it. "I didn't mean to offend you," I said.

"You didn't."

"But I promised Jonny I would try to help him find her."

"And you have to investigate every avenue?" he asked, his brow quirking.

"Something like that," I said. "How did Kay get on with her?"

"Okay, I think, but there's only a few years between them. They'd be more on a pop culture wavelength than me and Kay are." He grinned, sheepishly.

"Does Kay like it at Miller's Point?"

"She likes the calm and peace, because her part of Norwich is quite noisy."

"It wasn't peaceful the other night," I said.

He pulled a face. "Do you mean the scream on Saturday night? I'm sorry, that was Kay."

"It sounded like…" I stopped. I was going to say, in an attempt at humour, that it sounded like someone being killed, but that felt like bad taste now.

He smiled, as if he guessed what I hadn't said. "I can imagine. It was my fault, though. I told her about this old horror film I loved, and I found a cheap DVD copy in town. It's a proper eighties classic and cheesier than I remembered, but it got to her. We went to bed, I was out like a light, and suddenly she's screaming blue murder."

"It scared her that much?"

"No." He leaned forward. "She got woken by a noise."

I smiled, determined he wasn't going to scare me with some silly ghost story. "Is that right?"

"I'm serious," he said and looked it. "She's convinced it was rats or something moving around in the loft."

"What?"

"Yeah, it scared me, to be honest. I've never been in the loft but I checked the hatch and it was locked from our side, so I left it at that. I managed to calm her down, but I don't think she slept much after and she went back to her place in the morning."

"I saw her at the patio table."

He gave me a reserved smile. "You don't miss much from that window, do you?"

"It's hard not to," I admitted. "It's a much better view than I have at home."

"Anyway, once she'd gone, I went up to check and our section of the loft was empty, apart from some insulation foam and a few old boxes in one corner. There was an arch to get into next door, but I didn't think it was right to go through so I just shone my torch around and couldn't see anything out of place."

"And nobody else has mentioned hearing things?"

"No. One really odd thing though. After I checked the hatch on Saturday night, I happened to look out the window as I went back to bed and saw Will in his garden."

"I saw him too. What do you think he was doing?"

"He's told me there's a pregnant cat in there, so I assumed he was taking it some food but why he'd do that in the dead of night, I have no idea."

"And have you heard the rats or whatever since?"

"Not a peep."

We finished our drinks and he drove us home. I made him drop me outside his cottage, rather than drive down to the flat.

"Thanks for taking me."

"Not a problem," he said. "But do me a favour, Carrie. I'm not trying to be funny or frighten you, but make sure your door's locked. We kind of skirted the idea at the cafe, but if it wasn't an accident and you and I didn't do anything, it means somebody else did."

Chapter 30

I like to think I'm a rational woman but, with Boyd echoing what Jonny had said, I felt a little paranoid as I closed the front door and couldn't shake the feeling someone else was in the building.

The downstairs doors were locked and the skin on my arms prickled as I went upstairs.

"I'm coming in," I said before I unlocked the flat door and pushed it open. Everything was as I'd left it and, feeling a bit braver, I checked the rooms. The flat was empty. I decided a strong cuppa would settle my jangling nerves but then my mobile rang and startled me.

The number was Seagrave police station. "Hello?"

"Hi, Carrie, this is Trish. DS Samuelson spoke to me and mentioned you had an interest in a missing person report."

"That's right, for Flo Adler."

"I obviously can't give you details, but I can answer questions up to a point."

"I understand. Her boyfriend, Jonny Stewart, asked me to help him try to find her."

"Mr Stewart filed a missing person's report concerning an IC1 female named Florence Adler. There's no further information as yet, although my colleague, who's involved with the case, is a little sceptical about it all. Her family lives in Seagrave and haven't raised any concerns and nobody else has been in touch."

"Nothing from her friends?"

"No. Seeing as you're in social services, Carrie, you know the runaway statistics as well as I do. Flo's an adult but still in her teens and if she wants to leave, she's perfectly entitled to, even if that means not telling her boyfriend or friends. Does Mr Stewart have any reason to be worried about her?"

"Nothing concrete, it's basically suspicion and speculation, but I've witnessed a couple of things that might potentially be issues."

"I'm listening."

I told her about Will at the party and how I'd dealt with it.

"I agree it sounds untoward but, as you say, there might be a rational explanation, even if that's not apparent to either of us. And, bearing in mind the current situation, I'm sure Will wouldn't be up to answering questions, even if I got permission to do so."

"Probably not."

"You mentioned a *couple* of things?"

"Yes, there's a man called Harley, but I don't know his surname. I only saw him twice and, on both occasions, he was having a go at her. There's a romantic history, but she wasn't interested and he was trying to intimidate her. It wasn't pleasant."

"Okay," said Trish. "I'll make some enquiries and try to figure out who Harley is. But we can't put any real resources into this. I'm not saying we aren't going to try and find her, but a lot of young women get fed up with a tough life at the seaside and want to try somewhere new."

"I know," I said.

"Well, if you think of anything else," she said.

Something sparked in my mind. "Actually, there is something else and I don't know if it's relevant or just stupid."

"Tell me and I can be the judge of that."

I told her about the firepit and the smouldering wood and the person in the trees.

"I'm not sure that's anything to concern ourselves with," she said. "You'd be surprised how many people breeze through Seagrave with little more than a tent to their name. They're transients, mostly, and tend to keep out of the way, so as not to cause any trouble."

"That's what I thought," I said, "but then I noticed something the other night." I told her about the person on the footpath, from the night of the scream.

"You didn't see their face?"

"No, or which way they left because I lost them in the shadows. It might have been the transient I saw before, or one of my neighbours."

"It's curious, certainly, and if you spot anything like it again, please get in touch. I mean, it's more than likely nothing, but we can't be too careful. I tell you what, I'll see if I can swing over there or get a colleague to do so and just check out the trees."

"I'm sure the tent had gone the next day."

"I believe you. I'd put money on the person in the trees being someone passing through. And if it was them on the path, maybe they heard the commotion and decided to have a look for themselves."

"That makes sense," I said, though something was still nagging at me.

"It sounds like there's a 'but' coming."

"Yeah," I said. "It's probably nothing but, is it a little weird that whoever was camping in the trees left over the same weekend that Flo decided to go."

She clicked her tongue against the roof of her mouth for a moment or two. "I'd say it's more of a coincidence than weird, but we'll have a look around."

"Okay, thanks."

"I have to go, Carrie, but can we agree to let one another know if we hear anything?"

"Of course. Thanks, Trish."

"You're welcome. I hope everything's okay because Flo sounds like a nice person and it's never good if something happens to them."

"Tell me about it," I said.

Feeling slightly off, I went into the office and switched on the laptop. Work, as well as that strong cuppa, would focus me and draw my mind away from Jonny's theory.

I glanced out the window and saw Scott on his patio, looking deep in thought as he read through some papers. Zoe came and stood behind him, her hands on his shoulders as she spoke. He tilted his head back to reply and she kissed his forehead then went back into the cottage. Scott put the papers on the table and, after glancing through the patio door, took out his mobile and walked into the garden with it pressed to his ear. He had a short, subdued conversation then went into the cottage.

I noticed Boyd on his patio looking directly at me and felt a quick jolt of surprise. How long had he been watching me?

He grinned and waved. I waved back then he disappeared behind the fence.

I sat down, feeling a little ashamed that he'd caught me spying on the neighbours again. Then I stopped, as something nagged at me.

Boyd used the word 'spying' when he told me about Flo and, even though he denied it, what if there had been an element of him watching her? If he paid the wrong kind of attention to Flo, that might have pushed her to leave.

I liked Boyd and he seemed thoroughly pleasant and charming, but was that just his salesman charm obscuring whatever it was Flo and Rita had an issue with? Then there was the question about who was in Miller's Point when Amanda died. I know I wasn't in her cottage, I'm pretty sure Will wasn't, but could Boyd have been? It wouldn't take long to get back to his and jump in the shower, to give himself an alibi.

Or was I trying to make something out of nothing?

Chapter 31

I rang Rita and told her about the police, so she invited me for an early dinner at a small seafood restaurant she liked in Seagrave. We were quickly shown to our table and she chose Dover sole, while I had cod. After the waitress had brought the drinks, Rita leaned forward with her elbows on the table and rested her chin on the back of her hands.

"Go on, then," she said and listened intently as I told her what happened with DS Samuelson.

Our food came and looked as wonderful as Rita had said it would be. I tried my cod and found it was deliciously flaky.

"For someone recuperating," she said, "you seem to be doing a lot of things."

"I can hardly say no to the police, can I?"

"No, but you can take it easier than this." She ate some of her fish. "Speaking of which, have you heard anything about Flo?"

"Not really. PC Moss at Seagrave station says it's only Jonny that's reported her missing."

"As we've said, she's a grown woman and maybe she wanted to leave her boyfriend behind. Do you really think there's foul play somewhere?"

"I honestly don't know. If it wasn't for the Roxy situation, I'd happily concede she'd left, but..."

"Something's amiss, isn't it? You can feel it."

I shrugged and ate a chip. "What do you think of Jonny?"

"I think he's decent; a bit unfocussed and childish, perhaps, but he doesn't seem prone to flights of fantasy, either." She speared the last of her fish and popped it into her mouth then put her knife and fork on the plate. "If she didn't run away of her own volition and, so far as we're aware, wasn't bundled into a car, could she have been taken by someone she knew?"

"It happens."

"But at Miller's Point? That's a very limited field of suspects."

"One of whom," I said and looked at her intently, "happens to be Boyd Manning. I know he and Flo had a run-in, because he told me and I know Jonny doesn't like him. I also know you have an issue with him but, so far, you've avoided telling me what it is."

"Do you like him?"

"He's only ever been pleasant to me, which is what makes me curious."

"And when you're curious, you never give up, do you?" She twirled some hair behind her ear absently. It was a nervous tic she had, when she was unsure of how best to proceed. She took a deep breath and exhaled slowly. "I reacted because I've been an idiot and embarrassed myself." She dragged her top teeth over her lower lip. Her eyes had reddened.

As much as I wanted to know, this seemed to be upsetting her badly. "You don't have to tell me," I said.

"I think I should. You remember last summer, when Patrick was busy and we had the Anselmo thing going on and our stress levels were through the roof?"

"I do." It was just before Luca moved to Paris and I'd offered for her to stay with me for a while.

"Well, I moved into the flat and got to know Amanda and Will. Scott and Zoe weren't there then, but I did notice Boyd."

"He's a handsome man."

"He is, plus friendly and charming, with charisma to burn. He wasn't seeing Kay then and, one day, he said he had a meeting in Seagrave and was going to grab an early dinner there and I told him about this great little Italian place I know, so he invited me." She paused and tapped her lips with a finger. "I completely misread the situation, Carrie. I thought the younger women I saw at his place were his nieces." Rita shook her head. "God, what a fool."

"What did you say?"

"Every stupid fucking thing I shouldn't have. The table was intimate, we were talking quietly, and I was an idiot. I told him straight me and Patrick were separated and that if he, Boyd, wanted to take things further that evening, then I was very happy to do so."

"Oh," I said.

"He let me down as gently as he possibly could, but it cut me to the quick that I was too old for him. Much too old, as it turned out. I'm almost thirty years older than Kay." She shook her head. "I was crimson with embarrassment and the car ride back was the longest journey I think I've ever experienced. In fact, if I was ever that stupid again, I'd walk home. But he was really nice about it and so I think I turned my own embarrassment onto him and started to avoid him. It was easier that way, even though he was never less than pleasant. I don't know what Flo's issue was because I never asked, but I got the feeling he was a one-woman man, so I doubt he came onto her. I could be wrong, of course, but it's hardly a question we can ask him, is it?"

* * *

"Looks like you've got company," Rita said as she drove towards the flat.

Jonny was sitting on the bench and his moped was in front of my car. She pulled up alongside him.

"Just remember," she said to me. "You're not Nancy Drew and you shouldn't be doing anything strenuous."

"Thanks for bursting those bubbles," I said, and she laughed. "Thanks for dinner, too."

"You're welcome," she said. She waved to Jonny then reversed back to the corner.

"How's it going?" I asked as I sat at the other end of the bench.

"Pretty much the same as before," he said. "What about you?"

"I'm knackered. I had to go to the police station today and took the chance to ask them about Flo."

His face lit up. "Really? Wow, thank you! What did they say?"

I told him and his expression faded somewhat. "It could be worse, I suppose."

"It really could. I don't want you to think I agree with your conspiracy theory, but something's wrong. It seems like we're missing something, and I don't know what it is; although, if she was here, don't you think we'd have seen her by now?"

"Not if she was hidden."

"Hidden? Are you suggesting that professional people have effectively kidnapped a young woman and are holding her against her will?"

"You hear about it on the news," he said. "Never in Seagrave, granted, but I've heard things where they keep people in cellars and make them do really shitty jobs and don't let them go."

"That's slavery, Jonny," I said. "Nobody is hiding Flo to make her clean more."

"So what if it was something sexual?"

"Go on," I prompted.

"How about if someone fell in love with her and wanted to keep her all to themselves? They tuck her away and everything was fine until Mrs Ross discovered what was going on so they hurt her."

It didn't sound realistic, but it did make a bit of sense. My mind kept going back to that blood splat and how it linked in. If Amanda's death wasn't an accident, why wouldn't Jonny's theory hold at least some water?

"So, what do you think?" he asked.

"I think we need to find plenty of proof before we can speak to anyone about it."

"Really?" He sounded excited and surprised. "So you think we can find some proof?"

"I have no idea, because the logistics don't make sense. Holding her in a cottage would be ludicrous, which would only leave the boathouse, and unless she's bound tight, she's going to be banging on walls and screaming, isn't she?" I thought of Kay. "Even if she was tied up in a loft, we'd have heard her."

"We could check the boathouse for evidence."

"I doubt Will would let us look, especially if he knew why."

"Could we get in without him knowing?"

"Probably," I said, "but not today. I'm tired. We could try tomorrow, when no one's around."

"Good thinking. And I took your advice and got hold of Emily, Flo's best friend. She's okay with you calling her."

"Why would I call her?"

"Because Emily's at Sheffield Hallam and Flo's been up there a couple of times to stay in her flat."

"Okay," I said. I had no idea what I'd say but trusted myself to be able to bluff my way through it.

"What time tomorrow then? I work half a day on Friday."

"We'll meet after lunch then," I said.

He held out his fist and it took me a moment to realise he wanted me to bump it. I did and he grinned. "You're a star, Carrie."

Chapter 32

Friday morning dawned bright and clear, and I reached the river having managed to shave a further five seconds off my personal best. Thrilled, I did my warm-down stretches and looked over towards the trees. I got no sense of movement, and I couldn't see any flashes of colour amongst the trunks, so either the mysterious traveller had changed camping spots or left altogether.

I walked back to the breakwater and hoped Zoe would be running this morning. While I waited, I sat on the steps and watched a boat sail towards Seagrave with a pack of seagulls dive-bombing the wake. She appeared around the bluff ten minutes later and ran with ease and fluidity towards me.

"Hey," she said. Her forehead and cheeks glistened with sweat. "How did you do today?"

"Another five seconds. How about you?"

"I'm knackered, so I'll take that as a win."

"How are things?" I asked as she started to do her warm-down exercises.

"He's still cut up but I'm wondering now if it's a combination of guilt and loss walloping him."

"That would make sense."

"Should it feel like he's closing me out though?"

"What do you mean?"

She bit at the corner of her lip. "I know this sounds horribly selfish, but I've thought he was closing me out of his life for the past month or so and now it's getting worse."

"I'm not sure about before, but people do sometimes close up with grief."

"I know, but I have this feeling that something isn't right."

I felt sorry for her but didn't know what to say for the best. Dante had closed me out, when he believed the grass was greener on the other side, and it really hurt. Now didn't seem the time to share that, though, in case she was wrong.

She sighed. "He tells me he loves me, so I'm probably making a fuss about nothing."

"Don't forget you're grieving too."

"You know," she said, "you're the first person who's said that and I am a bit conflicted. She called me a gold-digger once and that kind of thing isn't easy to forget."

"No, I'm sure it's not. As for Scott, did you ever discuss things before Amanda died?"

She shook her head.

"In that case, my unsolicited advice would be to support one another through the grieving and then talk it through. You seem a strong couple and hopefully you can both get on the same page."

She touched my shoulder gently. "You've got a wise head on those shoulders, haven't you?"

"I try."

"It just feels like everything's all over the place now. I mean, we're in Seagrave at ten to meet with the solicitors."

"That's quick."

"That's what I said, but Scott's been making a lot of calls and him and Amanda were having all those secret chats, so perhaps there's other business they were dealing with."

I thought it best to change the subject. "Have you heard anything from Will?"

"Only that he's staying in a hotel in Seagrave until they release the cottage back to him, which could happen tomorrow. That's what the police told us, anyway. Scott doesn't want anything to do with him, because he's convinced Will had something to do with her death."

"Is he?"

"Oh, absolutely, but they were never the best of friends. Scott used to say, 'if he stood up to the old cow, she might not be such a bitch to me'. Now he reckons he finally snapped and lashed out."

"Did he tell the police that?"

"Yes, several times. In fact, he's not impressed you gave Will his alibi."

The thought of Scott being annoyed wasn't going to give me a sleepless night. "I had to tell the truth."

"That's exactly what I said and then he accused me of backing you over him."

"I'm sure that's just his grief talking."

We reached my front door. "Thanks for listening, Carrie, I do appreciate it."

"Anytime." I watched her walk away then, although it felt like a betrayal, I texted Jonny.

> *Scott and Zoe are going out this morning and Will is at a hotel in Seagrave, so this could be our best chance to check out the boathouse.*

Chapter 33

Jonny arrived at noon and I ushered him in quickly.

"How many cars were outside Scott and Zoe's cottage?"

"Just one. Nobody was parked outside the other two, either."

"Excellent," I said. "We'll just double-check everyone's out and then get cracking."

"Are you coming with me, then?"

"What else am I going to do?"

"I dunno." He shrugged. "I just assumed you'd want to take it easy and keep guard, or something."

"I'm recovered enough to help you." I put my flip-flops on. "Come on."

Jonny left his helmet, and we walked away from the flat. "I need to give you Emily's number."

"I'll ring her later. She might be in lectures now."

I peered around the corner. As Jonny had reported, there was only one car outside Scott and Zoe's cottage. To be on the safe side, I knocked on their door.

"What're you doing?" he asked with panic.

"If they're in, I can make up a reason for being here, but that's going to be difficult if they catch us breaking into Will's boathouse, isn't it?"

"True."

I counted to twenty then knocked on Will's door. There was no answer, so I tried Boyd's. "Okay," I said, "we're on our own."

We walked back and jumped over the fence onto Scott and Zoe's patio. I saw us reflected in the patio doors and felt terrified and strangely exhilarated by what we were about to do.

Jonny climbed into Amanda and Will's garden and waited for me to join him.

"You know, I don't know what the job is, but I never expected a social worker to behave like you."

"Should I take that as a compliment?"

He grinned. "Yeah, probably."

As we walked towards the boathouse, I wondered if Boyd had CCTV on the back of his property too. It was, I decided, too late to worry about that now.

"Will's apparently got a stray cat in there which just had kittens."

"Did you ask to see them?"

"Why would I do that?"

He looked at me askance. "Who doesn't like kittens?"

The sensor light above the boathouse was cracked. The door was closed but an unlocked padlock sat in the hasp. I glanced back towards the cottages and half-expected to see a curtain twitch, but nothing moved. I manoeuvred the padlock out of the staple, opened the hasp then put the padlock back. Jonny looked at me as if I were a master thief.

"Have you done this before?"

"I've opened a padlock and hasp, yes, but I've never broken in anywhere before."

"Right."

He opened the door enough to slip through the gap and I followed him.

"I don't think there are cats in here," he whispered. "My aunt had a load of them, and it doesn't smell like her place at all."

He was right. I could smell water, engine oil and, faintly, polish. I pulled the door closed.

I'd never been in a boathouse before, so I wasn't sure what to expect, but it looked bigger than it did from the outside. The right side had a narrow wooden deck that led to a closed door at the far end. A sturdy workbench was fixed to the wall and had a toolbox, vice and a couple of wooden boxes on it. Above us, two skylights let in plenty of sunshine. The joists were open, with a couple of lengths of wood towards the back to create storage space. Two canoes and a bike hung from them by cables.

The remainder of the space was a dock. Water lapped at the pilings holding the deck up and a boat, with '*Merry Traveller*' painted on the side in a flowing script, was secured to a mooring post. It bumped gently against two old half tyres nailed to a couple of the pilings.

The double doors at the end were closed, but there was a gap of six inches or so between the bottom of them and the water.

"She's a nice-looking boat," Jonny said and reached over to stroke the highly polished wood.

"Is she?" I don't move in the right circles to know anything about boats, other than canoes and pedaloes.

"Yes. My dad would sometimes hire one to take us along the Broads. They're really expensive."

"So, what is this?"

"A four-seater launch, probably about twenty feet or so. Look at how beautifully it's been varnished." A Union Jack was mounted at the stern. "Somebody takes bloody good care of this."

"How do you mean?"

"Well, look at it." He kicked off his engineer boots and stepped onto the bow. The boat dipped in the water, but he maintained his balance. "The wood's glorious."

I looked around and couldn't see any kind of bedding. "If you had a boat like this, would you let cats in here?"

"Not bloody likely," he said. "They would claw the shit out of it."

"Can you see any marks?"

He knelt down and leaned over to check the hull. "Not that I can see."

"That's curious," I said. "He made a big deal about them being in here and brought food in."

Jonny shrugged. "Maybe he was escaping from Amanda."

"Maybe, or perhaps he was just trying to keep people out. You check the boat and I'll look along the deck."

"Are we looking for cats? We'd have heard them, by now."

"We're looking for anything that would suggest Flo has been in here."

I walked along the deck slowly. The toolbox looked expensive and was filled with equipment. Midway along was a wooden box that smelled of turps and had several rags in it. Beyond it was a paper dinner plate holding the congealed remains of a meal. A couple of cans of bitter were next to it, both open and empty. A black plastic bin bag was on the floor under the workbench, and I opened it. There were several plates in there, all of them dirty enough to make me wrinkle my nose as they smelled like they'd been there for a while.

There wasn't much else to see and there was absolutely no sign of cats being in here.

"There's some bedding," Jonny said. He was at the stern. I took my flip-flops off and left them on the deck then stepped onto the boat. Across the back seat was an opened sleeping bag, a slim pillow and a blanket. It looked as though the bedding was made, ready for someone to sleep there. I looked up in the joists.

"Is there anything on those boards?"

Jonny stood on the side of the boat, reached up to the nearest rafter and pulled himself up without any apparent effort. "Nothing," he said, dangling as though it was perfectly natural and not a strain at all. "A couple of cardboard boxes near the canoes and that's it."

He dropped back onto the boat, making it rock and I held the side to keep steady. I got off and put my flip-flops back on.

"So, no cats but someone's been eating in here and they're all set up to sleep."

Jonny knelt and sniffed cautiously at the pillow. "That doesn't smell like Flo's shampoo. That smells like a bloke's shower gel."

"Perhaps Will slept out here, to get away from Amanda."

"Having met her," he said, "that's probably what I'd do."

I didn't disagree with the sentiment. "What's out the back, do you suppose?" I asked.

"The river, I'd think."

I tried the single door and it opened easily. I pushed it wide and Jonny leaned out, holding onto the jamb. "That's what I thought. You push open those doors then back the boat out onto the river."

"Could you use the boat on the sea?"

"Probably, but I doubt it. With a cruiser, he'd probably head inland towards the Broads."

I leaned forward and saw a thin, grassy strip that petered out about six feet away.

"What's that track lead to?"

"Nowhere, it's just a bit of land." He leaned forward until I was convinced he was going to lose his balance. "What's that?"

"What?"

He sat down and eased himself over the edge. He toed the strip gingerly, as if to make sure it wasn't going to float away with him on it, then stood on it. It didn't move. He knelt to pick something up and turned to me holding what looked like a dirty iPhone. He laid it on the deck at my feet. Mud was caked and smeared over the screen and in the edges of the white case. It looked like it had been there a while.

My sixth sense tingled and the question was so obvious, I didn't want to say it out loud. I had no choice. "Is it hers?" There was no reason why it should be, like there was no reason for it to be on that narrow wedge of land.

"Maybe. I didn't pay much attention to her phone, apart from the fact it had a white case. But loads of girls have white cases." He pushed the phone towards me and I could see, now, it was in a terrible sate.

"I have an Android, I don't know how to switch an iPhone on."

He pressed some buttons on the side but the screen remained dark. "Maybe it's out of charge, or waterlogged."

"It's the only thing we've found that's out of place," I said.

He picked the phone up and turned it over in his hands. "Does that mean anything?"

"Not necessarily, because it could be his, or perhaps just washed up there. It would help if we knew who it belonged to."

He clicked his fingers. "A friend of mine has a stall on Seagrave market. If anyone could get into the phone and find out whose it was, it'd be him. Shall we give it a go?"

I didn't have a better idea, so I agreed.

Chapter 34

Jonny parked his bike alongside a dozen or more mopeds and motorbikes in a doorless garage on a narrow side street.

"A friend owns this place," he said as he chained the bike to a ring on the wall.

He locked our helmets against the handlebars as I ran my hands through my hair. He smiled and shook his head and his hair fluffed out naturally. He led us through an alley to a road with cars and delivery vans cluttering the kerbs. The buildings were old, with architectural flourishes mostly hidden behind gaudy signage.

"This is Broad Row," he said. "Do you know Seagrave at all?"

"Not really."

"Okay, we're at the top end now, away from the beach. This area is old town and I used to hate it here, because it was where my mum did her shopping and there weren't any arcades or toy shops for me to look in. But I like it now, because this feels like proper Seagrave, not all the lights and glitz."

He looked around wistfully and I enjoyed this newly shown depth. I wondered how many other people he'd let see it.

"Buildings are like people," I said. "When I was your age, I thought lines on a face were the worst thing ever. And don't talk to me about grey hairs. But as I've got older, I realised it was the lines and scars that made me who I am."

"You have scars?" He seemed surprised.

"A few, but mostly I meant metaphorical ones."

"Oh, okay," he said and led me across the road. "Market Square is along here. It's where they hold the fabulous Goose Fair every year."

I raised my eyebrows in query.

"You've never been to the Goose Fair?" he asked and sounded suitably astonished at my ignorance.

"Have I missed much? It feels like I have, seeing that you called it fabulous."

"It's a bit of a joke, from the town sign calling this place Fabulous Seagrave. A funfair takes over Market Square for a week and it's great fun."

"I'll look out for it."

"You should."

Ahead of us, two people came out of an alleyway and walked in our direction. One of them was Harley, sporting a fresh and painful-looking black eye. His companion was a young woman, wearing a short skirt, a vest top and too much make-up. Her shoulders were burned and she looked at him attentively, as if caught up in the first stages of attraction. As we got closer, I could see she wasn't as old as I'd originally thought, and I wondered if he'd snagged a holidaymaker for a week of fun.

"Well," he said, when he saw us, "look who it isn't."

Jonny looked at him curiously and I couldn't tell if his ignorance was real or a ploy to wind Harley up. If it was the latter, it succeeded.

"So what's going on here, then, Jonny? Are you going for the older model now?"

He laughed at his own wit, and it sounded horribly forced. The teenager laughed nervously, and I felt sorry for her.

"At least he's not trying to intimidate me into going out with him, Harley," I said.

The girl glanced at me and I quirked my eyebrows at her.

"You might want to think about that and be careful," I said, sotto voce, passing on secrets to the sisterhood. "He does like intimidating women."

Harley put his hand on the girl's arm. "You leave her out of this, you old cow."

"Happily." I smiled. "So, another black eye. Do I need to see the other bloke again?"

"Are you taking the piss?" he demanded.

"No, I'm showing some concern. That's one hell of a shiner."

"I know, and you should…" He stumbled, as if he realised his punchline wouldn't work but couldn't come up with any other scathing response.

"What's your problem, Harley?" Jonny asked.

"You, you dickhead. Like it's always been."

"How can I be your problem?"

Harley went to say something, then glanced at the girl. "You know full well."

"I think he means Flo," I said, raising my eyebrows at the girl. She looked confused.

"Oh, yeah," said Jonny, "that's right. Well, when I got together with her, Harley, mate, she wasn't seeing you or anyone else."

"You got in the way, you lanky bastard."

Jonny shrugged, as if to acknowledge that at least part of that statement was correct. "Listen, we've got stuff to do, so why don't you do us a favour and fuck off?"

"Are you threatening me?"

"Do you want us to?" I asked.

The girl looked very worried and touched Harley's arm. "Can we go?" she asked. "You were going to buy me a drink and I'm not enjoying this at all."

"Good thinking," I said to her. "Maybe, once you get away from us horrible people, you should find yourself another holiday romance."

Jonny laughed and Harley's cheeks filled with colour.

"Come on," said the girl. "Let's go."

Harley gave us both a look that suggested he wanted us to turn into pillars of stone and then the girl tugged on his arm again. He allowed her to pull him away and Jonny gave him a jaunty wave.

"See you around," Jonny said.

"Yeah," said Harley. "Maybe when you've found Flo."

Jonny stiffened and stepped off the kerb. I held his arm. "What does that mean?" he demanded.

"I heard you lost her," Harley said over his shoulder. "That was careless."

"You want to be careful what you say," I said. "The last time I saw you, you were threatening her."

The girl now looked terrified, and she let go of Harley's arm and kept walking.

"You don't know what you're fucking talking about, old lady." Harley didn't stop walking.

Jonny tried to shrug my hand away, but I held tight. "Leave it," I said. "He's winding you up."

"I know, he's been doing it ever since I met Flo." Jonny shook his head. "Anyway, how do you even know him? And what was that about him threatening Flo?"

I told him about the two occasions I'd seen Harley before.

"I wish you'd said something before," he said.

"But Flo dealt with both situations well. If she wanted you to know she'd seen him, she'd have told you."

"I suppose, so. She knows I don't like him."

"I don't either."

"He's a really dirty piece of work and I couldn't stand the way he'd come sniffing around Flo, as if she was a reserve girlfriend for him."

I watched Harley rush to catch up with the girl, but she ignored him when he called her.

"He's got a bit of a temper on him," I said. "Do you think he'd do something stupid, like lose his cool with

Flo?" He was clearly a bully and maybe he'd tried to intimidate Flo one too many times and snapped when she rebuffed him.

"I doubt it," Jonny said. "He's trash and he's weak."

His lack of concern made me wonder if I'd grasped the wrong end of the stick, but the thought was lodged in my mind now. What if he had something to do with her going missing? "Are you sure?"

"No, but she wasn't scared of him."

"That's not what I asked, Jonny."

We both watched Harley until he disappeared into another alley, chasing the girl who still ignored him.

"Come on," Jonny said, "let's get going."

Chapter 35

We entered the southern side of the square. A road edged the west side, lined with shops that all looked in need of some care. The east side was closed off by a big, brick-built piece of Brutalism that appeared to be a shopping centre. Of the three units on the ground floor, two were for Boots and the third was boarded up. A few people sat on the benches in front of them, eating chips from cardboard trays. The market itself was a straggle of stalls, with only a handful of customers milling around. A mobile chip shop seemed to be doing the most business.

"Amir's over there," said Jonny, and we walked to a stall festooned with neon tubing and small signs of flashing lights.

A couple of teenagers were loitering in front of a table that held an array of phones, most of which reconditioned if the sign was to be believed. One teen poked at a couple of older Nokia phones, as if they were part of a museum tour.

A man with jet-black hair cut to a fade on the sides and slicked into a sharp parting on top was sitting behind the table looking at a laptop screen.

"Hey, Amir," said Jonny.

"Hey, man, long time no see." He stood up and they shared a complicated handshake before Amir smiled broadly at me. "And who might you be?"

"I'm Carrie."

"Hey, Carrie, Amir Persuad at your service." He shook my hand briskly. "Are you looking to upgrade your mobile?"

"I'm afraid not," I said.

The teenagers had been watching us and now walked away.

"We'd like a favour, mate, if you can," Jonny said.

"Sure, what's up?"

Jonny glanced at me, as if he didn't quite know how to explain the situation.

"A friend of mine's gone missing," I said. "We found this phone, which might be hers, by the river on the road out of Seagrave. It's a mess." I took the food bag we'd used to store the phone out of my handbag. "Jonny said if anyone could get into it, you could."

Amir took the compliment as well as I'd hoped he would, though his expression dropped a little when I handed him the bag.

"Bloody hell," he said. "That's coated."

"I know and we're not sure how long it's been out in the elements."

"Can you help us out, mate?" Jonny asked.

Amir turned the bag over in his hands then undid it and slipped the phone out. Some of the mud had flaked off the case and he shook it away. He lifted the phone up and blew grit and dust out of the power point. "Of course

I can," he said. "Go and buy Carrie a tray of chips and come back in thirty."

* * *

The chips were nicer than I'd expected. We sat on a bench by Boots and Jonny seemed pleased we were doing something constructive. We talked idly and he explained he'd met Amir at school.

We went back to the stall thirty minutes later. Amir was selling a handset with larger-than-normal keys to an older couple and we hung back until he'd made the sale.

"How were the chips?" he asked me.

"Nice."

"Good stuff." He sat behind the table and gestured for us to stand behind him. His laptop screen showed a young Asian woman holding a baby. "I had to clean the points out and it was password-protected but," he said and waggled his fingers theatrically, "I have my ways."

Amir held up the phone so we could see the screen. "It belongs to woman called Lisa Ryland."

He looked at us but I shook my head and Jonny pulled his lips into a shrug.

"Oh, okay," said Amir. "Anyway, there's a lot of texts, a few voicemails and a lot of photographs." He looked at me and raised one eyebrow. "I'm glad you said you didn't know her."

"Why?"

"Because some of the pictures are–" he coughed "–for home entertainment, let's say. Once I realised what I was looking at, I went back to a gallery view, because it felt odd looking at them."

"Oh," I said, my sixth sense tingling again.

I didn't know Lisa and wasn't about to look at her risqué pictures, but I wanted to understand why we'd found her phone outside the boathouse. Something didn't feel right, and while it was a stretch that there might be a link between Flo and a phone randomly turning up out of the blue, it felt like a thread we should pursue. If I were in a Sue Grafton novel, I'd check the gallery to see if me or Jonny recognised anyone. That might give us another person to ask.

"They're not all like that though, surely?" I said.

"Only one batch, but it's quite extreme."

"Can we look at the regular ones?"

"Sure. I'll put them onto the laptop, so it'll be easier for you to see."

"Why are we looking at them?" Jonny asked, clearly frustrated. "This isn't helping at all. We don't know her and it's not Flo's phone."

"Let's just give it a moment," I said.

Amir attached a lead from the phone to the laptop, his fingers brushed the keyboard and then an image of a smiling woman filled the screen. She was standing on a beach, the sea and sun behind her, her long dark hair blowing in a breeze. Sunglasses hid her eyes and made it difficult to tell for sure, but I would have put her somewhere in her early thirties.

"Does she look familiar?" Amir asked.

"Nope," I said.

Jonny didn't say anything.

We went through half a dozen or so pictures, which showed the same woman and a man who might have been her husband and a small boy who might have been her son. They seemed to be on a foreign holiday, in what looked like a very nice hotel complex.

Then she was in a room, wearing a white jacket and sitting at a table against a bland, beige wall. She wasn't smiling. Her hair was straight and she wasn't wearing sunglasses. Her expression suggested she was saying something to the photographer.

The next photograph was a selfie, of Lisa and a man. The image was blurred so I couldn't see him clearly. The next photograph was crystal clear, though, as were the next half-dozen. It was the same woman with an older man she was touching in a way that made it clear they weren't related.

"That's Will," said Jonny.

Chapter 36

My mind buzzed as we walked back towards Broad Row and I tried to make sense of what we'd found. Jonny had lost interest because it didn't concern Flo, but I had that tingling sensation again, which told me I was missing a link somewhere. I kept circling back to Zoe, telling me about Will's job at the hospital.

I took out my mobile. "Hold up a second," I said.

Jonny frowned. "Are you okay? Am I walking too fast?"

"No, I'm fine." I thought he'd set a good pace and was enjoying keeping up with him. "I just need to make a call."

"Fair enough," he said and took out his own mobile.

I rang Helen Bignell, a reporter I'd known for years who worked for the *Norwich Evening News*. She answered on the fourth ring. "Carrie! Long time no hear."

We caught up quickly with each other's lives, though I didn't mention my heart attack.

"I wanted to ask you a quick favour," I said. "I don't suppose you could check through and see if a name comes up against any of your stories, could you?"

"Sure." I heard some quick typing. "What's the name?"

"Lisa Ryland," I said and spelled it. I heard more quick typing.

"Yes, there is something. She was a senior registrar at Norfolk and Norwich University Hospital until last year, when she was let go and left the area. She had an affair with an unnamed married colleague, who was forced to retire. I can't find a note as to why we didn't name him, so there must have been an agreement reached somewhere."

Bingo! "How old was she?"

"Thirty-four, at the time she left."

"That's great, thank you, Helen. We'll catch up soon."

I rang off and grinned at Jonny. "I think Will had an affair with Lisa and that's why he had to leave his job. I'll bet if we looked at those raunchy photos, he'd be in them."

"But he's old and she was hot." He pulled a face. "How could she?"

"Love can be blind to age."

"You're a weirdo. And we're no further forward than we were before we started."

"True," I said and put my phone away. But was it? If he'd had an affair and been caught, that could explain Amanda's treatment of him; she was punishing him for his misdemeanour. If she controlled the purse strings, perhaps he couldn't afford to walk away and had to endure her making his life a living hell. I had no sympathy with cheats, but I wondered if Amanda's desire to extract her pound of flesh had pushed him over the edge and caused him to crack?

With that line of thinking, it made sense why Samuelson was so keen to check if I hadn't fallen asleep. They must have known about Lisa and the affair, heard from me there was a terrible argument, only for me tell them that it couldn't possibly have been him. That could also explain why Scott was annoyed at me and convinced Will was guilty. Amanda, surely, would have told her brother what happened.

"Bloody hell," I said. "He's the perfect suspect."

"I know, I told you that. You said you'd caught him being horrible to Flo. That's why I wanted to check the boathouse."

He was right, of course, although we were on different pages. The death of Amanda didn't register with him.

There were more pedestrians on Broad Row now and a platoon of food delivery riders had gathered outside a pizza place, chatting to one another and checking their phones.

"What a waste of time," Jonny said and sounded crushed.

"I'll try Emily, later. She might give us something."

A young woman, who looked about Flo's age, came out of the Victoria Arcade in front of us. She was checking her phone and pushing a buggy. The child in it looked content as he sucked on an ice pop.

Jonny gave her a glance. "Hi, Lauren."

She looked up and seemed surprised to see him, then glanced at me for a moment before giving him a half-smile that didn't seem particularly friendly. "Hey, Jonny." She took another look at me and her eyes narrowed suspiciously. "Haven't seen you in a while."

"I've been about. How's the little one?"

"A right pain in the arse," she said and leaned forward to ruffle the child's hair. He tilted his head back and gave her a smile. She returned it then leaned on the buggy and looked at me again. "Aren't you going to introduce me to your friend?"

She said the word 'friend' as if it were poisonous. Did she think there was something between me and Jonny?

"This is Carrie," he said. "Carrie, this is Lauren, Flo's friend."

That meant I needed to keep her onside. "Carrie Riccioni," I said, with a smile. "I'm an old friend of the family." Lauren's expression relaxed slightly, so I pushed on. "It's been years since I was last in Seagrave and Jonny offered to show me around."

"You came on his moped?" she asked in surprise.

"I like to live dangerously."

"You must." She looked at him. "So, have you been away?"

"No, why?" he asked.

"Because I haven't heard from Flo in about a week and she hasn't replied to any of my texts or snaps."

"Did you ring her?"

"Of course I did, you muppet, but it went to voicemail. I thought you'd gone away at first, then wondered if she'd fallen out with me or something."

"I'm sure it's not that," I said. "Jonny said she's away for a few days and he thinks she's lost her phone."

"So long as she's safe," Lauren said. "When you hear from her, Jonny, tell her to give me a shout."

"I will."

"I've gotta go, I need to get this one to my dad's before my shift starts." She gave me a nod, then said, "Get Flo to call me, Jonny, yeah?"

"I will."

"Why did you say you were an old family friend?" he asked, as we watched her walk away.

"I thought it would help and it did."

"How?"

"We found out Flo hasn't been in touch with a friend she talks to regularly, which means your theory has gained some weight. If she'd gone away of her own volition, it's more likely she'd have spoken to someone, but there's a lot of people who haven't heard from her."

"So that's more proof, then! Shall we go back to the police?"

"No," I said, finding it hard to hide my exasperation. "If Emily hasn't heard from her either, that might be enough for us to speak to the police again."

"How is this so difficult?"

"Because we're not the police, or private detectives, and we can only work on what we have."

"And we don't have anything except a phone that doesn't connect to Flo at all."

"I know," I said. "But we can't go around accusing my neighbours of doing anything wrong, because that'll just get us into trouble."

He shook his head. "This isn't fair."

"Nobody ever said it would be."

* * *

Trish rang as I stood by the front door, watching Jonny ride away.

I said hello and we exchanged pleasantries.

"I just wanted to let you know one of my colleagues was out your way earlier and he went to check the trees between Miller's Point and the beach."

"Okay," I said.

"I'd told him to focus on the far end, as you said, but he worked his way up about a quarter of a mile, just to make sure."

"There's nobody there, is there?" I said. That's why I hadn't seen the tent this morning.

"It doesn't look like it. He found definite signs of a camp, which would be near the spot that you mentioned, and he also found a cooking pit dug into the sand, but the fire area was covered with sand. It appears the person you saw was a transient or traveller, making their way up or down the coast, as we said."

"Well, it's a relief to find out someone isn't hanging around," I said.

"I'm sure. But, you know, it's the seaside and the beach can be a giant, free campsite, if you're willing to put up with it."

"So, you think it's definitely a coincidence that this person was here when Flo went missing?"

There was the slightest of pauses and Trish clicked her tongue against the roof of her mouth. "I couldn't say for sure, but that's my thinking, yes."

I felt disappointed and frustrated, in equal measure. "Okay, well thanks for letting me know."

"Of course," she said. "Keep in touch and be careful, alright?"

Chapter 37

I had an early dinner and then sat on the patio to enjoy the early evening light and make my phone call to Emily. Jonny said she'd been Flo's best friend since infant school, so if Flo was going to tell anyone anything, it would be Emily.

It took her long enough to answer that I was planning what to say in my voicemail message.

"Hello?"

"Hi, is this Emily?"

"It is," she said cautiously.

"Thanks for picking up. You don't know me, but my name's Carrie. I'm a friend of Flo Adler's."

"You're who?"

"Carrie Riccioni. Can I have a quick word? I'm sorry to disturb you on a Friday evening, but I know you're good friends with her."

"She's my best friend. And you're not disturbing me, but I'm a bit worried. Do you know her boyfriend too?"

"Yes, I know Jonny."

"Fair enough," she said. There was no caution in her voice now, as if I'd passed a test successfully. "Is everything alright with Flo? I haven't heard from her all week and our Snapchat streak is crocked."

"You've heard nothing?"

"Nope. I thought maybe she's got caught up in something, either at work or with her mum, and her mind's drifted off. She's been a bit moony for a while now."

"Like her mind's elsewhere?"

"Yeah."

"Do you know why?" I asked.

"Maybe," she said and a note of caution crept back into her voice. "But why are you asking me?"

"I'll be honest, Emily. I'm not sure anything's wrong, but something seems a little out of the ordinary."

"That's a good way of answering without telling me anything. You sound like the lecturer in my law class."

"Sorry, I just don't want to worry you. Flo didn't turn up for work this week and her mum doesn't know where she is either."

"Have you been to the police?"

"Jonny has and he asked my help to see if we could find something out."

"Are you a detective or something?"

"I'm a social worker, I'm just speaking to people who knew her in case they know something we can take to the police."

"And nobody's heard anything at all? Not even Roxy?"

"No, I spoke to her myself."

"Okay, well that's definitely odd. Flo wouldn't leave Roxy in the dark at all."

"You don't think she'd go away for a few days, to get her head straight or something like that?"

"Flo never had any mental health issues."

"I didn't mean that," I said. "I mean, to give herself a break. She worked hard here."

"And she carried a few worries too, thanks to her mum. And Jonny at times, following her around like a little pet. But if she wanted a change of scenery, she'd have come to stay with me for a few days. Unless…"

"Unless what?"

"How well do you know Jonny?" She sounded concerned.

"About as well as you can after a week. For what it's worth, I'm a pretty good judge of character and he seems okay."

"I know that, but I don't know if I should tell you in case you say anything to him."

"If you think it could help then say it. I won't tell him if you don't want me to, though I might have to inform the police."

"Okay." She paused and I listened to ticks on the line. "Flo and Jonny might not be a couple for much longer, if you know what I mean."

I made a non-committal sound. I had a good idea of what she meant but I wanted her to make it clear.

"She met someone else," she said, after a moment or two.

"Oh," I said.

"I always thought she and Jonny were tight and would figure out a way to leave Seagrave and make a go of things, but then she started hinting she'd met someone else. He was older and she's always had a thing for older men, ever since we started going nightclubbing in town."

This could be interesting. "Do you know his name?"

"No. She said he seduced her off her feet, but it was complicated and better I didn't know his name until they'd got everything sorted out."

"How long ago was this?"

"About a month or maybe a little more. We talked a bit less after that, but I suppose that's normal when you've met someone new and she didn't want to make things awkward for me."

"How would she do that?"

"I've been struggling with my course this semester and I know Jonny, so I think she was trying to protect me."

"That makes sense."

"Well, it did until you asked me questions her best friend should know the answers to." There was a burst of noise and someone spoke at her end. "Yes," she said, but not to me. "I'm sorry, Carrie, I've got to go. Keep me updated though, yeah? If I think of anything, I'll ring you on this number. I tell you, all this worry, if she's just gone away for a dirty week with her new man, I'll kill her. Do me a favour, though."

"What's that?"

"Don't tell Jonny. It'll break him in half and I think Flo should be the one to tell him."

* * *

I couldn't settle and went to bed at ten to stare at the ceiling as my mind turned things over.

Flo's new man could, easily, be someone none of us knew who'd given her the spur to run away and start a fresh life. If that was the case, then we simply had to wait for her to get in touch with her family.

But what if both Jonny and Emily were partly right? Flo, by Jonny's account, spent most of her time here, cleaning the homes of three men, all older than her by some considerable margin. Plus, I knew she had issues with two of them.

Emily reckoned she'd gone with this man of her own free will, but who would have the most to lose if Amanda discovered the new relationship? Boyd wouldn't care, but Will certainly would. If his life was bad before, seducing a teenager would make things ten times worse. I hadn't thought of Scott as being part of the suspect pool before my conversation with Zoe this morning and he would have a huge amount to lose. He already relied financially on his sister and if she threatened to withhold funds, what would he do?

Or what if there was another angle we hadn't thought of? What if Flo had been seeing someone here, then met a new man somewhere else, and it was that which sent her original lover, from Miller's Point, into a jealous rage?

My head was starting to ache because none of these thoughts and theories would coalesce into a pattern that made any kind of sense. As I rubbed my eyes, I had a thought.

Another angle had opened, this one a bit more morbid than the others. I'd been working on the assumption that Flo had been swept off her feet by this new man and he'd taken her away, but what if that wasn't the case? What if there was somebody who wanted Flo all for themselves but couldn't compete with an older and wealthier man? What if it was someone who had no problem using intimidation as a seduction technique and had taken the next logical step and got violent?

Harley fit that description. He was keen to get Flo back and, if he knew she was about to leave Seagrave for good to start a much better life, he might have got desperate. And a desperate measure might be to snatch her and hide her away somewhere. That could explain the black eye – perhaps she fought back?

And then, if I was willing to entertain the idea that Harley had snatched her, what about the mystery man on the beach? Had he approached her, perhaps come onto her and then taken her by force when she turned him down?

My head hurt enough now that I had to get up and take some tablets. I got back into bed, not sure whether I was making progress or just turning in ever decreasing circles. Was it likely Harley had taken her? Could we apply pressure on him, to somehow find out? Even bullies have soft places and all we had to do was work out where his was.

My thoughts were tumbling over themselves and I knew I wasn't going to make sense of anything now. To distract myself, I picked up my book and read until I could barely keep my eyes open.

* * *

My eyes opened to darkness when I heard a patio door slide closed.

I reached for my phone and saw it was a little after two. Who the hell was mooching around at this time of the morning? My skin chilled. What if it wasn't someone going out but coming in? What if Jonny had decided to do some investigating on his own?

"Oh, no." I quickly got out of bed and pulled the curtain back slightly.

In the pale moonlight, I saw Scott climb into Amanda's garden and make his way to the boathouse. Torchlight showed briefly and he looked around then removed the padlock, opened the door and went in. I watched the light dance under the door as he moved around.

Did he somehow know me and Jonny had been in there, or was he looking for something?

He came out a few moments later, climbed into his own garden and went back into the cottage, closing the door softly behind him.

I let the curtain drop, got back into bed and lay awake for a long time, wondering about what I'd just seen.

Chapter 38

A shriek made goosebumps pebble my arms. Boyd rushed out of his cottage, pulling his dressing gown closed.

"Not again," he said and we ran into Amanda's cottage.

Muffled voices upstairs were interspersed with splashes. I led the way this time. My heart was thumping hard and it was difficult to draw a breath.

I pushed open the bathroom door and Will was knelt in front of the bath with his back to us.

"What're you doing?" I demanded.

Boyd wrenched Will back by his collar. Someone was lying face-down in the pink-tinged water. I reached in and turned them over. Flo stared at me with lifeless eyes.

The nightmare startled me awake and, when I leaned over to check my phone, I was surprised to see it was past eight o'clock. It had been a long time since I'd slept in this late.

I sat on the edge of the bed. My neck ached, so I massaged it then stood up and stretched. Parts of me popped that probably shouldn't have. I went to the toilet, made a cup of tea then opened the curtains. The gardens were empty.

After getting dressed, I went out into a morning that was bright and clear, with a warmth in the air that promised a good day. As I crossed the bridge, a couple of walkers coming down the hill waved to me. I waved back.

The tide was coming in, but I didn't want to give up on my morning walk, so I turned around and walked back by the flat and around the corner of Scott and Zoe's cottage.

Their cars were parked outside and I could hear music playing. A car I didn't recognise was parked in one of the guest spaces across the road. I wondered if it belonged to the walkers.

As I walked along the front of the cottages, a mobile rang. I glanced over my shoulder and realised there was a man in the car. His face was hidden by reflections on the windscreen. He answered the phone and it must have been on Bluetooth because I heard the soft rumble of a reply.

I stopped at the entrance to Miller's Point, selected my Donna Summer record and put on my headphones. After setting the timer, I set off towards Seagrave and walked to the beat. When I felt I'd done enough, I was pleasantly surprised to find I'd doubled my usual distance. Even better, I was only slightly out of breath.

I did a few stretches then walked home, pacing myself with every other beat so I hit a brisk pace without knackering myself.

When I got back to Miller's Point, the unknown car was still parked across from Scott and Zoe's cottage. Her car had gone. As I turned down towards the flat, a car door opened.

"Excuse me!"

I glanced over my shoulder. A man wearing a blue shirt and dark trousers was standing by the parked car. He looked like someone on his lunch break from an office.

"Yes?"

He pulled that face people do when they think they recognise someone. "Do I know you?"

"I don't think so," I said. He didn't look at all familiar to me.

He clicked his fingers, as if that would help him remember. "It's Carrie, isn't it?"

A chill drifted across my shoulders. He stood perhaps ten feet away and it didn't feel like far enough. I felt horribly vulnerable. "Do I know you?"

"Probably not." He smiled what I assume he thought was a non-threatening smile but it didn't make me feel any better. "My name's Trevor Evans, I'm a journalist for the *Seagrave Telegraph*."

That didn't reassure me at all.

"I appreciate this isn't the best introduction, but I'm not stalking you or anything. If you don't mind me coming over there, I can show you my press card."

"Anyone can have a card printed up."

"That's true." He took his wallet from a back pocket, opened it and took out a card he held up. "There's nothing sinister here, I promise. I recognised you from file pictures we used for the story when you had your heart attack at the Chesterton tower block."

Rita had shown me a clipping from the *Telegraph* while I was recovering. They'd used an old photo.

"How are you doing now?" he continued. "You're looking healthy, if you don't mind me saying."

"I'm walking a lot."

"Is that where you just went?"

"Uh-huh."

"Do you mind if I come closer? It feels odd calling to you from across the road."

"I'm not sure we have anything to discuss, Mr Evans."

"Trevor, please."

"Well, Trevor, it's our standard policy at work to not speak to the press."

"I understand that but I'm not here for you, per se. I didn't even realise you lived out here." He jutted his chin towards Amanda and Will's cottage. "I'm here about the business with Amanda Ross."

"Did you just say business? She collapsed in her bath, Mr Evans."

"So the official line goes, but I have a contact at the station who says there might be something else."

"I assume by 'something else' you mean something you can sensationalise?"

If my dig landed, he didn't show any sign. "I understand you and a neighbour found Mrs Ross and her husband. Is that right?"

I shrugged. "No comment."

"Ah yes," he acknowledged, "you don't talk to the press. But, off the record, I have to say I'm a little curious about the whole thing."

"It's very easy to say you're off the record, Mr Evans."

"It is." He put his phone on the roof of the car and turned out his pockets. "No recording devices."

I smiled at his pantomime. "You expect me to believe that?"

"Probably not, but it's true. I just want to understand about the accident, which involved a well-respected local doctor, with an excellent professional reputation. However, in her private life, she was known to be difficult, to say the least."

He paused, as if waiting for me to respond. I folded my arms and didn't say anything.

"I understand she had a difficult relationship with her husband, especially after what happened at the hospital."

"I don't know about any of that, Mr Evans."

"And why would you?" He scratched his cheek. "I also understand a young woman from around here has been reported missing."

"She didn't live here."

"That's right, she cleaned the cottages though, didn't she?"

"She did."

"Don't you think it's intriguing?"

"I don't follow."

"Well, she's nineteen and worked here, in close proximity to a man who was forced to leave the hospital after his affair with a much younger colleague was made public. His wife stood by him but, privately, it's alleged she made his life a living hell. And then she passes away, just after a young woman has gone missing."

His thought process made me uncomfortable. He was on the same track as Jonny, but it sounded wrong coming from Evans' mouth.

"That's a terrible conclusion to make, Mr Evans."

"Do you think so?" he asked, as if he'd expected my answer. "Oh yes, that's right. According to my source, you provided Will Ross with an alibi."

I felt my temper rise and knew I should walk away. "What has that got to do with anything?"

He shrugged. "For someone in your line of work, Carrie, you're remarkably naïve."

My temper rose faster so I turned on my heel and stalked away, digging my nails into my palms to distract myself. If I had reacted, he would have got what he was trying to achieve. The best thing I could do, for my blood pressure and sanity, was to walk away.

"It was nice talking to you," he called.

Chapter 39

Anger and adrenaline fizzed through me and I felt horribly on edge. I made a drink, in the hope tea would help me calm down, and went into the office.

The coverage of Amanda on the *Seagrave Telegraph* site was dry and stuck to the basics, which was unusual. I've been involved in a couple of cases that attracted national media attention and they were sensationalised to the extent I couldn't equate the written word to what happened in reality. I then clicked on the staff link and found Trevor Evans' page. The picture they were using must have been at least ten years out of date.

Movement caught my eye and I saw Will in his garden. He walked to the boathouse and paused at the door, checking the padlock. He looked around, saw me and nodded, as if in greeting. I didn't respond. He went into the boathouse and came out a couple of minutes later. He didn't look my way as he walked back to his cottage.

I looked out the window for a while, wondering if Evans was still there or if he'd managed to doorstep Will. I snapped myself out of it and shut down the *Telegraph* site. Winding myself up about the situation wasn't going to help and I should get on with some work to distract myself.

The doorbell rang. I grabbed my mobile and marched downstairs, the anger and adrenaline back.

"I have my phone," I said to the shape through the glass. "If this is you, Evans, I'm going to call the police."

"It's Will."

"Oh." My anger faded, even though I didn't really feel like opening the door to him either.

"Can I have a word?"

"What about?" I was intrigued but didn't want to make this easy for him.

"Different things. We can talk in your garden, if you don't want me in the flat."

That seemed a good compromise, so I opened the garden door before the front one. Will stood on the step and seemed to have aged five years since I'd last seen him, with dark circles under his eyes and hollowed cheeks. Grief is never pretty, even when your wife had been horrible to you because she discovered you were being unfaithful.

"Hello," he said.

"Hi." I stepped to one side so he could come into the hallway. "Through there," I said and gestured to the back door.

Will went into the back garden and I followed him. The day had fulfilled its early promise and the sun was warm and high in an almost cloudless sky. We sat across from each other at the patio table.

"Thank you for this," he said.

"Is this a social call, or are you back at the cottage for good?"

"I'm back home. DS Samuelson got in touch yesterday to say his people had finished and I was free to move back in. Since I'm not sure of my financial situation, I thought it best not to book any more time in the hotel."

'Financial situation' seemed an odd choice of phrase. "And how was it, going back?"

He rocked his head from side to side for a moment. "Not easy, because I can't get the image of Amanda in the bath out of my head."

I nodded in acknowledgement. "It must be awful."

"I stood in the bathroom, just to see if I could. The police had tidied up well, but it seemed very peculiar and I didn't like it."

"I'm not surprised."

"I'll cope," he said and tapped his index finger against the tabletop. "I wanted to thank you, too. I was told you'd provided my alibi and I know you don't have a high opinion of me."

"I told the police what I saw and heard."

"We did have a lot of arguments."

"I can imagine Amanda wasn't best pleased with you."

A frown crinkled his brow then he leaned back and tilted his face to the sun. "So you heard about the incident?"

"I did."

"She wasn't pleased with me for a lot of things."

"Did you tell her about Flo?"

He looked at me and his eyes were sad. "Not everything is how it appears, Carrie."

"Is that one of your favourite phrases? You said that before, then never explained."

"I can't, that's why."

"So where is she now?"

"Flo? I wish I could tell you." He cleared his throat. "I honestly don't know. I haven't seen her since you came into the dining room and took her away. I was as surprised as anyone when she went missing."

He sounded like he was telling the truth, but if he could lie so blatantly to his wife, he wouldn't have any trouble doing so to me.

"I understand we're never going to be friends," he continued, "but I wanted to let you know I appreciate your telling the police the truth."

"Samuelson asked if I'd nodded off and not noticed you going back."

"I can imagine but, as you can see, they didn't find anything incriminating in the bathroom."

His expression was hard to read, but had he just admitted something? "Should they have?"

"Of course, if she didn't die of natural causes."

"Do you think she did?"

"Are you asking if I think my wife was murdered?"

"Is that what you're trying to tell me?"

He looked at me for a moment too long, then watched his finger tap on the table. "I'm not trying to tell anyone anything, Carrie. I went out, I walked on the beach, I came home, and she was dead. I don't know what happened any more than you do."

"Like you don't know what happened with Flo?" It was a cheap shot and I saw the sting in his eyes. "You were right, before, about us not being friends, because I'm sure something's happened with Flo – I just can't prove it."

"I hope, for your own peace of mind, that some day you'll believe I don't know anything." He shrugged and stood up. "Thank you for letting me talk, Carrie."

He left and it was only when I heard the front door close that I realised how tense I'd been. I felt suddenly washed out and my neckache from earlier came back with a vengeance. I kneaded the sore muscles until they started to relax.

* * *

I wasn't hungry but I made a sandwich for lunch and took it down to the patio. A Cessna flew over, trailing a banner that announced a band I thought had long since split up were playing at the Hippodrome.

Jonny rang as I was eating.

"Hey, Carrie, how are you?" He didn't give me a chance to answer. "I'm sorry I haven't rung before, but I got called into work for a rush job and all I could think about was how you'd got on with Emily yesterday."

I'd meant to let him know, but then it slipped my mind after the meeting with Evans. "She hasn't heard anything since Flo went missing."

"Shit." He made a sound like he was chewing his lip. "Did Flo say anything about going away to get herself together?"

"Not to Emily."

"Shit. So that was another dead end?"

He sounded so lost my heart went out to him. When he found out about the other man, he was going to be broken. "Maybe."

"Well I'm not giving up," he said. "In fact, I was thinking more about the link between Flo and Amanda."

"Just be careful with that. There's a creep of a journalist hanging around here jumping to the same conclusion."

"Is he? What did you tell him?"

"Nothing. I'm not talking to someone like him who's only interested in the sleaze of it."

"But if he finds out what's happening, who cares if he's only in it for the sleaze?"

He was so eager I realised he'd missed my point completely. "Think about it, Jonny, you don't want him sensationalising this. Nothing good can come of it. What angle do you think he'll use if she's being held by someone like Will? She's an attractive young woman and he's a much older, disgraced doctor? She'd become the selling point and they'd make her look cheap."

"But he might find out the truth."

"You're not listening to me, Jonny. How would you explain that to Roxy, and how would Flo feel if she had gone away to get her head together, then discovered she was the front page of the *Seagrave Telegraph* because of what you'd told a reporter? If social media got hold of it, it'd become a real shitstorm for her."

He paused. "I didn't think of all that," he admitted. "But does the journalist really think it's Will?"

"I have no idea, I never asked him, but I'm finding it harder to believe."

"Eh?" He sounded both surprised and disappointed.

"Don't you think he's too obvious?"

"But it makes sense if we agree there's a link between Flo and Amanda."

"We don't agree, Jonny," I said carefully. "And you need to be careful talking about it."

"But what I else can I do?" he asked, exasperation cracking his voice. "I'm trying my hardest here."

"I know, but you're also obsessing about the Miller's Point angle and maybe overlooking something else." I hadn't intended to say anything, but he needed the distraction. "I had a thought last night, but if I share it with you, you have to promise you won't go off like a bull in a china shop with it, okay?"

"I have no idea what that means," he muttered.

"How can you not?" I asked. "It means that you have to listen to me and not react, okay?"

"So why didn't you just say that?" he asked sulkily.

"Because it wouldn't have annoyed you, would it? Do you promise not to overreact?"

"Yeah."

"I was thinking about Harley last night and the fact that I caught him trying to intimidate Flo a couple of times. I know you said that Flo knew how to handle herself and I completely agree, but what if he had something to do with her going missing?"

"You think he took her?" He laughed. "That bloke's all mouth and as weak as piss. She'd kick the crap out of him."

"You're probably right, but when I saw him, he didn't have that black eye."

"Holy shit," he said. "Do you think…?"

"I don't know," I said quickly. "You promised me, Jonny."

"Yes, yes, but you're right. What are you doing now? Are you free?"

"I could be," I said, cautiously.

"Good. I'm just about finished with work, so how about I come and get you and we pay Harley a visit."

"We need to be careful, Jonny."

"We will be, I promise. I'll see you in ten minutes."

Chapter 40

He had a couple of minutes to spare by the time he pulled up outside the front door. I was waiting for him, sitting on the bench, the sun warm on my face. I got up slowly and fixed him with a glare.

"You have to be sensible, Jonny. No jumping off the deep end, alright? We're asking some questions, that's all."

"Yeah," he said and handed me my helmet. "I'm not an idiot, I was listening to you."

"Good." I got on the pillion. "So do you know where he lives?"

"No, but I have him on Snapchat and he's been on the same street since we talked, so I assume he's at home."

We rode back into Seagrave at a steady pace, and he didn't try to talk to me. We followed Marine Drive past the pier, the Winter Gardens and the funfair and then cut through side streets until we were back in the Duncan Jackson estate. I remembered enough to recognise the street where Flo lived but we kept going, finally stopping in front of a small block of flats.

"He's in there," Jonny said and switched off the engine.

I got off the bike, he locked the helmets to the seat, and then we walked across the scruffy lawn to the main doors of the block. A woman with two young children hanging onto a stroller came through the foyer. They were singing lustily, and she looked harassed and tired. It gave me an idea.

"What's his surname?" I asked.

"Tork," said Jonny.

I opened the door for the woman. "Thanks," she said and gave me a warm smile.

"You're welcome. Listen, I know this might sound odd, but do you know someone called Harley Tork?"

The woman narrowed her eyes and that made me think she knew, but wasn't sure if she should tell us.

"Sorry, that sounds like a weird question, doesn't it? It's just that my boy's away at college, and Harley's got some bits that I need to take up for him, but I can't remember which flat he's in."

That seemed to reassure her. "Yeah, sure. He's in flat forty-five."

"Thank you," I said.

We went into the foyer, which looked clean and smelled faintly of bleach. There was a lift at the far end and a sign on the door indicated it was out of order.

"Why doesn't anyone live on the ground floor?" I asked.

"Eh?"

"Nothing," I said and went into the stairwell. It was dark and claustrophobic and the poured concrete walls had a kind of Artex pattern on them. The space smelled much worse than the foyer had. Jonny became more tense the higher we climbed and, by the time we reached the fourth floor, he was wiggling his fingers like they hurt.

I stepped out into the sunshine and took a deep breath as I looked along to landing. There were five doors and one of them had been covered with a steel mesh. The balcony looked out over the Duncan Jackson estate and cranes from the docks seemed to rise out of the buildings in the distance. A couple of dogs were barking, and someone was playing dance music loudly.

"Remember to take it easy," I said.

"Alright, mother, I promise."

I glared at him, and he glared back for a moment, then held up his fingers in a Scout salute.

"Okay," I said, and we walked along to flat forty-five. There were curtains drawn over the windows and I couldn't hear any noise from inside. We stood on either side of the nondescript front door. "Ready?"

"Uh-huh."

I knocked and waited, but nothing happened. I knocked again, louder this time. I heard the click of a deadlock then the door opened a crack. Harley seemed surprised to see us and I thought, for a moment, he was going to swear and slam the door in our face but, instead, he looked from me to Jonny and back again. His black eye looked livid in the sunshine.

"What do you want?" he asked, his voice quieter than I'd expected. "And how the fuck did you know where I lived?"

"Snapchat, mate," said Jonny.

"We need to speak to you, Harley," I said.

"Can't it wait?" He looked over his shoulder. "And we need to do this somewhere else."

"You don't need to let us in," I said.

"Good, because I wasn't going to."

"I'm happy to stand here on the landing and talk and I'm sure Jonny is too."

"I am.",

"For fuck's sake," Harley said, and he stepped out onto the landing, pulling the door closed behind him. Jonny stepped out of his way, but I didn't and we now stood very close to one another. "What do you want?"

"I want you to tell me how you got that black eye."

"What?" He seemed genuinely surprised. "What the fuck has my eye got to do with you?"

He was about a foot taller than me, so I stood as tall and straight as I could and leaned into him. "Everything, Harley. If you remember, I twice saw you being verbally abusive to Flo Adler and trying to intimidate her."

"You're an idiot," he said.

I leaned in closer and he took a step back, knocking the door with his backside. It swung open and bumped against the interior wall.

"And you're a charmer. So how did you get that black eye?"

"I think you need to fuck off."

"How about we go to the police, with our theory that it came from Flo hitting you?"

"What? Are you insane?"

"Did you threaten her one too many times, Harley? Or perhaps you tried to grab her and, when she realised you were planning to take her, she threw a punch? Was that it?"

"You're mad," he said.

I shrugged. "Maybe I am, but I'm happy to go to the police and tell them this."

A door creaked open from inside the flat and the colour drained from Harley's face.

"What the fuck is all this noise?" demanded a croaky male voice.

The hallway was dark and it took a moment or so before I saw someone coming towards us. The man was rubbing his face and his hair was a series of wild corkscrews across his head.

Harley gave Jonny a withering glare and then moved to one side so the man could stand next to him. In the sunlight, his eyes looked puffy and there was a white drool mark at one corner of his mouth. Whoever he was, we'd woken him up.

"What's going on?" he asked, without looking at anyone in particular.

Harley and Jonny kept quiet.

"We were talking with Harley," I said.

"I can hear that," said the man. He fixed his attention to me and ran a hand through his unruly hair. "And who might you be?"

"My name's Carrie Riccioni. Who are you?"

"Ooh," he said, "a lah-di-dah Italian." He pronounced it as *eye*-talian. "Well, I'm the man who owns this flat and I have no idea who you are, or why you're making so much noise."

I glanced at Harley and raised my eyebrows. He took the warning.

"They came round because they wanted to see if I knew where Flo Adler was."

"Flo Adler? She hasn't been around here in ages."

"I know that, Dad."

Tork senior glared at his son and moved his hand as if to brush hair from his eyes. Harley flinched and I knew, with that one reaction, we were barking up the wrong tree. Flo hadn't caused Harley's black eye.

"So why didn't you tell them that?" Tork asked. He put his arm over Harley's shoulders and the young man almost shrank away from the contact.

"I did, Dad."

I didn't know the dynamic of this household, though a picture was rapidly painting itself in my mind and I realised that not only had Jonny been right – Harley *was* a weak bully – but that we had created a real issue for Tork junior.

"He did, Mr Tork," I said.

Startled, Harley caught my eye, but I ignored him.

"He explained the situation," I continued, "and we were just leaving. I'm very sorry we woke you up."

"Yeah?" grumbled Tork. "Well, that ain't going to help me much when I'm knackered at work, is it?"

"It's not," I agreed. "I'm sorry though, all the same." I tapped Jonny's arm. "We'll get going."

"But we…" said Jonny.

I hooked my arm through his and led him away. He waited until we'd got to the stairwell before he stopped walking.

"What the hell was that, Carrie? We didn't find out anything."

"Yes, we did," I said. "Didn't you see how Harley reacted to his father? Flo never gave him that black eye."

"Didn't she?" Jonny glanced back along the landing and then shoved the stairwell door open. "Well, that's just fucking brilliant," he said. "Back to square one."

* * *

We rode back to Miller's Point in silence. I got the feeling that Jonny was really annoyed with me, and I couldn't fault him for that. I got off the moped and handed him my helmet, which he strapped to the seat.

"I thought Harley might know something," I said.

"Yeah, well he didn't." He shook his head. "So that just leaves Boyd."

"What? Hold on, just because Harley didn't know anything, it doesn't automatically mean you're right about Boyd."

"Why not? I told you from the start Harley was as weak as piss and we both know Boyd likes younger woman."

"You're clutching at straws, Jonny."

He turned the bike around. "I've got to go. I'll call you later."

"Jonny, please don't do anything rash."

"Of course not," he said, yet I didn't believe him for a moment.

Chapter 41

Unable to focus on work or reading, I decided to get out for a while but didn't want to walk to the beach in case either Evans followed me or Will wanted another chat.

I looked at my car keys, sitting in a bowl on the shelf by the door. I wasn't supposed to drive but I felt better and my fitness was improving, so surely one quick run out wouldn't do any harm.

I put on my flip-flops, got my keys and went downstairs. I opened the door cautiously but no one was around, so I strolled over to the car and got in. It started first time. I switched on the CD player and Earth, Wind & Fire blasted out.

Tapping my fingers to the beat, I drove out of Miller's Point. Evans' car had gone. I turned towards Seagrave and took it steady but, rather than push my luck and go through the town, I saw a sign for Seasons Garden Centre and called in there.

I quickly found a space and got out. Across the way, where a line of trees formed the boundary of the car park and whatever was beyond it, was a small group of teenagers. They'd formed a circle and were laughing as they looked down at something, but there wasn't much humour in the sound. Fearing the worst, I stepped around the car to give me a clear line of sight and hoped I wouldn't see legs on the floor from whoever they were bullying. But there was nothing. One of the teenagers, a boy with a long face and acne around his mouth, saw me looking and said something. The others then turned to look, and the circle broke up, the teens ambling away towards the road. Maybe I was giving out social worker vibes or something.

It took a moment to realise they'd been standing around the messy remains of a seagull. It appeared to have been stamped on and some feathers drifted in a light breeze, while others were stuck to the tarmac by the gory mess.

I looked towards the teenagers again. One of them glanced over his shoulder, gave me a jaunty wave then laughed before turning back to whatever his friends were saying.

There was nothing to suggest the boys had killed the bird, but their clear joy at its destruction was unpleasant. I turned away from the mess and walked into the garden centre.

It was wide and spacious, with piped music, and the strong smell of coffee and bacon filled the air. I wondered, idly, how hungry anyone would be if they found themselves parked next to that seagull.

I browsed with the Saturday afternoon shoppers, admiring plants that, should I buy them, would be dead within weeks, and then did a quick tour of the outside. It occurred to me, not for the first time, how big a garden you'd have to have for some of the statues on sale.

When I went back inside, I saw PC Trish Moss walking towards the door as she talked into the radio pinned to her lapel. I adjusted my route so we intersected and, when she noticed me, she smiled.

"Hello, Carrie."

"I take it you're working?"

"Possible shoplifting," she said, "but the perpetrator had gone before I arrived. It's the end of my shift, so I'm happy."

"Do you have to go back to the station, or could I buy you a cup of tea?"

"I rarely turn down the offer of a cuppa."

At the cafe, I ordered the drinks and somehow managed to resist the temptation to buy a bacon butty. Trish got us a table by the window and I took the cups over.

"So, what brings you out here?" she asked.

"I just needed to get out of Miller's Point for a while," I said and told her about Trevor Evans.

"I know Mr Evans," she said, in such a way I gathered he wasn't her favourite person in the world. "He could be a good journalist if he didn't think he was working for *News of the World* during the eighties."

Her comparison made me laugh and she smiled at my obvious enjoyment.

"I take it," she said, "you experienced that version of him?"

"Absolutely." I didn't want to put her on the spot but decided to take a chance. "You don't suppose there could be a link between Amanda and Flo, do you?"

She pulled a face. "I didn't realise this was a cup of tea with strings attached."

"It isn't. I don't want you to tell me anything you shouldn't. Think of this as two friends chatting."

"You're good," she said and smiled. "In that that case, then, I doubt there's a link."

"Jonny agrees with Evans' theory."

"Why wouldn't he? He's probably grabbing anything that makes sense to him, even if he has to squint to see it."

"You've heard nothing else?"

"You remember that bit about me not telling you stuff I shouldn't?"

"Fair enough. I spoke to a friend of hers last night." I told her about my call with Emily.

"And you're telling me, unofficially, the following afternoon?" She didn't sound happy or unhappy about it.

"I'm sorry, I should have thought. Does it help at all?"

"You don't give up, do you?"

"Not really. I'm worried about her, Trish."

"Okay," she said and spread her hands. "She doesn't appear in any assault reports. It could be that she was taken but, if so, it was done without witnesses and still nobody, other than Jonny, has reported her missing. So, as an adult, if she chose to go away with a new man, as her friend suggested, then she can. At least that makes sense."

"Oh, I know. I've been swept off my feet and had my head turned for a while, so why shouldn't it have happened to Flo?"

"It's a story as old as time," Trish said.

"Do you think that's what happened?"

Trish finished her drink and shrugged. "Why not? There's no hint of anything suspicious, however much Jonny might want there to be."

"Thanks, Trish, I feel better for talking that through."

"I'm glad. You've done your best here, Carrie, and that's more than most people would have done. Jonny seems like a good lad, but people fall out of love for all manner of reasons. Maybe he knew the relationship was slipping away but couldn't face facts. That happens a lot too."

"It does."

"Anyway," she said and finished her drink, "I'm going back to the station, then home. Thanks for the tea, I appreciate it."

"You're welcome. And thank you for being candid with me."

"Always. Now get yourself home and relax."

* * *

I took her advice and spent the rest of the afternoon reading and listening to music. I made a bacon butty for tea, which was delicious, and Luca FaceTimed me as I washed out the grill pan.

I enjoyed watching his and Françoise's easy way with one another and just being involved in their conversation and laughter made me feel so much better.

He was keen to make sure I was okay and I told him about my improving fitness and that seemed to please him a lot. We were on the call for the best part of an hour and I really didn't want it to end, but they were going out and it wasn't fair to hold them up.

I reluctantly, but brightly, said goodbye and blew them kisses, which they returned.

Chapter 42

"I think there might be someone else."

Zoe and I were sitting on the breakwater, looking out towards the horizon. I glanced at her but she didn't shift her gaze and her watery eyes caught the early morning light. I waited for her to continue. If she had something to tell me, it was better she did it in her own time. Instead, I watched gulls circling under the heavily overcast sky. Some clouds were the colour of a bruise and it looked like we'd have rain before the day was out.

I hadn't slept well but forced myself out of bed and, happily, managed to shave another couple of seconds off my walk.

"I'm sorry," she said, after a while. I glanced at her but she was still looking out to sea. "I don't mean to offload on you."

"It's not a problem. It often helps to get things off your chest."

We faced one another. A tear shivered on her eyelid then tracked down her cheek before she palmed it roughly away.

"After we saw the solicitors yesterday, we went to visit friends in Sheringham. It'd been long planned and we'd talked about cancelling, but he said absolutely not. We hadn't seen Steve and Andrea for ages and he thought it would do us some good, so we went." She rubbed a finger over her lips. "I love it there and I love them, so I agreed."

"You had nice weather for it."

"Yeah," she said absently. "But he was so distracted and unhappy. Not with Steve and Andrea, but he was off with me and it wasn't something specific he was annoyed about, just a general air. Do you know what I mean? Where even if you're perfect all day, you still manage to get under someone's skin and on their nerves? Plus, he kept getting texts and would go off to reply to them, so I couldn't see him."

I felt for her, remembering my own sense of unease watching a husband receive and send texts he wanted to keep private. "Did you ask who they were from?"

"Yes, after it got so obvious even Steve said he wasn't paying attention to me. Scott said they were all work-related."

"Is that likely?"

"I don't know. They could have been, or it could be someone else he wants to be with."

"But you don't know for certain?"

"Of course not," she said. "He's hardly going to admit it, is he?"

It was a good point. "So how did it go with the solicitors?"

Zoe shrugged. "Very well, from Scott's standpoint." She threw a pebble towards the beach and watched its arc. "Amanda changed her will at some point and he's going to inherit her entire estate."

That surprised me. "All of it?"

"Uh-huh. I take it you know what happened with Will at the hospital."

"I do."

"Well, once that came to light, she apparently cut him out of her will altogether. I don't know how he'll take it, though I'm sure Scott will let him know in the worst possible way. In fact, it wouldn't surprise me if he just tells him to get lost. The cottage is in Amanda's name, after all."

"Do you really think he'll tell him to go?"

"Why not? He doesn't want the bloke he blames for his sister's death living next door." She took a deep breath and let it out slowly. "Scott's happy, though, because it'll settle all his debts and still leave plenty."

"Do you believe Will had anything to do with Amanda's death?"

"I don't think so. Everybody who came into contact with that toxic couple knew that they were bad news for each other, so it was obvious he'd be the prime suspect until you gave him that alibi, of course. And the police don't seem to be pursuing Will either."

"I know, I spoke to him yesterday. Plus, there was a journalist hanging around outside yours."

"What did the journalist want?"

"Information about Amanda, and he's trying to make a link between her and Flo going missing."

Zoe's frown was so complete it looked as if she'd flinched. "How on earth did he make that connection?"

"I didn't ask."

"Well, if he turns up today with that kind of conspiracy theory, Scott won't be very happy." She offered me a wan smile. "Like I'd notice that, eh?"

"It might be nothing, Zoe. Like I said before, grief works differently on different people."

"Yeah, I'm probably misreading the whole situation and Scott's suffering in silence, even though I've told him he can talk to me about things whenever he wants to." A hopeful look flitted across her face. "Perhaps we'll be better today."

"I'm sure you will."

"Shall we go? I don't know if I'm sweating a lot, or the stone's cold, but my bum's freezing." We got up and she rubbed her backside briskly. "I need to get out of these clothes."

We walked along the breakwater and she stopped me, on the bridge, by touching my arm. "Thank you for this, Carrie. It really helps to talk things through."

"You're more than welcome. Listen, why not come over for a coffee when you've got sorted?"

She checked her watch. "That sounds lovely. Would ten o'clock be okay?"

"Ten'll be fine."

Chapter 43

Jonny knocked on my door an hour or so later. His eyes were red-rimmed and he seemed agitated.

"Hey, Carrie; this isn't too early for you, is it?"

"Not at all. How are you?"

He held his hand flat and rocked it a little from side to side. "Been better, been worse, you know how it is."

"I do." He really didn't look well. "Did you get much sleep last night?"

"Not really."

"Did you want to come in?"

"I don't know." His agitation seemed to be growing, like he was a spring coiled one turn too many.

"What's the matter?"

He pouted a shrug. "I asked a question I shouldn't have and didn't like the answer I got."

That was too cryptic for me on a Sunday morning. "Eh?"

He turned his head away. For a moment, I thought he was going to leave but, instead, he put his helmet on the moped saddle then leaned against the wall. He exhaled hard, his cheeks puffing out. Whatever he wanted to say clearly wasn't coming out.

"How about I get us a drink?"

"Have you got a beer?"

"Nope. You can have tea, coffee or water. Why don't you come in?"

"Can I have some water and we sit in the garden?"

"Sure." I opened the door for him then jogged upstairs, made a tea for myself, got him some water and went down to the patio. I put his drink in front of him and sat across the table. "So, what's up?"

"I'm sorry, Carrie, I didn't know who else to talk to, but I feel guilty about laying all this on you."

My day was starting to follow a pattern. "Don't worry about it."

He took a long drink of water and put the glass down carefully. "I went out on a pub crawl with my mates and we ended up at a club called Tigers. The boys were trying to cop off with the honeys in there but I was too busy looking around, in case I saw Flo."

I sat forward. "You saw her?"

"No." He shook his head, as if I hadn't been paying attention. "But I saw Lauren, out with her crew."

I remembered Lauren, the young woman with the pushchair. "Right."

"She'd had a bit to drink, and we're not the best of mates anyway, so she starts telling me I'm not good enough for Flo. That she needs to spread her wings and doesn't want me being a weight around her neck, dragging her down."

That sounded harsh, but I didn't know the cause of ill ease between them, so I kept quiet.

"She was in my face, Carrie, it was horrible, and then she laughed at me because I was looking for Flo."

"Why would she laugh at that?"

"Because she says it's a waste of time. She reckons she doesn't know where Flo is, but knows she wanted someone else."

I felt a quick chill. "Did she say who?"

"No, just that she'd got the hots for someone who was older and better than I could ever be."

"Were they having a relationship?"

"Lauren didn't say, but Flo said he had money and could give her the life she deserves."

It sounded so painfully close to what Emily had told me, I didn't doubt it was the truth. So, had she gone away with him or had Jonny's theory been right from the start? If Flo misunderstood the situation and showed her hand, had she inadvertently forced the man to do something to keep her quiet?

"You're thinking the same as me, aren't you?" he said. "She fancied one of the fuckers here, and when she made a fool of herself, they had to act."

"We can't be sure, Jonny. It could have been any older man, from anywhere."

"But she doesn't go anywhere else, I already told you that." He shook his head, angrily. "No, it's one of these bastards. They've kidnapped her and we need to find her."

"We don't know that, Jonny."

"I have to believe it though," he said and his voice cracked. "Because I don't want to think of anything worse, do you know what I mean?"

I could see in his eyes what he was trying not to acknowledge and I didn't push him on it.

"She's been gone almost a week, Carrie. What if they're not feeding her properly?"

He was working himself up, his anger papering over the holes of logic in his theory.

"Jonny," I said gently, "we don't know any of this for sure."

"Then how else did she know him? You saw Will being horrible to her."

I thought back to that night but I couldn't remember any kind of sexual desire in Flo's attitude or body language. "She wasn't waiting for him to make a move, Jonny, she was trying to get away from him."

"So, what about Boyd? You know as well as I do that he likes them young."

Jonny's anger and fear were clearly blinkering him. "That doesn't necessarily mean anything, and Kay is probably ten years older than Flo. It's not like he's got a harem of teenagers running around."

He took another sip of water and looked at me like I was a stranger. "I didn't expect you to close everything off like this, Carrie."

His tone surprised me. "What are you talking about? I thought we were discussing this."

"So did I, but now it feels like you're taking the piss."

I felt a kick of anger. "How am I doing that?"

"Making jokes about teenagers and whatever." He got up so quickly his chair rocked back and he had to catch it before it fell over. "I don't know, I'm knackered and angry and sad at what Lauren said and I'm ruining everything. I can't get her out of my mind, Carrie."

My anger faded at his openness. He was lost and didn't know how to cope. "I know, Jonny."

"I keep looking all over town and I can't afford to fuel up the moped and the fucking thing is on its last legs anyway. But I know it's this place, I feel it in my bones." He glanced over my shoulder. "Do you think I could crash in the empty flat? You wouldn't know I was here and I'd be able to snoop around."

The thought of him snooping around in this state didn't fill me with joy. "It's not my place," I said, diplomatically. "I'd need to ask Rita."

"Great, I'll kip on the floor and it won't be a problem. I appreciate this, Carrie, I really do. I'll call you later, is that alright? Perhaps we can talk some more then, when I've had some sleep."

"You should definitely sleep," I said. "And I'm about all day to talk."

I followed him through to the hallway and opened the front door.

"Thanks," he said awkwardly. "I'll speak to you later."

He walked over to his bike, shook his head then pulled on his helmet. He started the moped up, then got on and rode away. I was about to close the door when the engine stopped abruptly and I heard shouting. Had he fallen off, or hit someone? Had Evans turned up and waylaid him? With the mood Jonny was in, he might lose his temper and that wouldn't end well.

The other voice was Boyd's and that made me move. I jogged towards the corner steadily but was soon running as the argument got more vicious.

Boyd's car was in front of his cottage with the boot open. He stood beside it, glaring at Jonny, who was squaring up to him. Jonny's moped was lying on its side behind the car, the front wheel still spinning slowly. Boyd had a suitcase in his hand.

"Who the hell do you think you are?" Boyd demanded.

"You know who I am, you disgusting pervert. You should be ashamed of yourself, ogling little girls when you're almost sixty."

Boyd was clearly taken aback. "Who's ogling little girls? What are you talking about, you moron?"

"I'm talking about you, you fucking pervert." Jonny took a step towards Boyd and raised his fists hesitantly.

I waved my arms as I ran to get their attention. "Hey!" I needed to stop this from escalating. "Hey, Boyd!"

He glanced at me before looking back to Jonny. "I don't suppose you have any idea what's going on here, Carrie, do you?" he asked.

"Yes," I said, stopping a few feet from them. "Jonny, what're you doing? Boyd's not the answer."

Jonny ignored me. "Where is she?" he demanded and took a step closer.

Boyd slowly put the suitcase down without taking his eyes off Jonny. The threat of violence was almost tangible and it turned my stomach.

"I've already told you," Boyd said, "I have absolutely no idea."

"You're a fucking liar. She told me you tried it on with her."

"She told you what?"

"You heard me, you lying pervert."

Boyd jerked his thumb towards me. "And you'd better be careful, talking like that in front of witnesses."

"Calm down, Jonny," I said.

"I'm not scared of you, Manning. Tell us the truth."

"I have been, you idiot, you just don't want to listen."

"So what's with the case? Are you taking it to where you've stashed her? I know about her man friend and I know you're a dirty old man who chases young girls. It doesn't take a genius to put all this together."

"For your information, smart-arse, this belongs to Kay."

"Oh, is she in on this too?"

"Jonny," I said, "you're being ridiculous."

"Am I? Maybe they're weird. Flo found handcuffs in his bedroom once, so maybe Kay likes–"

Boyd shoved him. Jonny grunted and staggered back but managed to keep to his feet.

I put a hand on Boyd's shoulder, but he shrugged me off. "Boyd," I said, tension and anxiety making me angry. "Leave it."

"Yeah, listen to Carrie," mocked Jonny.

"And you can knock it off, too, you idiot," I said, directing my anger at him. "You're making this worse."

"He shoved me first."

"What are you, a child?" Boyd demanded, his lips pulled tight against his teeth. "Come at me if you want, because I can defend myself, but don't drag Kay into your sick fantasies."

"Yeah?" Jonny sneered and lurched forward.

Boyd planted a foot, braced himself and punched Jonny quick and hard in the belly. Jonny's breath whooshed out and he had to grab the car for support. He leaned forward, gasping as he struggled to take a breath.

"Boyd," I said, sharp and even. I tugged at his shoulder again and he moved back willingly now.

"I didn't want to hit him," he said, "but I'm not having him talk about Kay like that."

"He didn't mean it, he's wound up."

"And I'm not?" Boyd asked in disbelief. "He meant everything. We're all wound up because that's what happens to adults. It doesn't mean you can throw your weight around and slander people's girlfriends."

Jonny finally took a deep breath and coughed.

"Get out of here, Jonny," Boyd said, his voice rough with anger. "And don't come near me again or I'll call the police."

I took Jonny's arm and he tried to shrug me off. "For fuck's sake," I muttered. "Don't make things harder for yourself."

He let me support him back to the moped and I had to help him lift it. He put his helmet on then sat on the saddle.

"You need to be careful, Jonny. You can't go around accusing people like that. Boyd could report you."

"Who cares?" he muttered and shrugged. "But I suppose the police will come for me because I insulted the young girlfriend of a bloke old enough to know better, but they won't look for my girlfriend."

"Stop feeling so sorry for yourself. That's not how it goes and you know it."

"And what do you know, Carrie?" He glared at me. "Are you just trying to be my social worker now?"

I stepped back, surprised at the venom in his words. "I'm trying to help, Jonny."

"Well, you're not."

His words stung, even though I knew they were said in the heat of the moment. "I never said I was a detective and I didn't cross any lines, but you're just a loose cannon now. I think you'd better piss off."

"I'm going," he huffed and started the bike.

"Your bike sounds like shit too," I shouted.

He tapped the side of his helmet then rode away. I felt angry, defeated and frustrated.

Boyd closed the boot of his car and looked at me. "That wasn't pleasant," he said, calmly.

"I'm sorry you got dragged into it."

"Why are you sorry? It was that dickhead who started on me." Boyd rubbed his knuckles. "I haven't hit anyone since I was at school."

"I'm glad you didn't punch him in the face. You'd have knocked him out."

He shook his head sadly. "I don't like violence, I really don't, but he pushed me too hard."

"I don't think anyone would blame you. He's lost, Boyd, and he's clutching at straws."

"Well, he picked the wrong straw to clutch at." He looked at me intently. "For what it's worth, I am taking this back to Kay's and I don't have any idea where Flo is. I was never that big a fan of hers, to be honest, and I certainly never came onto her." He rubbed his hand again. "I hope they find her, though."

"Me too." I was annoyed at myself, feeling like I hadn't handled any of this well.

"Before you go, Carrie, I need to make you understand I never did anything with Flo and I didn't lead her on. Whatever that idiot thinks, I'm not a pervert. Yes, Kay's young enough to be my daughter, but she's a lot older than Flo."

"You don't have to explain yourself."

He shrugged with one shoulder, as if he understood but couldn't comply. "I think I do, if you're willing to listen."

"Sure."

"I was married before and for a long time. She was my teenage sweetheart and we met on the first day of college, when we were both nervous students. I loved Bella so much, it made my stomach flutter to think of her. Have you ever been in love like that?"

"When I first met Dante, yes. It wore off after a while."

"Ours didn't and we were perfect for each other. In fact, the only bump in the road was when we found out I was sterile, but we managed to get over that too. And then" – he clicked his fingers – "as if by magic, she contracted cancer. One day she was fine, the next day she wasn't." He took a deep breath. "It was horrible. We knew it was terminal fairly quickly and she needed a lot of care and it's the worst thing I've ever experienced, watching her fade. Just…" His voice tailed off and he bit his lip.

"She passed and, after a few years on my own, I accepted a well-meaning friend's offer of a blind date. Bella had made me promise I'd start again and so, finally, I carried out her wish. It wasn't easy because, although I found women in their early fifties attractive, I kept thinking about health issues, so I went younger. I wanted someone in the prime of their life, so I wouldn't have to go through the same situation again." When he looked at me, the light caught the shine of tears in his eyes. "I know that makes me selfish but…" He waved his hand.

"Not at all," I said.

"I'm sorry to blurt this out now, I should have said something earlier, but you're the nicest person here, Carrie, and I need you to understand. I've never told anyone here the truth." He checked his watch and looked conflicted. "Look, I'm sorry, but I need to get going."

"Of course."

"I'm sorry I hit him, but he pressed all the wrong buttons."

"Don't worry, he dragged you into it."

"Yeah, well I'm sorry you got dragged into it too." He smiled weakly. "I hope, at some point, we can find the time to have that drink together. It'd be nice to talk rubbish and share stories of the same pop culture."

"I'd like that too," I said.

Chapter 44

By the time Zoe came round, the colour of the clouds matched my mood. My anger at Jonny for confronting Boyd simmered, as well as his insinuation I hadn't done enough to help Flo.

"I think we're going to have a storm," she said, looking up at the sky.

"Looks like it," I said and gestured for her to come in.

"Speaking of storms, did I overhear you trying to referee between Boyd and Jonny earlier?"

"You could say that."

We went up to the flat and she sat at the dining table, looking out towards the hill. One person was walking there, wearing a bright-yellow cagoule.

"Coffee?" I asked. When she agreed, I went into the kitchenette and put the kettle on.

"So, what happened?" she asked, and I told her how rash Jonny had been and what he said.

"Ouch," she muttered. "That must be tough."

"It was." I noticed she was rotating her wedding ring around her finger. "How are you feeling?"

"Better, because our talk this morning helped me put things into perspective and I asked him outright what all the phone calls and text messages were."

"And it wasn't what you'd thought?"

"Nope," she said and her smile was hopeful. "Apparently, they're all to do with a business deal. He's been talking to some people in Norwich about a start-up and they were looking to rent space, but it got snarled with financing, which he's obviously now got." She spread her hands. "It's all so obvious and there was me, putting two and two together and making nine, driving myself nuts in the process."

Someone shouted outside, the sound drifting through from the office. Both of us looked at one another and raised our eyebrows. There was another shout.

"Is that Scott?" she asked, getting up from the chair.

She followed me into the office and we stood by the window. Scott and Will were facing one another in Will's garden, about ten feet apart. Neither of them looked happy.

"You're a fucking idiot," Scott shouted.

"Shit," said Zoe. "Scott's so mad at him, he's going to do something stupid."

Will said something but the sound didn't carry. Scott didn't reply but flexed his fists, his arms so rigid at his sides they might have been carved from wood.

"I need to get down there," Zoe said.

We rushed downstairs, got our shoes, and then she was out the door with me right behind her. The clouds were navy blue now and racing across the sky.

She vaulted the fence into her garden and I tried to keep up.

"Scott!" she shouted. "What're you doing?"

He glanced at her and his thunderous expression lifted slightly, but not enough for my liking. "This little fucker's back in the cottage."

"I live here," said Will, quietly but forcibly.

We climbed into Will's garden together. I stood next to her and could almost feel the tension coming off her in waves.

"No, you fucking don't," Scott said. His body seemed to vibrate, he was holding himself so solid and still. His lips were tight against his teeth. "You're fucking out of here."

"No, I'm not," said Will. He seemed unnaturally calm to me and that, in its own way, was almost as frightening as Scott's obvious anger.

"Scott," Zoe said, holding her hands out. "You need to calm down."

"I am calm," he said, his voice clipped. "He needs to go."

Will looked at each of us in turn. "You can't throw me out of my own house."

"And you can't kill my sister, then wander in like nothing's happened."

"I didn't kill her and Carrie knows that."

Scott glared at me. "Yeah, you can fuck off too," he snarled. "Why would you lie to the police and give him an alibi?"

His anger was frightening but I held my ground like I'd been trained to. If you gave ground, it was almost impossible to regain it. "I told the police what I saw."

Scott shook his head, as if he'd got a fly buzzing in his face. "I don't know what you're getting out of this, but we all know he did it."

"The police went over their house with a fine tooth comb, Scott, you know they did," Zoe said. "They spoke to us. There's nothing to link Will to what happened. It was an accident."

"Of course there's nothing to link him to it, his DNA is all over the fucking place."

"Scott," she said, sounding like a woman well-used to talking her way out of a potential confrontation. I wondered how many times she'd seen him lose his temper. "Amanda slipped. It was a horrible, tragic accident."

"No, that's not it at all. She hated him and made his life hell, and he finally snapped."

"If you want to talk about who made her life hell," Will said, "shouldn't you be looking closer to home?"

Scott made a sound deep in his throat that sounded almost like a growl.

"Winding Scott up isn't going to help anyone, Will," I said, as I felt the first spot of rain on my forehead.

He looked at me sympathetically. "I'm sorry you had to get tied up in all of this, Carrie."

"You should be sorry to me and to Amanda's memory, you arsehole," Scott said and took a step closer to Will. "I want you gone. Amanda didn't want you here and neither do I."

"But Amanda didn't know everything, did she?" Will said. "I wonder if Zoe does?"

Scott launched forward and punched Will on the jaw. Will's head snapped to the side and he staggered back, tripping on one of the gnomes and falling into the pond.

The sudden violence shocked us into silence and Zoe looked frightened. I felt more rain on my face. Scott was breathing heavily and Will groaned in pain. Zoe grabbed Scott's arm and I went to check Will wasn't going to pass out and drown.

"Are you okay?" I asked him.

"No," he said and touched his jaw. He winced. "Fucking bastard," I think he said, because the words didn't come out right. "He broke my jaw."

"Maybe he dislocated it," I said. "You need to keep calm and we'll call an ambulance."

He slapped my hand away and staggered out of the pond.

"Zoe," I said, grabbing for him and missing. "Try and get Scott inside."

Will picked up one of the gnomes, then squared up to Scott again. Scott shrugged Zoe off but didn't otherwise move.

"Will," I said then repeated his name, louder, until he glanced at me. "Put that thing down. Don't make this worse."

"He's too fucking weak to do anything," Scott sneered. "He only picks on defenceless women in baths."

Will swung the gnome quickly and it hit the side of Scott's head with a horribly loud crack. Scott's eyes rolled up and he fell in a heap.

Zoe screamed and bent over her husband.

I needed to get Will away from them so he couldn't do more damage, so I shoved him as hard as I could. He dropped the gnome and lost his footing, then staggered sideways and fell back into the pond.

"You twat," I yelled at him as he dragged himself out of the water and sat on the grass. "Stay there, if you know what's good for you." I pulled my mobile out of my pocket then turned to Zoe. "How is he?"

She was crying. "He's breathing and making sounds, but there's blood behind his ear."

"I'll get help," I said and dialled 999.

* * *

The rain came down heavily.

I found an umbrella in Zoe's cottage and she used it to protect Scott's face from the downpour. I helped her put him into the recovery position then she knelt by his side, stroking the top of his arm as she told him, over and over, that she was there.

He was making a peculiar mewling sound, almost as though he was having a bad dream. I stood between him and Will to make sure Will didn't do anything to make things worse. He sat by the pond, looking despondent and occasionally touching his jaw and wincing. He wouldn't make eye contact.

Apart from Zoe, nobody spoke. I listened to the rain and occasionally brushed hair out of my eyes.

When the ambulance arrived, Will looked at me for the first time and I jabbed my finger at him.

"If you move a muscle," I said through gritted teeth, "I'll tell the police you went for me and Zoe too. Do you understand?"

He nodded and I went into the cottage to let the paramedic in.

"Are you Carrie Riccioni?" he asked.

"Yes, the man I rang about is still unconscious. He was hit in the head with a stone garden gnome ornament. The neighbour got punched in the face and reckons he's broken his jaw."

"Thanks." He said something to the driver then went through the house. I was about to follow him when the police car rolled in. PC Digby got out of the passenger side and waited for the driver before they both came to the door.

"Hello," he said, when he saw me. "I thought I recognised the name."

"Hi. You need to go through."

The lead officer came through first. "Did you call in?" he asked.

"I did."

"I'm Sergeant Fitzgerald and we'll need to speak to you before we leave." He looked at my sodden hair. "Do you want to get dried or anything?"

"No, I'll wait."

"Fine, we'll get to you presently."

He went through.

"It's been a weird week around here, hasn't it?" Digby asked.

"You could say that."

He went upstairs and got a towel from the bathroom for me. I stood in the kitchen so I didn't get in the way. The paramedic tended to Scott, and Fitzgerald stood with Zoe. Digby helped Will to his feet.

The ambulance driver came through with a stretcher and a foil blanket he handed to me. I wrapped it around my shoulders and watched them load Scott onto the stretcher and carry him out to the waiting vehicle. Zoe went with him, wearing her own blanket.

Fitzgerald came into the kitchen, leading a handcuffed Will who had his head down and didn't so much as cast me a glance. They went out too.

Digby and I were left in the kitchen, both of us dripping onto the tiles.

"When can I go back to my flat?"

"Let me get your statement, then you can." He clicked on the kettle. "How about a hot drink?"

He made us both a very strong brew and I put plenty of sugar in mine. We sat at the dining room table as I gave him my statement. It didn't take too long. I finished my drink, then he said I was free to go.

I walked out into the rain and around to the flat. It was late afternoon but dark enough that it looked like early evening.

Chapter 45

I peeled my clothes off and put on my dressing gown, then ran a bath. I needed warming up but also thought it would calm me down to soak a while. I found some bubble bath that promised to relax me and poured in a liberal amount, then went into the kitchenette and put the kettle on.

The doorbell rang and I groaned. I didn't want to see anyone, I just wanted to be left alone, so I ignored it. It rang again and droned on for longer this time. I growled at the intrusion. Whoever was out there, it seemed, was desperate to see me.

What if it was Rita? Had she perhaps heard about the altercation and wanted to find out the details? I checked my phone but there were no missed calls or messages received. I put it on the counter and made my tea.

When the doorbell rang again, I went downstairs and pounded hard on each step, in the hope my mystery caller would hear and know I wasn't happy to see them.

The doorbell rang again.

"For God's sake," I shouted. "I'm coming." If it was Jonny or Evans, I decided I'd swear enthusiastically at them before slamming the door in their face.

I pulled open the door.

Flo stood on the step, cuddling herself as she looked at me through her eyelashes. Her hair was flat to her head and her clothes were sodden. She was shaking. It took me a moment to react and then I grabbed her elbow and pulled her into the hallway.

"Oh, Flo," I said.

She started to cry and opened her arms. I pulled her into a hug and rubbed her back until her breathing calmed down.

"I'm so glad you're here, Carrie," she said into my shoulder. Her breath hitched. "I managed to get away. I don't know where he's gone, but I was able to get away."

"Of course," I said, rubbing her back as she shivered against me. My thoughts raced but I knew we needed to get her warm and dry first, then inform the police and, probably, get an ambulance to attend. "Let's get you upstairs," I said.

"I'm so cold."

"I know, love. I have some towels; we can dry you off." I couldn't let her get into my bath, in case she washed away some vital evidence. "Are you okay to go upstairs?"

"Yeah," she said and took my hand. She gripped it tight as we went up the stairs with her slightly in front.

"Go in," I said when she paused on the landing.

She did and stopped in the middle of the lounge, under the light. She wiped her face and I quickly looked her over. The skin around her eyes was dark and she'd lost enough weight that I could see the change in her face.

"I'll get you some towels and then we need to call the police."

"No," she said and shook her head. She looked frightened.

"We need to tell them, Flo. If you've been held against your will for over a week, you have to report it."

"I just want to have a bath and get warm and eat something then go home. I must stink."

"You don't, and I can't let you do that. The police would kill me. I'll get some towels and you can strip off and get dried and have a hot drink."

"Okay," she said reluctantly.

I found three big towels in the bathroom cupboard and gave them to her. "You can get sorted in the bathroom, if you want, but please don't get into the water."

"I won't."

She left the door open and I rushed into my bedroom and quickly put on a pair of shorts and a vest top. When I went out, I knocked on the door jamb of the bathroom.

"Are you okay?"

"Yeah," she said, from the lounge.

Confused, I walked along the landing and saw she was standing in the kitchenette with her back to me, still wearing her wet clothes. She was leaning on the counter nearest the window and her head was tilted down.

"Flo? Are you okay?"

"Uh-huh," she said. It didn't sound like she was.

"You need to dry yourself off then get warm." I looked on the counter for my phone. I checked the pockets of my shorts, but it wasn't there either. "Have you seen my phone?" I asked.

"Yeah," she said and turned slowly. She was holding a kitchen knife in front of her stomach. A chill brushed my neck and shoulders and I shivered. Surely Flo didn't regard me as an enemy?

"Did you want to put the knife down?" I asked, trying to keep my voice level. "You're safe now, Flo."

I didn't think she'd turn it on herself, but I couldn't take the risk of looking away. If she slashed at her forearm or wrist, then I'd need to move quickly.

Chapter 46

"Not really," she said and brought her arm up, the blade flashing in the dull light. She tapped the blunt edge against her shoulder a couple of times and then pushed away from the counter. She walked past the window and into the lounge, as if she didn't have a care in the world.

I suddenly had the horrible idea I'd been sold a dummy. "Flo?"

She faced me and smiled as she pushed wet hair off her forehead. "You're not as smart as you look, Carrie, are you?"

"You were never really missing, were you?"

"Bingo," she said and clapped her hands a couple of times, holding the knife awkwardly. "When did you figure it out?"

"Just now."

"Because I didn't want you to call the police?"

"No, that happens a lot when people have been violated or hurt in some way. Calling the police makes it real and they don't want to accept it, which is understandable."

"So, what was it?"

"The way you walked with the knife."

"Was I too cocky?" There was amusement in her voice, as if she was taking direction in a play.

"Just a bit."

She walked to the office door and back to the sofa.

"So," I said, "what now?"

"I need you to drive me into Seagrave, so I can pick up some stuff."

"Can't you walk?"

She pulled a face and gestured towards the window. "It's fucking pissing it down, in case you didn't notice."

"I did."

"And anyway, I'm not really here, am I? I'm a missing person."

She sat on the sofa and gestured for me to sit on the chair across from it. She regarded me with a steely gaze and her expression was sharp but unreadable.

"It's okay, I'll stay on my feet."

"Suit yourself." She shrugged. "So, I need you to drive me into Seagrave."

"I heard you the first time," I said and nodded towards the knife. "Do I have much choice?"

She chuckled. "I liked you from when I first met you, do you know that? You had a good attitude and you were pleasant to me."

"I'm so glad," I said sourly.

"And, weirdly, even though we'd only just met, you were really concerned about me. From what I can gather, you and Jonny were the only people who were worried about where I was. Everyone else seemed more concerned their places wouldn't get cleaned. And I doubt my fucking mother even realised I wasn't there."

"She did know," I said. "I went to see her."

Flo seemed surprised. She licked her lips nervously. "Did you see Roxy?"

"I did."

For a moment, her face seemed to crumble. "Was she okay?"

"She seemed to be, though she was really missing her big sister."

"Oh." There was a flicker of uncertainty in her eyes.

"Because, you know, she didn't expect her big sister to tell her lies."

Flo blinked away the uncertainty. "She'll be fine, I'll make it up to her." The sharpness came back into her expression. She held the handle of the knife with her thumb and index finger, letting the blade swing naturally like a lethal pendulum.

"So where were you?"

"In the loft," she said, and her tone was so calm and collected it was scary. For anyone listening who didn't know, we might have been discussing career options or where she would move to.

"You were never in the boathouse at all?"

A frown kinked between her brows. "Out in that stinky, cold place? Not on your life."

The penny dropped. "This was never about Will, was it?"

"Oh, I wish you hadn't said that, Carrie. You don't want to slip out of my good books, do you? I thought you were lovely, until I realised you weren't on my side."

"What are you talking about? I was never not on your side."

"Of course you were. What else do you call giving Will his alibi, even after you'd heard him in the dining room."

"I told the police the truth about that day, not because of what I'd heard." I stopped. "Or what I thought I'd heard."

Flo leaned forward, eyes wide, as if waiting for me to make the final connection.

"Will wasn't lying, was he? He didn't have you trapped in the dining room; you somehow contrived to make it look like that."

She clicked her fingers. "Bingo, Carrie! You're pretty good at this, aren't you?"

If she'd lied about that, the rest of her tales folded like cheap paper cards. "It's not Boyd either, is it? You were hiding in Scott's attic. He's the older bloke your friends Emily and Lauren mentioned."

"You're getting better at this guessing game."

I shook my head. "Do you expect me to believe that you willingly hid in a loft for a week?"

"Why not? Scott boarded the place out and told Zoe she wasn't to go up there, because he kept his work spread out." She laughed. "Actually, he put a camp bed up there for me and a chemical toilet."

"And you lasted a week in those conditions?"

Now she shook her head. "Hardly, Carrie. I spent the nights up there, but Zoe works in Seagrave. When she left in the morning, I had the run of the house and Scott was there too, most days. We had the best time. I started using her shower gel and perfume, so she wouldn't smell someone else in the house. I loved it, though I didn't enjoy climbing back up and knowing that she was going to be sleeping beside him."

"But you couldn't go outside. You were still a prisoner."

"That's a harsh word," she said, "especially when it was my choice. And I watched you, too, looking out of your window and spying on the neighbours, like you were invisible. I saw so much."

"So, all the time Zoe was worried about him seeing someone else, she was right. Except that the other woman was living right above her all the time."

"Zoe's such a tight-arse bitch, she doesn't deserve him."

"And you do?"

"For now, at least, we're made for each other. Amanda kept telling me about her brother, who was always getting into trouble, and then I saw a picture of him. Fuck me, I thought, he was a real man. Not like Jonny and the weedy shits I've had to suffer around here. When I met him, I knew we were going to be together. He wasn't happy with Zoe, she's too fucking strait-laced for him, but I was willing to do what he wanted. And he was happy to have a teenager all over him." She grinned at me. "You know how men are."

"And you were just going to run away?"

Flo laughed. "You really don't have much of an imagination, do you?"

"But you do?"

"Oh, I do and what I couldn't figure out, Scott did. It was all laid out for us, because Will fucked up with that woman at the hospital. Amanda hated him for what he'd done and was determined to make his life a misery, she didn't care who saw how badly she treated him. And he's so pathetic, he didn't do anything about it. Did you know that he sometimes slept in that horrible boathouse, rather than be in the same room as his wife? I caught him one day, taking some supplies in there, and he was so embarrassed, I think he did it after dark from then on. What an absolute wimp, and the whole world knew it. So when Amanda told Scott about willing her estate to him, that was the opening we needed. A pathetic husband, known to like young women, holds the lovable cleaning lass against her will then decides to kill his wife too. I mean, they make documentaries about that kind of thing all time."

The chill brushed my neck again as I realised I'd just heard a confession. "Did you kill her?"

"You really should be a detective, Carrie."

"That's why my alibi was a problem, isn't it? Boyd was in his house with the CCTV you probably knew about, but you wouldn't know what area it filmed. With Scott and Zoe away and you missing, that only left me, Will and Amanda."

Flo gave me a quick burst of applause. "Got it in one," she said. "But it wasn't really a problem, in the end. It all looked like an accident, didn't it? Even if Will hadn't had an alibi, she still might've slipped."

Anger flared, deep in my belly. "You're fucking heartless."

"Nope, just sick and tired of living here with absolutely fuck all to my name and a stupid boyfriend who thinks he can take me away from it all but never will. And, you know what? It wasn't even difficult. Scott told me he was going out, I heard the Rosses argue and knew that was my chance. I waited until Amanda was in the bath then let myself out of the loft. It wasn't too difficult, after that."

"What did you do?"

"I made her stand up then shoved her. Her head bounced off the wall and her eyes began rolling."

"That's why there was blood on the tiles," I said.

"I was going to wipe it away but then thought I might accidentally leave some kind of clue behind, so I left it there. I'm pleased you noticed."

"So did DS Samuelson."

"Who cares, because it didn't matter much." She was gloating now. "And when the people found my DNA all over the place, it didn't matter because I'm the cleaner and I got into every room."

"You had it all planned, didn't you?"

"Not really, though I wore some Marigolds so I didn't touch her bare skin. After she started to fall, I grabbed her head and aimed for the taps." She smiled, almost dreamily. "It made a weird noise when she hit them. I think she was dead straight away, but I held her head under the water for a few minutes, just to make sure."

"And Scott knew you were going to do it?"

"He didn't quite know I was going to do it like that, but his surprise worked well. He was genuinely shocked. Not that he really cared about her. Amanda made his life hell and he couldn't wait to see the back of her."

"But what about when the police searched the place?"

"I was already out. I'm not an idiot, Carrie. Once I'd finished with Amanda, I was back in Scott's place and into the loft as quick as you like. When he boarded the floor, he put up a dividing wall between his and Amanda's house, so all I had to do was keep quiet for a while. I heard one of the officers up in Will's loft, bumping about and I just lay on the camp bed and waited until they'd gone."

I couldn't believe how callous and calculating she sounded, but my anger was tempered by fear. Taking a life didn't seem to have affected her, nor did the fact that she'd attempted to frame Will. If she could be this unfeeling, then I didn't stand a chance. "You're sick."

"No, I'm just tired and pissed off. Scott's been feeding me and now he's in hospital and I don't know how he is or when he's coming back. So, I can't stay here, can I? Which means you're going to drive me into Seagrave, while I figure out my next move."

Fear crept over me like a heavy blanket that pinched my shoulders and threatened to smother me. I was convinced that if I drove her anywhere, I wasn't coming back – I knew too much for her to let me live.

I was so scared, it was hard to take a breath and I needed to calm myself down. I'd been trained to deal with situations like this and had to apply that knowledge now, but it was difficult to focus. What helped me was the anger brewing through me, that I'd managed to survive a heart attack and now found myself at the mercy of a heartless killer.

The best way to deal with getting trapped together in the car with her, I realised, was to refuse to go. I couldn't worry about what would happen then, because I couldn't control that. In this situation, I only had to worry about how to deal with the immediate future and I had to be flexible. If she came at me with the knife, I would do my best to fight her off even though she had youth on her side and I was recovering from a fucking heart attack. If I didn't fight her off, then I was as good as dead.

But, on the other hand, if I agreed to drive her, that might give me some more options because we'd be outside. I might be able to improvise something. The thoughts raced around my head like an angry trapped wasp and it was difficult to focus on them with any clarity.

"What if I refuse?" I asked, playing for time.

"Then I kill you," she said simply. "You've got clothes here and some money, so I could order an Uber. The driver wouldn't pay much attention to me if I was wearing a hood and some sunglasses, would he?"

"Probably not."

"Or maybe Jonny will come back, sniffing around and trying to get back into your good books, then I'll force him to take me." She tapped the knife against her knee. "I didn't enjoy killing Amanda, but it wasn't as horrible as I thought it would be. I'm sure I could do it again."

She sounded so believable, I knew my only chance was to get us both outside. "Okay."

That seemed to surprise her. "You're going to drive me?"

"That's what you want, isn't it?"

"Yeah," she said. "So come on, lead the way."

Chapter 47

My heart raced as I opened the front door. I stepped into my flip-flops and took my hoodie off the peg and put it on.

"No coat for you," I said, without turning to face her. "Boo hoo."

I opened the door and the rain hit me immediately. It was coming down hard now and I could barely see the hill through the gloom.

"What're you waiting for?" she asked.

"Nothing," I said, but I was hoping for a great escape plan to present itself.

"Then get outside. The quicker we get going, the quicker we're done."

She shoved me and I stumbled over the door frame. The rain pelted the hood of my jacket and soaked across the shoulders. My feet were instantly wet as I splashed through a puddle.

"Christ, it's chucking it down," she said, then shoved my shoulder. "Get to the car."

The rain was loud but, above it, I could hear the ridiculous and wonderful sound of Jonny's moped. I glanced towards the cottages and she did the same.

"The fuckwit did come back," she said.

"You don't need to hurt him, Flo. He's tried so hard to find and help you."

"Don't tell me what to do," she said and held up the knife, as if I could have forgotten she was armed. "Get to the car."

"What're you going to do?"

"I don't know yet."

She pushed me on and I'd just reached the car as Jonny came around the corner, the moped headlamp casting a beam filled with sparkles of rain. Flo squatted out of sight beside my leg and pressed the tip of the blade into my thigh. She put her other hand on my foot so I couldn't move it.

"If you move or signal him, I'll slash your leg," she said.

"Okay."

Jonny waved and pulled to a stop in front of the car. He got off the bike and pushed up his visor. He was only wearing his T-shirt and it looked black with the wet, sticking to his chest and belly like a second skin.

"Hi," he said and gave me an embarrassed smile.

"Hi."

I had to get rid of him quickly without revealing Flo was here. I could tell him to fuck off, but doubted he'd react to that. If I let him come closer though, Flo might stab the pair of us.

"I'm sorry about before," he said. "I shouldn't have said what I did, but I was angry, even though I know you're on my side. If I could take it all back, Carrie, I really would."

"Don't worry about it." I quickly widened my eyes, hoping he'd notice, but I don't think he did through the rain.

"So will you keep helping me to find Flo?"

"Of course," I said. The point of the blade pressed my leg and I had to fight the urge to look down and ask what I'd done wrong. "I'm happy to help you, Jonny. So why don't you get off home now and come back tomorrow and we'll start again."

The tip pressed in harder and now I did look down at her. She glared at me and bared her teeth. "Get rid of him."

"So where are you going?" he asked.

"Into Seagrave."

He frowned at me. "You're driving? But why are you standing by the passenger side?"

"Just because," I said. "Listen, Jonny, I'm getting soaked here. You take off and I'll see you tomorrow."

"Yeah," he said and took a step forward. He took off his helmet, his curls instantly flattened to his head. I could see in his face that he'd twigged something was wrong and he was going to come around the car.

"Please don't come any closer," I said and the blade pressed so hard into my thigh I was sure it must have broken the skin.

"Get fucking rid of him," Flo hissed.

"Is it a problem with the engine? My mum's car won't always start when it's pissing down."

"The car's fine," I said. "Honestly, I'm just about to leave."

He clearly didn't believe me and walked around the front of the car. "I don't mind checking if you pop the bonnet for me."

Flo turned and shifted herself forward, which meant she not only moved the knife away from my leg but took her hand off my foot.

As Jonny came closer, I nodded my head towards Flo, hoping he would realise. She duckwalked a couple of steps to the front of the car and they were perhaps six feet away from one another now.

I kicked her between the shoulder blades as hard as I could. "Run, Jonny!" I screamed.

Flo fell forward but got quickly to her feet and stood in front of him. The look of elation that lit up his face faded quickly when he saw the knife. Confused, he looked from her to me and back again.

"Run, you idiot!" I shouted.

"Flo," he said. "Where've you been?"

She took a step towards him. "It was Will," she said. "He took me and tied me up in his loft and said if I made a noise, he'd kill me."

His face twisted with confusion and I realised she was good. Even after seeing the knife and me kick her, he still didn't know whether to believe her or not. "How did you get away?" he asked.

Flo made a noise deep in her throat and lurched forward, slashing the knife towards him. Jonny tried to move back but wasn't quick enough and the blade buried itself into his left shoulder. He shrieked with pain and fell back, the blade slipping out of him. He staggered away but managed to keep to his feet. Flo jabbed with the knife again and he raised an arm. The blade cut a deep line on the underside of his forearm and he howled with pain.

Chapter 48

I grabbed two handfuls of her hair and yanked her backwards. She screamed and her feet slipped so, for a moment, I was holding her up. I spun around and she couldn't stop herself as I slammed her into the passenger door. She hit it with a thud and a cry but managed to keep hold of the knife. I grabbed for her again and she swung at me wildly, the blade missing my legs by inches. She pushed herself away from the car and I backed up, trying to maintain the distance between us.

"Get in the fucking car, Carrie."

"We need to help Jonny." I didn't know how badly he was hurt, but I had to get her away from him.

She swapped the knife to her left hand and ran her right hand down her face, sluicing the rainwater away. As she moved the knife back, I took my chance and hit her in the face as hard as I could.

I'd meant to slap her but it became a weak punch that hurt my knuckles. Her head snapped back with the impact. She steadied herself and I was going to throw another punch when she held the knife towards me. Her left eye twitched.

"You fucking bitch," she said and touched her eye gently. She winced at the contact.

I reacted without really thinking. Relaxing my toes, I kicked up my right foot and the flip-flop slid off at speed. She put her hand up to shield her face and it bounced off her forearm. I kicked the other one at her too then turned to run.

There weren't many options. I couldn't go up towards the cottages because she was in my way and we'd have to pass Jonny. My car was out because she'd be on me easily if I tried to get into it. I might be able to reach the flat before she did, but if I didn't manage to slam the door on her then I'd be trapped in an enclosed space.

All I could do was head towards the beach. I ran and, very quickly, regretted my choice of kicking my flip-flops at her. I sprinted across the tarmac, my feet jarring so much that I knew I'd have to change my gait.

Running on the balls of my feet was better but the small stones and gravel underfoot burned against the sensitive skin. I gritted my teeth and kept going, past the fence and onto the path.

"How are you fucking running away?" she shouted in surprise. Then she was after me. "You can't outrun me, Carrie. I'm going to get you."

She was probably right, but I wasn't going to give in easily. I tried to ignore the pain from my feet and regulate my breathing, which was already burning in my throat. I'd worked hard to build my fitness this past week and now I needed to take advantage of that. Heat spread across my chest and I hoped it was exertion and heartburn, rather than another heart attack.

By the time I got to the bridge, my breathing was ragged but so was Flo's. She'd been cooped up for a week and this sudden burst of exercise clearly wasn't doing her any good at all.

I crossed the bridge, the wooden slats feeling wonderfully smooth against my poor soles, and then I was on the path. The tide was in, water lashing against the breakwater. That only left the hill which, from this angle, looked like a horrifying prospect. It must have been forty-five degrees in places, with lots of grass and exposed rocks. The summit was lost in the mist of rain and sea spray but I knew I wouldn't have the energy to reach it. The question was, how much energy could Flo muster? She was running on anger and the fact that if she let me go, she was doomed, and I couldn't discount that.

I glanced over my shoulder. She was about twenty yards from the bridge and running with an awkward, almost stiff-legged gait that was slowing her down. It might buy me a bit of time, but not a lot.

There was no choice but to go up the hill, so I stayed on the grass but followed the track the walkers had naturally formed. The soft surface soothed my feet but the angle didn't do my calves much good.

"How are you doing this?" Flo demanded.

Ignoring the pain in my chest and legs, I pushed on. The path kinked around an exposed rock and I slipped, almost losing my footing. Something brushed my shoulders and I heard Flo's rasping breath. She was virtually on top of me. I tried to speed up but there was no more energy in my legs.

I got around the rock and then something tangled in my feet and I fell forward. I flung my arms out and the grass was soft enough that it didn't hurt as I landed on my knees. Fingers curled into my hair and, with a yank, Flo pulled me into a sitting position. My scalp burned. There was blood on her cheek and a streak of mud across her forehead. Her eyes were wide and it looked, terrifyingly, like she'd lost control.

She let go of my hair and staggered back a couple of steps. She was breathing heavily and leaned forward with her hands on her knees. I watched the knife, gripped solidly in her right hand.

"How did you do that, you cow? When I saw you last, you got knackered going upstairs." She glared at me. "How the fuck did you outrun me?"

"I exercised," I gasped.

"Not enough."

"Maybe." I watched her face, seeing the confusion and cunning in her eyes. We both knew where this was going but, now we were here, perhaps she wasn't so sure she could go through with it. And in instances where you could exploit that kind of uncertainty, you kept people talking. "So, what happens now? Do we walk back down the hill, or are you going to kill me here?"

"If I have to," she said and looked at me blankly. "It wouldn't take much to get you closer to the edge and then you're just another person who fell off the summit of the hill."

She said it without emotion, but I could see something behind her eyes and then it clicked into place. "My God," I muttered. "Merry didn't take a wrong turn, did she?"

For the first time, she looked away as if I'd hurt her.

"What did you do, Flo? Merry loved you."

"She was in the way," she said, but her heart wasn't in the argument. She sounded like a kid denying she'd broken a vase while still holding part of it. "I didn't really want to do it, but I couldn't risk her talking."

"You killed her to stop her talking?"

"She saw me, Carrie," Flo said, and an edge crept into her voice now. "She saw me coming out of Scott's and I knew, once I went missing, that she would tell someone about it. And I couldn't take that risk."

"So, what did you do?"

"I talked to her and made up some shit about why I was there and then she went on her way, up the hill in the darkness. I waited for a few minutes and then followed her."

"You walked after her, knowing you were going to hurt her? That's bloody cold, Flo."

She shrugged. "What else could I do? She would've ruined everything. So I went up behind her and, when she reached the top, I grabbed her. Scared her half to death and it might have been easier if she'd just keeled over from a heart attack, but she didn't. She tried to defend herself, Carrie. She was throwing slaps and trying to kick me."

"You pushed her over the edge?"

She shook her head. "I didn't mean to."

"Don't fucking lie to yourself, Flo. You're a cold and calculating little bitch. You followed her up the hill and you must have known she was never coming down again."

"It's not like that. I never wanted to hurt her, or you, or Jonny. That wasn't my plan, but there's no other way out now. I need to get away, to start again."

"What about Roxy?"

The faintest hint of a smile played at the corners of her mouth for a moment. "She'll be safe. Once we're set up, I'll take her away and give her a better life than our bloody mother could ever manage to do."

"And how are you going to do that? Scott's badly hurt, don't you realise? He went away in an ambulance. He won't be going anywhere."

"You're lying."

"And how're you going to get Roxy? There'll be a hunt for you."

She was moving, ever so slightly, as if struggling to keep her balance. I edged back to increase the space between us and put my hand on a palm-sized rock. I grasped it, without really thinking through what I could do with it.

Flo shrugged. "I'll think of something, like I always do. Like I always fucking have to do." She wiped her face again. "Get on your feet, Carrie. I'm sick to death of this weather and I just want to get sorted out. We're going back to the car."

"No." I wasn't going to let myself get caught up like this. I'd worked too hard to make sure my heart attack didn't rob Luca of his mother to let some vicious bitch finish the job now. I slowly got to my feet, making sure to keep the distance between us and hiding my right hand, holding the rock, behind me. She didn't seem to notice.

"I'm not kidding, Carrie."

"Scott got hit in the head, you idiot. He was bleeding and is probably badly hurt. He's not going to be able to run away with you so you won't have access to his money."

There was a moment of doubt in her face but she shook her head. "I'll kill you, here and now, then. I can always steal Jonny's moped if needs be and get away on that."

"Go ahead," I said. "I'm not kidding either. You haven't got any money and you haven't got a chance."

We both heard the sirens at the same time and I looked over her shoulder in the general direction of Seagrave. She glanced around but needed to keep her attention on me. Through the gloom, I could just make out the flashing lights on the road.

"They're coming this way," I said.

"No they're not."

I wasn't telling a lie. "Yes, they are. Perhaps you didn't hurt Jonny as badly as we both thought. Maybe he rang the police and they're coming to arrest you."

"Don't be so fucking stupid," she shouted and looked over her shoulder again, her movements brisk and jumpy. She was scared, as if she couldn't work out where this latest twist in the plan would take her.

"They're coming for you," I said, as clearly as I could. I wanted to rub her nose in it and wind her up even more. If she panicked now, I might have a chance. I gripped the rock tighter in my hand. "You're a murderer, Flo. They'll make sure Roxy never sees you again and she'll grow up feeling horribly let down, thinking that her wonderful big sister deserted her after doing all those terrible things. You killed one woman in her bath and you pushed a pensioner to her death. You can't explain that away and come out of this some kind of heroine, however hard you try."

"Shut up!" she screamed.

"Think of how sad she'll be, when she finds out you ran away and deliberately left her alone. The poor little girl will cry herself to sleep."

"Shut up," she shouted. "Shut up, you horrible witch."

"They're almost here, Flo."

She looked behind her then and I closed the gap between us with a couple of steps and swung my right hand as hard as I could. She must have caught a glimpse of me, because she turned and leaned back at the same time, to avoid contact. My blow glanced off her shoulder and the impact made her cry out. She kept to her feet and, as my momentum pushed me forward, she lunged at me. I arched my body out of the blade's path, but only just. She lunged again and the blade sliced my arm, leaving a trail of fire.

I swung for her again and caught her in the chest, but there wasn't enough force in it. She staggered back and her right leg slipped out from under her. I brought the rock down as hard as I could, aiming for her knife hand, but caught the same shoulder as before. There was a very loud snapping noise as her collarbone went and then she began to shriek.

Flo dropped to her knees, pressing her knife hand to her damaged shoulder. She looked at me with red eyes.

"Stay where you are," I said and held the rock up so she could see it. "I don't want to hurt you, Flo, but I will if I need to."

We stood that way, the rain pelting us for what felt like an hour, but it was probably no more than ten minutes before the first policeman made his way up the hill.

"My name's Carrie Riccioni," I called to him. "This is Flo Adler. She's armed with a knife, but I think I've broken her collarbone."

"What are you armed with, Carrie?"

"I have a rock in my hand."

"Did you hit her with that?"

"I did."

"Drop it then," he instructed and I did. "Where's your knife, Flo?"

She didn't respond.

"It's in her right hand," I said. "The one she's holding to her shoulder."

"Thank you," he said. "Put the knife down, Flo."

She didn't move.

"Flo," I said. "It's done. It's over. You can't get away from this."

She looked at me through her eyelashes. "You've ruined it all," she said. "I only wanted something better for me and Roxy."

"I know, so don't make it worse."

"Put down the knife, Flo," the policeman said again. "Or I'll be forced to use my Taser."

"Put it down, Flo," I said. "Think about Roxy."

She blinked and then her head dropped. For a moment, I thought she was going to move and took a step backwards, but she let go of the knife and it dropped into the grass.

"She's let it go, officer," I told him.

"I saw. Step back, Carrie."

I did as I was told and watched as the officer took care of the situation. By the time he'd finished, two more officers had come up the hill after him. They carried insulated blankets and handed me one, and one of them pressed something against the cut on my arm.

I pulled the blanket over my shoulders and allowed myself to be led back down to the bridge.

Epilogue

I woke before the alarm but lay quietly until it went off, then got up and walked to the window. Even though it had been five days since Flo chased me up the hill, my calves were still sore and there were a lot of painful little cuts on the soles of my feet.

I opened the curtains and looked down onto Aldwych Street, where cars were parked nose to tail at the kerb. Across the road, some of my neighbours were already up, while a lucky few still had their curtains closed. The only pedestrian was a young woman, running at a steady pace along the pavement.

After putting on my dressing gown, I padded downstairs, being careful not to bump my arm on the banister because that did hurt. The police took me to Seagrave Diagnostic Centre because the slash Flo inflicted was bleeding so badly, but the doctor who checked me over said that was down to the blood thinners of my heart medication. He cleaned me up and used Steri-Strips to close the wound, before bandaging it up.

I went into my narrow kitchen, put the kettle on and leaned on the counter, gazing out of the window as I waited for the water to boil. My thoughts drifted back to last Sunday.

Rita was outside the flat in her car when the police took me home, after I'd given my statement at the station. She checked my arm was okay then embraced me tightly. Tears glistened in her eyes and on her cheeks.

"I'm so sorry," she said.

"What for? None of this was your fault, Rita, just like my heart attack wasn't your fault."

"But if I hadn't offered to let you stay here, you'd never have met Flo."

"No, but she'd still have done what she did."

"And might have got away with it too," she said, then we went inside and she made me a strong cup of sugary tea.

I didn't sleep well that night, because Flo chased me in the vivid dreams that kept waking me up, so I moved out of the flat on Monday. It was a relief to get back to my own house. The dreams weren't so scary after that. On Tuesday, I set up my office in Luca's old bedroom and tried to get back to normal with things.

Jonny texted that afternoon and I went to see him. He greeted me at the door with his arm in a sling and a bandage padding out the shoulder of his T-shirt. The coffee table in his lounge was awash with brightly coloured cards, which surrounded a straggly bunch of sad-looking flowers in a vase and a tub of Celebrations chocolates.

"Make yourself at home," he said. "Did you want a chocolate?"

"No, I'm fine, but thank you. You've got a lot of cards."

"I was surprised to get so many. My mum gave me the flowers, but I think she must have bashed them about on the way here, because they were half dead when she arrived." He grinned. "It's the thought that counts though, eh?"

"Of course. How're you feeling."

"I've been better," he said and moved his shoulder gently. "The doctors reckon the knife didn't touch anything too important, so I should be fine."

He asked about my arm then made us a cup of tea and we avoided talking about Flo, even though she was the main thing we had in common. I stayed for about an hour and, on impulse as I drove home, I called into a newsagent shop and bought a copy of the Seagrave Telegraph. The story was still on the front page, with Trevor Evans in full News Of The World mode. Since the story was even more juicy than his suspicions when he cornered me at Miller's Point, he must have thought all his Christmases had come at once.

Flo was charged with the murder of Amanda and Merry, as well as assault charges for her attacks on me and Jonny. Scott was still in hospital with a fractured skull and his condition was said to be stable. Not much had been said about Will, but I assumed he must have been in some level of trouble.

It was Zoe I felt most sorry for. When I rang to see how she was, I almost didn't recognise her voice because the emotion was so thick in it. She'd gone back to Filton to stay with her parents and it seemed she didn't have any plans to return. Her marriage, she told me, was dead and buried. I couldn't blame her.

After I drank my tea, I had a shower then sat on the bed in my dressing gown as I dried my hair and looked out the window. There were fewer cars at the kerb now and schoolchildren on the pavements. Life went on.

I was getting dressed when my phone rang and Rita's smiling face was on the screen.

"Hey, you," I said.

"Hey, Carrie, how're you feeling?"

"Better every day," I said. "How're you?"

"Me? I'm fine, you know that."

"Yeah," I said. "I know that."

Neither of us spoke for a few seconds, and I looked out of the window again. A young mother stood outside my front yard, leaning on a stroller as she glanced over her shoulder and shouted at someone to hurry up, or they'd be late for school.

"I'll see you later," she said. "Don't forget we've got that Zoom meeting at ten."

"I won't."

We said our goodbyes. Outside, the young mother was walking away, now holding the hand of a small boy. I watched her go, happy to see life going on in my cramped and crowded residential street.

It might not have had the views and space of Miller's Point, but I was glad to be home. And I couldn't see myself heading back to Seagrave in a hurry.

Acknowledgements

Mum, Sarah, Chris, Lucy and Milly; Nick Duncan, Sue Moorcroft, Julia Roberts, Jonathan Litchfield and Caroline Lake; Steve Bacon, Wayne Parkin, Peter Mark May and Richard Farren Barber; The Crusty Exterior; my Con family; Ian Whates and the NSFWG gang; Ross Warren and Penny Jones; everyone who's bought, read, talked about or reviewed one of my books; the entire team at The Book Folks.

David Roberts and Pippa, for the Friday night walks and many other various adventures and laughs.

Alison and Matthew, who make everything worthwhile.

If you enjoyed this book, please let others know by leaving a quick review on Amazon. Also, if you spot anything untoward in the paperback, get in touch. We strive for the best quality and appreciate reader feedback.

editor@thebookfolks.com

www.thebookfolks.com

Also by Mark West

All FREE with Kindle Unlimited and available in paperback!

DON'T GO BACK

Beth's partner Nick can't quite understand why she acts so strangely when they return to her hometown for the funeral of a once-close friend. But she hasn't told him everything about her past. Memories of one terrible summer will come flooding back to her. And with them, violence and revenge.

ONLY WATCHING YOU

After separating from her cheating husband, Claire begins to feel watched. She nearly gets run over and someone daubs a hangman symbol on a wall near her house. As letters begin to get added to the game, she'll need to find the identity of her stalker before they raise the stakes.

THE HUNTER'S QUARRY

Young single mother Rachel has no idea why an assassin is trying to kill her. Have they confused her with someone else? Did she do something wrong? Whatever the answer, it looks like they'll carry on trying unless she can get to safety or turn the tables on them. But first she'll have to find out what they want from her.

STILL WATERS RUN

A short holiday at the end of summer should be a chance for sixteen-year-old Dan and his recently divorced mother to unwind. Yet despite quickly striking up new friendships, their break takes a nasty turn when a holiday worker is murdered. Dan becomes embroiled in events. Can he get out or is he in too deep?

A KILLER AMONGST US

When her husband invites Jo on a couples' hiking weekend, despite disliking camping she accepts, hoping they'll rekindle their former closeness. But her hopes are shattered when the group starts to argue amongst themselves, and then the unthinkable happens… a happy holiday quickly turns into a desperate fight for survival.

WE WERE SEEN

A professional woman who is opposing the development of a golf course on a local nature site finds her life falling into turmoil when someone begins to blackmail her with compromising photographs. Will she succumb to their demands or can she deliver the extorter into the arms of the law?

Other titles of interest

THE THINGS WE HIDE by Vanessa Garbin

Desperate for work to fund an operation for her injured husband, Nadia accepts a job offer from a successful estate agent. However, lured by the promise of a hefty commission, she accepts a very indecent proposal. Though ashamed of her actions, she earns enough to put their lives back on track. That's until there is a knock on the door, and the past comes flooding back.

FREE with Kindle Unlimited and available in paperback!

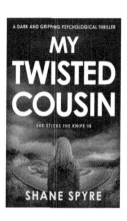

MY TWISTED COUSIN by Shane Spyre

Teenager Harper hates her younger cousin Audrey, who is always getting into trouble. So when she is sent to stay with her, she decides to make the visit as difficult as possible. She goads Audrey, winding her up into a frenzy. But Harper has underestimated the effect of her actions, and as matters escalate, she'll be lucky to escape alive.

FREE with Kindle Unlimited and available in paperback!

Sign up to our mailing list to find out about new releases and special offers!

www.thebookfolks.com

Printed in Great Britain
by Amazon